[Leave a message]

Cat Connor

The third Veronica Tracey Spy/PI novel.

I0640813

For Granddad, Constable Thomas William Illes (NZ Police no.1700), who was always reading and Nana who never read a book in her life.

For information regarding permission email the publisher at 9mmPressNZ@gmail.com, subject line: Permission.

Editor: Nicky Hurle
Formatting: 9mm Press
Publisher: 9mm Press, New Zealand
Publication date: June 2022
Country of first publication: New Zealand.

ISBN paperback: 978-0-473-62804-8
ISBN ePub: 978-0-473-62806-2
ISBN Apple Books: 978-0-473-62809-3
ISBN Kindle: 978-0-473-62807-9
ISBN Hardback: 978-0-473-62805-5
ISBN PDF: 978-0-473-62808-6

[Messages]

"Cat Connor delivers again. Her marvellously unique undercover intelligence team in sleepy Upper Hutt, New Zealand frustrate an international biological weapons attack using techno-age spy craft, and family connections in a retirement home. It is an exhilarating mix."
- Professor Brian Stoddart; Screenwriter — winner of TMFF (UK), KIIFFA (India), Feel the Reel (UK), Bridge Fest (Canada) and Siren international (Australia) competitions; Crime novelist — the four Superintendent Chris Le Fanu novels set in British India

"Fans of crime fiction will love Cat Connor's fast-paced and entertaining spy thriller."
- SL Beaumont; Winner IRDA Mystery / Suspense / Thriller Award
Semi-finalist Publisher's Weekly BookLife Fiction Prize
Long-list Ngaio Marsh Award for Best Novel

Chapter One:
[Ronnie: Messages]

The answer machine kicked in before I disabled the door alarm. By the time I got to the phone, the caller was leaving a message. I listened as I flicked the lights on and powered up the computers for the day. Romeo flopped on his bed by my desk, cocked his ears, and watched the answer machine.

"She's not in there," I said, giving his head a rub as I moved around him. "Can you imagine the horror of Nana living in the answer machine?"

I swear that Romeo nodded. He's a wise old hound.

Nana's feeble voice spilled from the device on the front desk and filled the room.

"Veronica, dear, the girls and I were wondering ..."

Nothing good ever came from those particular words. What she said next stopped me in my tracks.

"Donald and Enzo are stopping in to discuss wedding plans."

Of course they are. The golden boys were letting Nana run the wedding planning. I opened the blinds and let the winter sun into the room. It felt warm despite the day expecting a maximum of twelve degrees. Nana continued, "We would like you to be here."

I looked out the window at the railway station across the road. All quiet on the eastern front.

The deceptively feeble voice continued, "We value your input, Veronica. Perhaps you could bring Ben with you?"

Oh, right. It's a wedding ambush. No thanks. Once Donald and Enzo tie the knot, she'll be full steam ahead trying to railroad me and Ben into a wedding.

"I'm not getting any younger, Veronica. It would make your old Nana very happy. We shall expect you at eleven-thirty. Bring Romeo."

She hung up.

Buggery bollocks. It was all going swimmingly until she played the age card. Right up until then, I could throw down the 'busy with work' card. But, old age trumps work, every bloody time. My name is Ronnie Tracey, and I live with my crazy cousin Donald and Romeo, my retired-racing greyhound, in Trentham, Upper Hutt. I'm a full-time private investigator and part-time Nana wrangler. This wasn't always my life. Once upon a time I was an intelligence officer for the New Zealand Security Intelligence Service. As much as I like to pretend the spy lark is in the past, it is pretense. A few years ago, my two best friends and I opened our own private investigation company, *Wherefore Art Thou.* It's mostly wayward spouse and theft as a servant jobs for Jenn, Steph, and I, until it isn't. Until my old vocation comes knocking.

The message from Nana bounced around in my mind for a few minutes before Jenn and Steph arrived at the office.

"What's that look?" Steph asked, waving a hand in my

direction.

"Nana," Jenn interceded.

"Correct." I sat at my desk.

"Do we need to know?" Steph asked.

"Just the usual. Wedding nonsense. It's quite the production."

Steph looked up from the open diary in her hands. "New client meeting in thirty-minutes and the case reports need finalising before I do the billing."

I nodded. "What do we have on the new client?"

"Not much. His name is Terry O'Sullivan. He worked for Defence for thirty years and then worked for a logistics company until his retirement two years ago."

"He was forthcoming then?"

Steph smiled. "Not really, I did a bit of background. Wanted to see what, was what."

"And he wants?"

"Wouldn't say except that it's personal. He's retired so it isn't going to be business is it?"

Could be marital. Usually is when it's personal.

"Okay. Flipping for it?"

"Not this time," Steph said. "He asked for you. And he called pretty early."

Jenn laughed. "Awesome. I've got enough personal cases at the minute." She picked up her iPad and some files. "Surveillance this morning. See you when I get back."

I waved as she left.

"There wasn't a message on the machine when I got in,

except Nana's," I said.

"I drew the short straw. My cell phone number is on the after hours recorded message this week," Steph reminded me.

We take turns having our cell numbers on the answer machine for midnight emergencies.

"It's serious then, whatever he wants," I said.

"I'd say so."

"Probably not a cheating spouse in that case."

Steph and I looked at each other for a split second before the phone rang. I moved my head in the smallest shake. She grinned and let the call go to the message bank.

The usual spiel spilled from the direction of the phone: We're not available right now, leave your name and number and we'll call you back when one of the team is free. I busied myself, opened files on my computer, and settled in to work mode.

A male voice stopped and started, then forged ahead, "Um ... I'm looking for Ronnie Tracey. I need help."

Steph snatched up the phone, and said, "One moment caller, she's right here."

She handed me the phone and hovered near my desk.

"This is Ronnie. Who are you, and how can I be of service?"

"I'm Luke O'Sullivan, and I don't know where I am, but I need help."

Isn't that interesting?

"But you knew my phone number?"

4

"I saw it once."

"Okay, and what would you like me to do?"

"Find me."

"You're using a phone. Why call me? Why not call someone you know?"

"Because whatever is going on here is not something I want my family involved in. Tell me you'll help me."

"I will." Because I'm like that. "Is your father Terry O'-Sullivan?"

"Yes. How do you know that?"

"He's coming in soon to meet with me. I'm guessing you're the reason."

"Shit. Don't tell him anything."

"Look around. What do you see?"

"I'm in a building of some type. There are no windows. Someone's coming. I can hear footsteps."

"Can you get out?"

"No," he whispered. "I managed to get into a hallway and that's how I found the phone, in an office."

"Anything with an address on it?" Offices usually have windows unless it's a basement office. I could hear him shuffling through papers. "P.O. Box."

"Give it to me," I picked up a pen and wrote the number and location of the P.O. Box on my desk pad. "Anything else? Usually letters and bills are addressed to a person or company, not just the P.O. Box."

"They're addressed 'Manager' but no name." The shuffling of papers continued. "There are some invoices for vegetables and meat." The sound changed, more muffled.

"I have to go. I just saw goat cheese on an invoice and that said 'Manager' as well."

"Stay safe."

He hung up. I had no idea why he was where he was, or what would happen to him, and I didn't like it. I looked up at Steph and handed her the P.O. Box info. "See what magic you can do. I need a name or a business name. He said everything is addressed Manager."

She smiled. "I do love snooping." She trotted over to her desk and got to work.

I wondered briefly how messy the situation would get and if I'd need to reach out to either Ben or Crockett. I felt a smile on my face as I logged into my work laptop and began the arduous task of writing the final report for a wayward spouse case. Ben's name popped up on my screen. Think of the devil ... he must have felt the Nana vibes. I opened iMessage.

Ben: Dinner?
Me: Sounds good.

Who in their right mind would turn down dinner with the actor Ben Reynolds? Although Ben wasn't your typical actor. He was also an American intelligence officer. We were kind of a thing. Sometimes we weren't a thing, but today we were a thing. Ben was typing; I could see the dots moving in iMessage.

Ben: I'll pick you up from home at seven.

Me: Okay, see you then.

Steph looked over and smiled at me. "You look pleased with yourself, what happened?"

"Ben is taking me out tonight."

"That's nice. Wonder if I can get Jenn interested in a meal out ..." her voice trailed away as she typed.

"Have you heard from Crockett?" I said, while typing the date into the template.

"I'm not the right person to ask. If anyone has heard from Crockett, it'll be Emily downstairs in the bookshop."

"Of course, Emily would know."

That's not exactly true. She would know, but she wouldn't know she knew without checking her diary. Emily runs our bookshop; she's amazing and everyone loves her. I liked that Crockett and Emily were close. We'd known Emily a long time; she wasn't half bad as an investigator until her accident. She doesn't remember those days, but we do. Every now and then, we get a glimpse of the Emily who ran surveillance operations and had our backs in sticky situations.

Crockett worked with me and Ben a couple of times in recent history. He had an interesting skill set from his years undercover in a biker gang. He wasn't bad for an Aussie and handy to have around if things went sideways. His special skills are not like mine. My expertise is finding people. Once I even found a collection of garden gnomes hidden across Upper Hutt. That was nearly the end of life as we knew it. Well, pre-COVID it was considered nearly the end. Post-COVID life is not so easily up-set. We've hardened up a bit since then. And what's a lost garden gnome or two?

Chapter Two:
[Crockett: Makes no sense]

"Look, pal, you may as well just come clean and save me all the aggravation." I leaned back against the wall behind me and eyeballed the uncomfortable looking bloke sitting in the chair in front of my desk. Little beads of perspiration gathered on his forehead.

"She's been following me." He rubbed his hands together, then scrubbed his palms down the thighs of his jeans.

"And why would she do that?"

"How would I know? Maybe she likes me?" His line of sight faltered mid-chest then dropped to the surface of my desk.

"Course, that'll be it."

"What did she tell you?" He attempted eye contact but again fell short.

"She told me nothing."

That did it. He snorted. His eyes blasted mine. "Then what the fuck is this all about?"

I pushed off the wall, took two steps around my desk, tipped the chair with one hand, until he was balanced on the two back legs, while he struggled and panicked. "Messages you left her you piece of garbage." I pressed play on my phone.

His voice blasted from my phone and overrode the

ridiculous commotion he was making in my office. He shut up.

"Emily, Emily. You don't remember me do you? I can do whatever I want, and you will never know."

The silence in my office was deafening as I hit play again. "Emily, Emily. You don't remember me. You don't remember anything. No one can stop me. I'm going to have some fun with you."

I pushed the chair up a bit then let it go with a shove. He went down like a fat kid on a seesaw. There was a sickening thud when the back of his head smacked into the floor.

"Get up you sack of shit. We're not done here."

Toby rolled over, rubbed his head, and then dragged himself to his feet. "No one can take a fucking joke," he muttered, holding the back of his head.

"It wasn't a joke, pea-brain." I popped him square on the jaw, and as his head came back, I smacked him again. Once more for luck, and I knew I had to walk away. I took a deep breath and stormed out of my office. "Art!"

"Crockett?" Art said from the couch in the reception area. "What's going on?"

"The bloke in my office needs ..."

"To disappear?"

"To sling his hook and never be seen around here again."

"Close enough," Art said. He stood and walked purposefully into my office. "Don't know what you did mate, but you're not doing it again."

I made a beeline for the door. What I needed was air. If that air took me by the bookshop I wouldn't mind at all. The Harley waited patiently for me at the curb. Nothing beat a ride on a sunny day after smashing a dickhead in the face for misbehaving. I roared up to the curb outside the bookshop and climbed off the bike. As I hung my helmet on the wing mirror and over the throttle, I peered past the glare on the window trying to see if Emily was inside. I locked the bike, pocketed the key, and strode through the open sliding door.

"Hey!" I called into the back of the shop, spotting Emily shelving books.

She turned. A smile slowly graced her lips. I waited.

"Hello, Crockett."

"Hi there, Milo."

Her smile radiated. "I like Milo."

"I know," I said with a grin. Shame they don't have it at the café. "I'm going to grab a coffee from *Cake & Kitchen*. Want me to get you a hot chocolate?"

"Yes, please. I like hot chocolate."

"I won't be long." I could hear voices coming from the interior door. "What's happening in there?" The daybook was open on the counter. I could read it from where I stood, so I glanced over and read Emily's handwriting. "Writing group."

"Yes," said Emily. "That is what it is." She stopped. I could see a struggle on her face. "Um."

"Crime writing," I said, as I read another detail.

She nodded and smiled. "Yes."

"I'll be back."

"I will be waiting."

When I returned with Emily's hot chocolate and my coffee, Jenn was in the bookshop sitting at the desk in the back corner of the room.

Emily stood behind the counter, looking up as I walked in. "Hello, Crockett," she said brightly.

"Hello, Milo." I smiled and handed her a takeout cup. "It's hot chocolate. Be careful."

"Thank you."

"You're welcome. I need to talk to Jenn. I'll be right back." I smiled and left my coffee on the counter by Emily. "Hey, Jenn, can I have a word?"

Jenn turned the screen off on her tablet. "Sure. What's going on?"

I lowered my voice so Emily couldn't hear me, "I had a chat with a low-life called Toby Cartwright. He thought it was funny to leave threatening messages on Emily's phone. He left a few on the bookshop voicemail as well."

"Jesus. Is Emily all right? She hasn't said anything."

We both looked over. Emily was sipping her drink and watching out the big front window.

"She's okay, I think. I don't know how much she remembers, and I don't want to remind her. I copied the messages and then deleted them from her mobile, and the shop phone."

"How did you hear them to start with?"

"I was here when she opened the shop the other day and pushed play on messages on the shop phone. I asked her about other messages, and she handed me her phone so I could look."

"What's wrong with people?"

"This pecker-head knew her. He knew she wouldn't remember if he did something, so I guess he's been into the shop."

"Okay, we need to increase her security. Put cameras inside the shop."

"I can have one of my guys do that, if you think Ronnie will be okay with it."

"She'll be fine with it. We talked about putting at least one camera in here pointed to the back wall after that bullshit with the cryptographer. I can sign off on extra security so no worries there." She pointed to the back wall and then the door. "I'd want one pointed near the back and one covering the entrance."

"Great. What about the back room?"

"Just shop floor. General public doesn't go out the back."

"What is going on out there?"

"One of our surveillance operators is a crime writer and she's put a crime writing group together that's now meeting weekly."

"Upper Hutt has enough crime writers to warrant a group. Wow," I said. It was hard not to be both impressed and a little scared. "Considering what's gone down with this latest creep, it's got to be a good thing that there are more people in and out of the shop."

"I agree," Jenn replied. "I can work more from this

desk. No reason why half my paperwork can't be done here, it's mostly on my tablet anyway. Interviews I'll do upstairs, but the other stuff I can happily do down here."

"If that works for you, then it'd be great." And a load off my mind.

"You really are worried aren't you?"

I couldn't deny it. "Don't let her hear. Use the earbuds, press play." I unlocked my phone and opened the audio app before I passed the phone and ear buds to Jenn. The look of disgust on her face as she listened, and the way she ripped the earbuds from her ears, told me all I needed to know.

"I'll be working from the shop floor as much as possible," she said. "This is not okay."

"You're right there. I had a chat with him before coming here."

"Chat?" Her eyes drifted to my hands as I put the phone in my jacket pocket. "You always rough your knuckles up talking?"

I shrugged. "Maybe I speak with my hands."

"Make sure it doesn't come back to bite you on the arse, Crockett. You won't be much good to Emily if you get locked up."

"I know." She was right. But he damn well deserved a couple of pops to the chin. "I'll be around a bit. Have a new job starting, but it shouldn't keep me away too long."

"Between us we can cover Emily. I'll make sure Donald, Enzo, Steph, and Ronnie, know that they need to keep an eye out."

I nodded. Jenn's response reaffirmed my decision to stay in New Zealand and remain part of this crazy mixed-up team situation. They might be Kiwis, but I didn't let that cloud my judgment when it came to their character. They were good people.

Chapter Three:
[Ronnie: What's going on?]

A tall, thin man with a yellowish pallor walked into the office. I placed him at around the sixty-five-year mark, maybe closer to seventy. Romeo met him by the front desk. As soon as Romeo was acknowledged, he sauntered back to his bed by me, lay down, folded his right foot over his left, and rested his chin on his long limbs.

"Good morning," the man said, into the room.

"Good morning," I replied, and stood. "Terry O'Sullivan?" He nodded. "Join me under the window, it's more comfortable." I pointed to the couch and armchairs as I walked toward him.

"Thank you," he said. "Are you Ronnie Tracey?"

"I am," I replied, and shook his outstretched hand. "Have a seat."

I sat in my usual armchair and watched him sit on the couch. Sun filtered through the blinds and cast striped shadows across the coffee table. I waited for Mr O'Sullivan to speak. He didn't seem to know where to start.

"What is it that brings you to us?" I said, with a smile. "You said it was a personal matter?"

His head nodded. "It's about my son. He didn't come home last night and he's not answering his phone."

If I hadn't had a call from the son, I'd be suggesting he was on a date that went well, and we shouldn't worry for at least another twenty-four hours.

"Why are you concerned? I presume he's over twenty-one."

"He came back from overseas yesterday. He said he was going to the supermarket, and he didn't come home."

"Where overseas was he?"

"I don't really know. He's in the army."

"So, why not talk to his commanding officer. Perhaps he knows where he is?"

"He's part of Army Intelligence. They won't tell me anything. There's a number to call and then someone rings back. I called. No one has rung back."

That's probably not a good sign.

"I need to tell you something, Mr O'Sullivan." Time to deal my meagre cards. "Your son rang me this morning. We are trying to track his location through the limited information he could give us before he had to go."

Mr O'Sullivan rubbed his face with both hands. "He's all right?"

"He didn't say otherwise. He did say he doesn't know where he is."

"How did he get there? What happened? He was just going to the supermarket."

"What supermarket?"

"Countdown."

"Which Countdown?"

"The one just along from here."

"Maidstone," I said, quietly. "Okay, they have cameras. I'll see if I can get someone to give me access."

Sonya. I'd talk to Sonya.

"Are you sure he's all right?"

"As far as I could tell. He asked for my help," I said. If he's military but asking me, not his unit, then there are more questions. Hard questions that would upset the unwell looking man in front of me. I collected my thoughts and found a question that might help. "What time did he go to the supermarket?"

Mr O'Sullivan thought for a few seconds. "Before dinner. He was getting me ice-cream." He stopped speaking and looked at me. "It's a five-minute drive. He left home at five-fifteen."

I wrote that in my notebook. It was good to have some idea of times for the security video. "That'll help."

"Why didn't he ring home?"

"I can't answer that, Mr O'Sullivan. All I know is, he rang me." And that to me means he knows this is bad, and someone wants something from him. "Leave it with me. I have some contacts and resources that might get us some answers." I gave him a reassuring smile. "I'll do my best to find Luke and bring him home safely. Did you bring a recent photo?"

"Yes. The lady I talked with told me you'd need one." He reached into his jacket pocket and handed me a photograph."

"Thank you, this is great. When was it taken?"

"Two months ago, overseas."

"Okay." Recent is good.

"Thank you, Ronnie." He stood and turned to leave.

"Do you think this is related to his work?"

"That's a possibility. Unless it's a kidnap for ransom situation. Have you received any demands?" I walked with him to the door.

"No."

"If there's no ransom demand, and he's not off with a friend, then I'd hazard a guess that this is somehow connected to his job."

"Bring him home Ronnie. I'd like to spend what time I have left with my son."

"I'll be in touch. If you hear anything, call me." I picked up a card from the front counter and pressed it into his hand. "That's got my cell phone number on it."

I watched Terry O'Sullivan close the door behind him as he left, then I turned to Steph.

She was still working. Sometimes it takes a bit of digging to trace people who own P.O. Boxes.

I picked up the phone from the desk and dialled star fifty-two. A robotic voice said, "The last number that called was private."

Oh well, it was worth a shot.

Steph must've seen me with the phone. "I tried that before."

"How's the search coming?"

"Shell company, owned by another shell company, owned by ..."

"Another shell company," I finished. "Like a shell game on steroids."

"Exactly. Someone doesn't want people finding out

who they are."

"Could it be a state?"

"Yes."

I sat at my desk and did my own digging. This time I attempted to poke a wee bit into Luke O'Sullivan's military records. No doubt flags flew as I came up against blocks and sanitised/sketchy army records. He was intelligence. Who did I know who could talk to me about Luke O'Sullivan? Bill. I needed to reach out to Bill.

I scrolled through my cell phone contact list until I found Bill. Then tapped in his phone number. He took a while to answer. Didn't surprise me. They were probably scrambling to find their man.

"Ronnie, can I ring you back?"

"Nope. This is about O'Sullivan."

There was a hiss, a click, then a door shut, and Bill's voice returned. "What do you know about him?"

"I know he's missing."

"And?"

"Your turn ..."

"He didn't check in last night or this morning."

"Why was he off-base if he's that important?"

"He was visiting his dad; the man is ill, liver cancer."

That explained the jaundiced appearance.

"We need to meet," I said.

"I think we do," replied Bill. "Briscoes, kitchen appliances. Ten minutes."

"See you there."

I hung up, put my cell phone in my jacket pocket, and

took Romeo's lead from the hook next to my desk. He stood and ambled over so I could clip it to his harness.

"You're coming shopping," I told him. "Best behaviour please."

I swear he nodded before giving my leg a nudge.

"How long will you be?" Steph asked, she didn't look up. Her eyes remained on the screen in front of her as she worked.

"Not more than half an hour," I said. "Bring you back coffee?"

"And a cake," she said.

"And a cake."

Chapter Four:
[Ronnie: Army Intelligence]

Romeo peed on a tree in the small park between our office and the railway station. When he was done we walked down the ramp to the subway that led under the tracks to Briscoes. I loved walking with him. It was reassuring having him glance up at me every few steps. "Good boy, Romeo. You're a very good boy." His chest puffed up, and he held his head a little higher as he strutted along next to me.

We followed the concrete path around to the entrance to the carpark. I scanned for anything out of the ordinary before we crossed to the footpath by the store. The automatic doors opened. Romeo and I stepped into the interior. Always felt a bit dark in the store to start with, and it took a second for my eyes to adjust.

A sales assistant called out from behind a register, "Hi Ronnie, hi Romeo." Romeo looked over and wagged his long thin tail.

"Hi, Alice," I said with a smile.

"Can I help with anything?"

"Not today. Just browsing really. Thinking about replacing my toaster sometime soon," I said.

"Let me know if you need a hand, Ronnie."

"Will do."

Romeo and I walked past the checkouts and into the

store itself, turned right, and moved slowly to the kitchen appliance area. Browsing. No rush. Just a woman and her greyhound looking at kitchen stuff. Nothing to see here. Romeo nudged me when I paused for too long in front of anything. Hounds like to keep moving or sleep. Standing around isn't his favourite thing. Over the top of a stand of kitchen beaters, I saw Bill. I made my way past him to the toasters. He followed, casually.

"Why the secret squirrel bizzo?" I said, while looking at the price of a toaster that I quite liked the look of, although at two-hundred and ninety-nine dollars, I could live without it.

"We've got one of ours missing."

"I know."

"Why are you involved in this?"

"Good to see you too, Bill," I said with a smile. "Can you believe the price of this?" I pointed to the crazy expensive toaster.

"It'll be on sale in a week for fifty-bucks," he replied.

We chuckled. It's Briscoes; of course it would.

"Luke's father came to see me," I said, checking the price of a similar toaster and finding it half as dear, but still ridiculous. "He's worried."

"We're all concerned. What do you know?"

"I know Luke hasn't called you." That was true. If he had, they'd know something, and Bill said he missed both his check-ins. I wasn't prepared to say that Luke spoke to me.

"Why do I think you know more than that?"

23

I shrugged. "Question for you, Bill, is there a reason why Luke wouldn't want to contact you, or someone else from his unit?" I let the implications of my question surround him.

Bill's expression soured. "I don't know."

"I think you do. You need to clean your house, Bill. It feels like there is something wrong there."

"What about this toaster?" Bill said, pointing to a black enamel four-slice.

"That's nice," I said, inspecting the multitude of buttons on the front. Complicated. "Where was Luke before he came home?"

"You know I can't tell you that."

"Is it relevant?"

"Perhaps."

I scoured my memory banks. Where were we active? Everywhere wasn't helpful. Luke said something about goat's milk cheese on an invoice. How did that fit? Greece? That general area? Or he's being held in a random place with no connection to wherever he was overseas.

"The Balkans?"

"You know I can't say," he said, and nodded with the slightest movement of his head.

"Greece was beautiful last time I was there," I said. It truly was. I opted to mention the country that was at the southernmost part of the Balkan peninsula.

"I always liked Montenegro myself."

And Albania sat between Greece and Montenegro.

Thank you, Bill.

"It's a very special place."

"If you hear from him again, let me know."

"There is no reason for me to hear from him. I have no connection to the man. Find the problem, Bill." I looked at the patient hound, who huffed quietly. That was as close as he ever got to expressing his displeasure at standing still. "Come on Romeo, let's go." Nothing here but lies.

Romeo and I stopped into the bookshop. Emily was shelving books at the back of the shop. A couple of customers were browsing the children's book section.

I called out, "Hi, Emily!"

She turned and smiled. "Hello, Ronnie. Hello, Romeo."

We passed the customers who both smiled and asked to pat the hound. He was delighted with the extra attention. It slowed my progress to Emily. She continued to work until we joined her.

"Busy today?" I asked.

We walked back to the counter together. Emily went behind the counter and looked at the daybook. I stayed on the public side with Romeo. Her finger traced her own writing before she looked up and said, "The morning was busy, yes. That is good."

"Very good." The bottom line will appreciate the sales. I saw a frown flicker in her eyes. "What's the matter?"

Her finger was still on some text in the daybook. I can read upside down and it was a note to remind Emily to tell me about an email.

"An email arrived this morning. I do not know what to do with it."

"Can I see it?"

"Yes. My computer is under the counter."

"Okay. Pass it to me, please."

She reached under the counter and picked up the laptop. "You want him to stay with you?" I tipped my head at Romeo.

She smiled. "Yes."

I walked him around the counter to her and dropped his lead.

"Stay with Emily, Romeo." He didn't even glance at me as I walked away. I took the laptop to the vacant desk at the back, sat down, and opened the lid. The shop email account was already signed in and an email was open on the screen. A quick glance told me it was the email in question. I read it carefully. Then read it again. It wasn't our usual type of email. No wonder Emily didn't know what to do with it.

Kia ora,

I felt I must write to you as you are the only bookshop in New Zealand who stocks this series, and I am unable to locate the author. Please, forward this to her if you can:

You are a powerful writer, and you create strong worlds. It has taken me nearly three weeks after finish-

ing Vaporbyte to calm down enough to take the uncommon action of writing to an author.

I am still very angry at your total breach of the "social contract" which writers have with readers. As readers, we allow writers into our personal mental space to create worlds of imagination, and in order for us to allow you into that very private space, our mutual 'contract' is that you will not breach that Trust.

In your Byte series you created a strange and powerful figure in Ellie. In the final volume you set her and US up for her retirement. We understood, even though we were sad to see her go. Then you totally breached our Trust by killing her off. I doubt you have any idea just how severely you wrenched our emotions. I am assuming ignorance, rather than arrogance, hence this email.

I thank you for the Byte series. However, I no longer trust you, so I won't be reading or purchasing any of your new books.

Nga mihi

Sue

I clicked on raw source and found the origin ISP. I forwarded the email and a note with the ISP typed in it, to myself. What was it with today and messages?

I closed the email program, shut the laptop lid, and strolled back to the front of the shop. I handed Emily the laptop and picked up the dog's lead from the floor.

"It's okay Emily, I'll handle that email."

"It was strange?"

"Yes, it was. The reader seems to have confused creative non-fiction with fiction. I'm going to have a look at some books," I said, and took Romeo down the back to the crime wall. I reached up and pulled a copy of Vaporbyte from the shelf and read the blurb. Why hadn't I noticed the name of the main character before?

There was no way these books were all written after Ellie Iverson's death. Twelve books in five years? Hardly seemed likely. Perhaps Crockett could shed some light on the author and the subject of the series. He knew Iverson, whereas I'd never met her. He might know something about whoever the person is who wrote the books.

As for the crazy fan email, I'm sure Ellie thought she *was* going to retire and didn't expect to be blown to smithereens. I pushed the book back into its rightful spot and wondered how anyone could write with such detail about the life of an FBI agent. Guess there were interviews and access to people who knew her. Perhaps not for the last book though. My understanding was that the entire team perished in the drone strike. All except Crockett. He didn't seem like the type of person to blab for the hours it would take to get this story together, and I doubted he knew it all anyway. Guess that's why the genre is creative non-fiction. I pushed the email and the series out of my mind.

Emily was serving customers. Romeo nudged me and huffed. He was bored. I wasn't moving fast enough for him.

I walked slowly around the shop with the dog, browsing titles, and waiting for Emily to finish. As the last customer left, I joined her at the counter.

"Has Crockett been in recently?"

She smiled but continued writing in the daybook. When she finished writing she carefully put the pen back in the cup on the counter and made eye contact.

"He brought me a hot chocolate. Then he talked to Jenn." She frowned for a moment before picking up the next recent memory. "He had his coffee with me."

"Is he picking you up later?"

"Yes."

"You always smile when Crockett is the subject," I said with a grin. "It suits you."

Emily frowned for a split-second, then her smile returned. "Crockett is a nice man."

"Yes, he is." I remembered a conversation about cameras. "Is there anything written in the daybook about a technician coming in to install cameras?"

Emily turned back one page reading carefully. Her finger traced word by word over sentences. "A man from Crockett's company," she said without looking up. She looked from the book to the calendar on the wall beside the counter. "Today. At three."

"Who will be here with you?"

She read the entry again. "Jenn."

Good to know they could organise things without too much drama. Perhaps I should get Crocket and Jenn to take over the planning of Donald and Enzo's wedding. I smiled. "We better get back to the office. Bye Emily."

Emily waved as we passed the large front window.

Memories of the Emily I used to know tugged at me. She'd lost so much. Emily and I used to do late night surveillance gigs, regularly. We'd had some fun on those long nights. I missed my friend Emily. The last time I'd seen that Emily was during a dangerous job when I threw her a handgun and her muscle memory kicked in, like I believed it would.

Chapter Five:
[Ronnie: Exodus]

I settled behind my desk and retrieved the peculiar book-shop email. I decided I'd get that out of the way before getting on with finding Luke O'Sullivan. I pinged the ISP and watched as the results appeared. Upper Hutt. The person used a well-known, but dreadful carrier, and lived in Upper Hutt. Interesting. The email was really nothing to do with the shop or Emily, and I couldn't help her find the author. No, that's not true. I could. That's what I do. I didn't *want* to help her find the author.

Dead is dead. If the woman didn't understand that the stories she read were true crime, albeit written in a creative non-fiction manner, then she wasn't super in touch with reality. No one needs that in their lives.

"What's got you smiling?" Steph asked, setting a cup of coffee on my desk.

"Thanks for that," I replied, with a nod at the steaming cup. "I'm sorry I forget to grab you a coffee and cake."

"I thought you might've been distracted. Now what's happening here that you got you smiling?

"The bookshop received an odd email from a reader. I've decided not to pursue it because it's ridiculous non-sense."

"Show me?"

I moved sideways so Steph could read the email on the

screen.

"Reality and that woman seem conflicted," she replied. "That's true crime, that series?"

"Sure is."

"What the hell is she on about with that social contract malarkey?"

"Another break from reality ... no doubt she's sent similar emails to Stephen King?"

Steph's laughter bounced across the desk. "Hope the author is unreachable; could be a *Misery* situation developing."

I picked up the coffee mug and took a sip. "This is good. What is it?"

"Gregg's hazelnut." She perched on the edge of my desk. "I'm still digging into that P.O. Box. It has more layers than Donald and Enzo's wedding cake."

"That's suspicious."

Steph agreed with a nod. "Right, back to it."

A few minutes later I took my coffee into my private meeting room down the hall. Carefully, I closed the door behind me and flipped the lights on.

I stood still for a moment and breathed in the scent of candle wax, incense, and warmth. Yes, warmth has a smell. It's comforting and pleasant. The opposite to the smells surrounding the retirement home Nana lived in; that smelt of lost hope, lavender, and death. One last deep breath got me moving. I removed candles and a map from the cabinets that lined the walls. This time I chose a map of the entire Wellington Region. Not the easiest thing to spread on one table. I pushed both big tables together then spread the map carefully, smoothing out the creases as I went. I leaned over to make sure I could still reach the middle comfortably. No sense having the huge map over the tables if I couldn't hold my pendulum over the map. Satisfied I could reach, I opened the windows. No breeze. That was good.

One by one, I lit the candles and positioned them at the four corners. Quietly, I called the corners and asked for spirits help to locate Luke O'Sullivan. I held my tiger's eye pendulum between my thumb and index finger and let it swing at will for a moment. When it settled and stopped, I asked my first question.

"Show me yes."

The pendulum swung clockwise in big fat circles.

"Stop."

It stopped dead. Hanging straight down.

"Show me no."

The pendulum swung out from my fingers in a straight line and back.

"Stop."

It stopped dead.

"Show me seeking."

The pendulum swung in lazy circles anti-clockwise."

"Stop."

It stopped with a jerk.

"Thank you. Now, help me find Luke O'Sullivan."

I moved my hand to the bottom right edge of the map and waited. The pendulum swung in large slow circles, anti-clockwise. Tugging my hand as it reached the outermost limits of the circle, I moved ever so slightly in the direction it dictated. The process continued until my arm felt as if it no longer belonged to me. Over Newtown the circles dropped from large slow circles to smaller tighter circles but were still anti-clockwise. Near Wilson Street and Riddiford Street in Newtown, the pendulum suddenly stopped and reversed its swing, making the circles tighter and more urgent.

"Is he there?"

The pendulum stopped dead at the intersection. Then swung a clear wide yes.

"Thank you for your help." I placed the pendulum on the map and watched as it rolled to the Riddiford Street intersection and stop with its point facing Wilson Street.

That was the location. No doubt about it.

I packed up the room. Carefully snuffing out the candles last. I gave it a few minutes before I closed the windows. With one last check of the room, I left.

Back at my desk, I wrote Riddiford and Wilson on a piece of memo paper, and opened Safari. I looked for restaurants in the vicinity. There were a few. One in particular had a menu that suggested eastern European and Mediterranean cuisine, and a name that had me shaking my head in disbelief. I wrote the address on the same piece of memo cube. *Manger* could easily be autocorrected to Manager. The mail Luke found all had the word Manager, so maybe it was supposed to be *Manger*. Maybe it was Manger, and his brain autocorrected his eyes.

"Hey Steph, fancy lunch in town?"

Her head swivelled so she could make eye-contact with me. "Depends where."

"A place called *Manger*."

"Really, it's called *Manger?*"

"That's what it says."

"What kind of food? Do they serve hay? Is straw a food group?"

"Don't you have a lot of questions?"

Steph laughed. "You've been known to have shit ideas when it comes to lunch and dinner. Don't know if eating at a place called *Manger* is going to improve your hit rate!"

Rude, but true.

"The menu says, Mediterranean, Eastern European. No mention of hay or straw."

"Might be all right."

I rolled my eyes. "Free lunch, yes or no?"

"Yes."

Romeo nudged me. "You too, boy," I replied giving his bony head a pat. "Got any further with the P.O. Box?"

"Not really. I've never come across something so well-hidden. But now that we know it's *Manger* not manager, I can look for the owners of the restaurant on the New Zealand Companies Register."

"I'll make some notes then we'll hit the road."

"Sounds good. I'll let Jenn know we're out for the afternoon."

Steph rang Jenn and I made some notes in the O'Sullivan file. That was when I heard it, the tap-tap-tap of a cane on the stairs. My heart lurched. Surely not! Steph's eyes widened as they met mine across the room. Romeo was on his feet at the main door, head cocked, ears akimbo. I knew that look. She was here.

Good grief. This was my sanctuary. That could not be Nana tapping her way up the stairs! Shit. I forgot I was supposed to see Nana. I brought this on myself.

"No! Can't be," Steph said, disbelief filling her words. "Not Nana, not here!"

There was a wooden knock on the door. The handle turned.

"Romeo, darling boy," crooned Nana. Her bony hand petted his head.

Like the well-mannered gentleman he is, he waited for her to enter the office door, and escorted her to my desk. Bustling in behind her were Ester and Frankie. They completed the trio that I referred to as *The Cronies of Doom*. Ester was a former police officer who worked with my grandfather. She was a canny old thing.

I rose to my feet. "Nana, what a lovely surprise. Would you like to sit under the window on the couch?" I pointed over to the comfortable seating area. Anything to get her away from my desk. I certainly did not want Ester near my desk.

"That's very kind, Veronica, dear." She turned to the oldies behind her. "What do you think, girls?"

They nodded. The about shuffle began. Steph tried

sliding down in her chair to avoid eye contact. It was too late.

"Is that you, Stephanie?" Nana said, waving her cane toward Steph's desk. "Do come and meet the girls."

She looked at me for help, I smiled and shrugged. She glared.

I gave a wide-eyed innocent look and shrugged again.

What could I do?

Steph's glare intensified as she drew a line under her chin with her thumb.

"Steph's just leaving, Nana," I said.

Steph mouthed the words 'Thank you' and rushed out the door calling, "Lovely to see you, Nana. Next time. Sorry, got to rush. Busy, busy."

"Mask!" I yelled after her.

She ducked back, leaned over the front desk, and pulled the drawer out. Her fingers rummaged around for several seconds then with a huff she straightened up. A mask dangled from her hand. "I'll be back."

"I might be here," I replied.

"Veronica," Nana said.

The door closed. I took a deep breath. Be nice. It's my fault she's here. I should've gone to see her. I touched Romeo's head as I stepped around him and took a seat. "How can I help Nana?"

"You need to try on your dress."

Panic surged. Dress? I didn't see any bags or boxes. Three old ladies. Three sensible old-lady handbags. Nothing that looked like it would hold a dress.

"What dress?"

"For goodness sake, Veronica. Keep up. You *are* the best woman. What were you planning on wearing to the wedding? Jeans?" Nana tutted her disapproval. The cronies joined in.

Just what I needed. Old people tutting in surround sound. I'd be delighted to be able to wear jeans and Doc Martens to the bloody wedding. If we could throw in a flannel shirt and a baseball cap, I'd be in heaven. But it's not my wedding. A loud internal laugh took me by surprise.

"Veronica!"

"Sorry, Nana, my mind is elsewhere."

"When are you going to try the dress on?"

"Tonight?"

"Good. It is at my apartment. I will expect you after dinner. Don't disappointment me this time, Veronica."

"Yes, Nana." I smiled. "Did you really come into town to remind me to try on the frock?"

"Not exactly, dear."

Here we go.

"Don't tell me there is another mystery at the village?"

I scanned their wrinkly faces and noted immediately the sparkle in their aged and faded eyes. Nothing caused that like sticking their beaks into somebody else's business.

"A wee one. The girls and I ..."

And nothing good *ever* came from a sentence that began like that. "Nana ... I've got a lot on the books right now."

"We just need you to look something up on the inter-webs for us." Nana smiled. Her thin lips stretched wide over her false teeth. A terrifying sight. "It doesn't have to be you dear. Jennifer or Stephanie could help us."

Over their cold dead bodies, or mine, if I suggested it.

"I'll get my laptop and you can tell me what I need to look up." Best to just help. At least that way I'd find out what they were up to and could potentially head it off should that be required.

From the other side of the room *The Cronies of Doom* seemed like a group of innocent oldies. To the uninitiated they were. I knew better. Ester the former-police woman was still capable of detecting. My Nana was a career po-lice officer's wife, and she took the role very seriously. Frankie stood for absolutely no rubbish from anyone. I wasn't sure, but I think she was a headmistress once upon a time. That was the vibe. On their own they were quite manageable. As a trio, it was a different story. The lined faces and washed-out eyes looked at me as I re-turned with my laptop and settled back in the chair.

"Now, what am I doing?" I glanced over the screen at Nana.

"We think someone famous is living in Upper Hutt," Frankie said.

"You're kidding me? You want me to cyber stalk some-one?"

"Oh no, dear. Not stalk someone. Goodness. Young people these days." She flapped a bony wing at me. "Just tell us if they are in Upper Hutt," Nana responded.

An audible sigh escaped before I could check it. "Right then, who is this poor person?"

"Michaela Carlisse," Nana said.

"I don't think she uses that name, June," Ester said with quiet authority.

I glanced at Nana, waiting for fireworks. She just loved to be corrected.

Nothing.

What alternate hell is this?

"Should I search for the Carlisse woman?" My fingers were poised above the keyboard, browser window open and ready.

Ester spoke, "Try Michaela Carlisse, but when you don't find her, please, try Michaela Kennedy."

That took seconds. "Sorry ladies, no such person has shown up in a preliminary search."

Didn't mean she wasn't around, but I wasn't digging deeper without a jolly good reason.

"That's disappointing," Nana said. "You're quite sure?"

"Yes. Nothing."

"Goodness we must've been mistaken," Frankie said. "That's not like us."

My stomach sank. They weren't going to drop it.

"We shall continue our investigation," Nana said. "The old-fashioned way."

Ester smiled. Her lips taut over her yellowed teeth. "A little leg work won't hurt us."

"Best you three be careful and don't harangue anyone,"

I warned.

Nana smirked then changed tack and projected the sweetest voice possible, "Veronica, dear, how much haranguing could we three do?"

"I know you, Nana. Be nice."

"You'll be over after dinner to try the dress on, Veronica, won't you?"

"Yes, Nana."

Romeo stretched, the tags on his collar jangled. "You too Romeo, you're always invited," Nana said. He ambled over and encouraged Nana to rub his ears. "What a very good boy. You could teach Veronica a thing or two." With that, Nana rose slowly and motioned to her cronies. "We'll probably need to stop by the café for a cup of tea before we start our investigation."

"Good idea, June," Frankie said. "I'm parched."

Ester echoed the sentiment.

I escorted them out of the office and watched their measured descent of the stairs. Steph appeared in time to wave them off as they exited the door at the bottom.

"What are they up to?" Steph asked, as we went back inside and closed the door.

"No good. They're stalking some poor person, or at least trying to find out if this person is in Upper Hutt."

"I feel sorry for whoever it is."

"Me too."

We resumed our tasks at our respective desks.

"There's no business registered called *Manger*," Steph said. "They must be registered under a different name."

"Not making it easy are they?" I replied, adding the finishing touches to some notes to go with an invoice.

"I'll keep trying the P.O. Box, and do a few searches to see if I can cobble together enough information to find the company behind the restaurant."

"Great. I've got to write a report for a client who is not going to be happy with my findings." Her husband is a right scoundrel.

An hour disappeared like a minute.

The main phone rang. Neither of us moved to answer it.

My fingers froze above the keyboard when a male voice came from the answer phone and said one word. "Exodus."

I knew I couldn't get to the phone before the call ended, so I took a breath, picked up my cell phone, and rang Ben.

He answered faster than I expected. "Did you get a call?"

"Yes. Did it sound automated to you?" Ben asked.

"Yes. I'm coming to you."

"You know where I'll be."

The call ended.

Yes, I did know. We had a prearranged meeting place for calls like that one.

I unlocked my desk drawer. From behind a panel in the back I removed my handgun, which I kept in a paddle holster, and two spare magazines. I shoved them into my backpack before Steph noticed. Then I added other bits and pieces, including a tactical torch and a tactical pen. I gave Romeo a big pat. "Stay with Steph. I'll be back." I glanced at the memo on the desk, then picked it up and put it in my pocket.

Steph was at the main desk with her finger poised over the flashing message light on the phone base. "Do I delete?"

"Yes."

"Bugger about lunch," she said. "Keep in touch." She waggled the fingers of her left hand toward Romeo. "He's fine with us. I can drop him home to Donald if you're not back by close of business."

"Thank you." My hand wrapped around the door handle. Footsteps ran up the stairs beyond the door. I twisted the knob and pulled the door open as the footfalls stopped.

"Ready?" Crockett said, glancing past me to Steph. "Hey, Steph." She smiled in return.

"You too?" I asked.

Crockett nodded. Whatever this is, it must be big. I turned to Steph. "The new client, if anything crops up let me know ..."

"Of course. Take care out there," Steph replied. "We'll handle the day."

I motioned to Crockett to follow me and hurried to the storeroom.

"We need to ditch our cell phones," I said. "Turn yours off and hand it to me." I walked into the storeroom with both cell phones in my hand.

I located a metal box on the last shelf at the back of the room. The box was big enough to hold several laptops as well as smaller devices. I opened the box and placed the cell phones inside.

"Faraday cage?" Crockett asked.

"Yes."

From a case a few shelves below, I removed three cell phones. "These phones are registered," I said, handing one to Crockett. "But not to anyone that actually exists. Don't turn it on here."

I shoved one in my pocket and another in my backpack.

"You have iPhones as burners ..." Crockett said.

"They're secure." From another case I took four Air-Tags and dropped them into a zippered compartment inside my pack. They're handy to have and they were synced to my chosen phone. "All three iPhones have the other phones numbers already in the contacts, but that's all. No one else's numbers are kept stored in these phones. They're all on separate plans. Every few weeks we use them, during cases, just so they appear to be regular phones. They're never turned on near or in this building. Sometimes they're walked past it though, because if we completely avoided the area it would look suss."

"Smart."

"Hopefully. Give me a minute to talk to Steph, then we'll leave."

Crockett nodded. I firmly closed the storeroom door. Crockett waited at the top of the stairs while I went back to the main office.

"Steph?"

"Yes," she replied from the back of the room.

"Can you keep an eye on Nana. Let her know I've been called away on a job."

"Yes." She narrowed her eyes at me. "What else?"

"We're going dark. My phone is in the cage. I have the spares."

None of us had the numbers for those phones on our regular phones.

"Emergency protocol?"

"Yes."

"Are we starting with day zero or one?"

"Zero."

Day zero meant any necessary communication was achieved through the public discussion on the bookshop Facebook page posts. Day one: the comms moved to WhatsApp. Day two any communication was via a community page. And on it went. Always switching the method by which we contacted each other. It wasn't foolproof, but it helped. For anything that required screeds of information we used the draft folder of the *Wherefore Art Thou* email program. If you don't send an email there is no electronic trail. Handy.

Her expression changed to reflect a modicum of concern. "How long do you expect to be gone?"

"No idea."

Romeo ambled over for a pat. "You're a very good boy. Listen to Steph." I reached into the drawer of the main desk and removed a couple of disposable face masks.

I closed the door behind me as I left. Took a breath.

Then smiled at Crockett.

"Ready?" he asked.

"Let's go." I glanced at my watch as we walked down the stairs. Two minutes to cross the road and get on the next southbound train that should be waiting at the station. I doubted we'd make it. There's always another train. Only twenty-five minutes until the next one.

Chapter Six:
[Ronnie:Petone Police Station]

Crockett's car was parked out front. I was used to seeing his Harley not his car.

"My car," he said.

"I see that," I replied. "Drive to Heretaunga station and park your car somewhere."

"We're not driving?"

"Nope. Train." I handed him a face mask. "Make sure you wear it."

"Thanks," he said, dropping it on the passenger seat. "Going to Ben?" Crockett turned the ignition key.

"Yes. Get a move on. The next train is leaving in twenty minutes. Board at Heretaunga. I'll be in the last carriage."

I checked the traffic as I approached the crossing. I crossed the north and south bound lanes without a pause, hurried over to the railway station and skirted around the ticket office to await the train. Plenty of time to buy a ticket, but it was easier to do that onboard so I wouldn't appear on the ticket office camera. I hooked the mask over one ear, then the other, and adjusted the fit around my nose.

The wait seemed impossibly long. Not many people were gathered for the next train to Wellington. I leaned on the station house wall.

When the train arrived, people spewed forth from the

doors of all four carriages. I walked to the last carriage, but the door was closed. I pressed the button to open the door at the very back of the carriage. As I stepped inside, I checked for anyone taking notice. No one did. Most times commuters kept to themselves.

I chose my seat, turned left, and walked to the very back on the opposite side of the south facing carriage. Less chance of being seen in that seat. Except for Trentham Station. The Wellington-bound train used platform one, that was on the left. I gave an internal shrug. Masks were handy and surveilling someone on a train was hard. If someone spotted me from a platform then they were already looking, but they weren't on the train. Good luck to them. I'd see everyone getting on at subsequent stations, and spot anyone who checked me out. The train lurched away from Upper Hutt. No crew came through. The few people in the carriage were at the other end and engrossed in their phones. Wallaceville came and went, then Trentham.

I heard the announcement for Heretaunga. As the train stopped, I saw Crockett waiting. He boarded and slid into the seat directly in front of me. I could see the blue from his mask. Most stops would be on our right as the train travelled toward Wellington. Our seats kept us out of the view of randoms on the platforms. As annoying as face masks could be, they were pretty handy if you didn't want to be recognised. The train crew-person came through just after Heretaunga. As she approached from the other end of the carriage, I leaned forward and said,

"Ticket to Wellington."

Crockett gave a slight nod.

We purchased our tickets separately. My plan was to disembark at Ava and have Crockett do the same at Petone.

At Manor Park, I switched on my phone. Then I reached down to the bag at my feet, bringing me closer to Crockett. I whispered, "Turn your phone on at Waterloo."

Crockett replied with a very quiet, "Okay."

"I'm getting off the train at Ava. You stay put until Petone. I'll text you once I'm off with a location."

He nodded.

There was no one near us. The closest commuters were at the other end of the carriage. All of them were on their phones, earbuds in situ, face masks on. No one even glanced toward us. I spent the next few stops watching passengers come and go. No one noteworthy appeared. No one fidgety or unsure. Several older women, probably off out for lunch and a spot of shopping in the city. A few university students, or maybe they were Weltec. Students all the same. At Ava, I disembarked without looking back. I crossed the railway bridge and walked toward Petone. After walking two-hundred metres, I texted Crockett, deciding he would be clear of the train and platform at that point and needing direction. I had a longer walk than him.

Me: Meet at the old police station on Jackson.
Phone 2/Crockett: Okay

Me: Text when you arrive. I'm a little further away than you.

I shoved the phone in my jacket pocket and walked. Keeping my mask on made me look like a good citizen in these post-COVID, pre-next pandemic, times. Jackson Street came up faster than expected. Its arrival heralded by a hum of traffic and people. The street buzzed with life and that life spilled down the side streets and met me on my approach. I turned toward the police station and the phone in my pocket vibrated. I looked at the screen.

Phone 2/Crockett: Here
Me: Go around the back. You should see Ben waiting.

Weaving in and out of people on the footpath, I walked quickly to the nearest pedestrian crossing. A couple of minutes later I was walking down the side of the police station.

Ben and Crockett were in one of the back rooms. I saw their heads through the window before I opened the door. I pulled my mask off.

"We good?" Ben asked.

"Think so," I replied, dropping my pack onto a chair. I took the third phone from the pack and handed it to Ben. "Where's yours?"

"Off, and in my pocket."

"When we get a chance we should put your phone in the cage at the office."

"Now what?" Crockett asked.

"I was hoping one of you would know. Do you?"

Crockett smiled. "This is your town, Ronnie. I'm the outsider."

That wasn't a denial.

"We're off the usual grid. Whatever this is, we won't hear about it through regular channels," Ben said. "If the three of us received the same message, then something bad has happened. I wonder who else got that message?"

I sat down and studied Crockett for a moment. "You came to me, why?"

"When I went back into the field, MacKinnon told me if I ever get an *Exodus* message to go straight to you."

Of course, he did.

"Did he tell you what it means?"

He shook his head. "Not really, just that I should go to you."

Then it was up to me to tell him. "Someone, or possibly an entire operation, has been compromised."

"What does it have to do with us three?"

"I can only speculate." I fiddled with the mask on the table in front of me. "Could be something we are working on, or one or more of us are compromised."

Ben interjected, "Or someone we know and if they talk we're screwed."

Ben and I made eye-contact. It was as if I could read the word *'Genesis'* in his blue eyes. Couldn't be that, surely. Crockett wasn't part of it. Ben and I were though. *Genesis* was an operation that collected and analysed intelligence surrounding and pointing to weapons of mass destruction, and it included the development of bioweapons. There were a lot of recruited intelligence officers involved from various countries, but no single state ran the operation. It was a worldwide clandestine operation that fed intelligence to various countries if required, but usually, it dealt with the threat using tactical surgical strikes. It wasn't just analysts and collectors, there were also special forces teams. I didn't know where the money came from to fund a wide-spread and tactical organisation, but there always seemed to be plenty. Ben and I were collectors.

"I had a new job start with my tradies last week," Crockett said. "Installing more high-tech surveillance gear."

Ben nodded. "I did some data recovery from an embassy two days ago. Went like clockwork."

"That's all?" I moved in the chair. "Nothing else happening?" It was starting to look like O'Sullivan was the trigger.

"The tradie job is part of a long running operation. Could be something."

"Then you and Art would've got the *Exodus* message, not us three," I said, waving my finger between us. "I got a new client this morning. Have a feeling it could be related. We have a missing man and he's military intelligence. His father is my client."

Except he's not missing, because I'm pretty sure I know where he is.

"Sounds promising," Crockett said. "Who sent the message?"

I shook my head. "Don't know."

He leaned back in his chair. "MacKinnon?"

"Wasn't his voice, but he was my first guess. I think it was an automated message."

Crockett took the phone I gave him out of his pocket and looked at it. "Can we contact MacKinnon?"

"Yes. But not using our phones. There's a phone here."

He frowned. Ben stood, walked to a cupboard at the back of the room and opened it. He stepped aside to reveal a telephone on a small desk within the cupboard.

A cupboard phone. So very *Get Smart*.

"Anyone know his number?" Crockett asked.

I walked over to the phone, lifted the receiver and punched MacKinnon's number into the keypad then pushed the speaker button. The phone dialled, then rang. No one answered. The call rang off. I hung up and tried his home number. No one answered.

"His son?" Ben suggested.

Would be a lot easier to call him if I had my mobile phone with me. I saw James MacKinnon's phone number in a file once. I recalled the image and punched the number into the cupboard phone. Again, the phone rang and rang. This time it went to voice mail, so I left a message.

"Hey, Jay, got time for a coffee? It's been a while. Call me back on this number. I'm free for the next hour."

I hung up. Silence filled the crevices of the sunny room. Both MacKinnon's unreachable. The explanation

53

could be innocent. The only other person who sprang to mind was Chandler. I didn't like it and wanted another option.

"Who else?" I asked. "Please don't say Chandler. That man is the absolute last resort." He wouldn't take my call anyway. But, I knew, he'd take Crockett's. Chandler was an evil son-of-a-bitch and a full-on nightmare. We disliked each other with equal venom. I got his former boss fired which kind of made me the king maker for Chandler. He's the head of NZSIS. Or as I prefer to call him, the dickhead.

Ben and Crockett sat quietly. I could see the cogs turning. Eventually Ben said, "I might know someone. But, then again, I might not."

"Is it worth trying?"

"Yes." Ben walked to the phone and made the call. He put the phone on speaker. We listened to the ringing. And ringing. At the last gasp, a woman answered. "Who are you?" She sounded American.

"Ben Reynolds."

"Why are you calling me?"

"Thought you might've heard something?"

"I hear lots of things, Mr Reynolds. Be more specific."

Ben looked at me and mouthed the word, *Exodus*. I nodded.

"*Exodus*," he said quietly.

"I don't know what you're talking about," the woman said with a sigh. "And if I did, I wouldn't be talking on a telephone with someone I can't verify."

"Can we meet?"

"I don't think that's wise."

"Oscar mike?"

"Affirmative."

The phone clicked and beeped.

"Who was that?" I asked.

"Karen Osborne, CIA."

I sat back at the small table. "She knows something is going down. Otherwise, why is she on the move?"

"Be nice if we knew what the something is," Crockett said. He spun the phone in front of him. "Are we going to ground, or hunting, or are we the prey?"

"Your guess is as good as ours."

Chapter Seven:
[Ronnie: Now what?]

The sun slipped behind the buildings on Jackson Street as Ben and I went in search of food. We left Crockett at the police station. He was safe there. I explored that thought for a spilt second. He was safe there. We were out in the open. Maybe I should've sent him for food.

My mind turned to Nana. She was not going to be happy. I'd already let her down once by ducking out on her morning wedding planning session. Now I'd really be in the doghouse for not trying the frock on tonight. No doubt Donald would be a miffed as well.

Ben tugged my hand as he led me into a bakery. I'd forgotten we were even holding hands. The smells of hot mince pies, seasoned chips, and cold cream donuts mingled in a custardy backdrop. My stomach rumbled. Pie, definitely a pie. I scanned the chiller cabinet. And a custard square.

Ben was already shoving pies into brown paper bags. I ordered three cream donuts and three custard squares to go with the pies. Brown paper bags of deliciousness were piled in front of me as I swiped my Eftpos card, thankful that I'd pocketed my alternate wallet while in the stock room at the office. Go ahead and try to trace this transaction back to Ronnie Tracey. Best of luck to you.

The lady behind the counter glanced at us, obviously

noticed we didn't have a bag to carry the food and produced two large paper bags from behind the counter. She
stacked the pies and handed the warm bag to Ben. Then
put the cooler food into another bag so nothing crushed
and handed it to me.

"Thank you," I said.

We didn't talk on the way back to the police station.
We watched in store windows as we passed by, looking to
see if anyone followed us, or took any notice of our presence. No one appeared to give us a second glance. That
was a bonus.

Ben knocked twice on the door. I heard the lock click
and then Crockett swung the door open.

"Something smells beaut," he said. "My mouth is already watering." He then resumed his position at the table. "Okay out there?"

"Yep," Ben said. "Quiet here?"

Crockett nodded.

Ben unloaded the pies in their individual bags and
passed them around. I sat the dessert bag in the middle
on the table. Silence ensued as we ate. They were good
pies. Not the best I'd ever had. But good. Broadway was
the best.

Ben wiped his mouth on a serviette that he fished from
the big bag. I never noticed the lady put them in ... super
observant.

"What time is it?" Ben asked, with a smile in my direction.

"Puzzle time," I replied without thought, while ripping the bag of pastries open. "Custard squares first though."

We devoured the custard squares in record time and then the creamed donuts.

"Know what we forgot?" Ben asked.

"Coffee ..."

"I'm on it," Crockett said, grabbing his worn black wallet and the new phone from the table. "Be right back."

"Don't get lost," I said, and almost meant it. "Don't leave an electronic trail." That I did mean.

"No problem. Got plenty of cash on me."

The door closed behind him. What was he even doing here with us? Why did Crockett get an *Exodus* message?

Ben reached out and touched my hand. "Problem?"

"Maybe."

"Crockett?"

"What do you think?"

"I was wondering why he got the message. It won't hurt having him along, as something is definitely up, otherwise Osborne would've wanted a meet."

"Good point." Perhaps I needed to ease up on the Crockett thing?

"All right, what is it? There's something. I know there is."

"I need to get into the city," I said, making eye contact with Ben. "The person I'm looking for might be in a restaurant in the city."

"In a restaurant. And why do you care?"

"I was hired by this person's father and also, the target

contacted me directly. He's not a nobody. The military are looking for him."

Ben leaned forward. "Could he be the reason for this secret squirrel business?"

I nodded. "Highly likely, I'd say. He's Army Intelligence, only been back home a short while and, my understanding is, that he was given leave to visit his terminally ill father."

"And?"

"He vanished. His dad is concerned."

"Anyone else bothered by this?"

"Absolutely."

"And you want to find him before they do." It wasn't a question; it was a statement. Ben continued, "We're going to the city to find this person. What about Crockett?"

"I doubt we can get away from him, and I don't know why he's involved. I want him close. Who knows what the hell is going on?"

"Something bad, that's all we can be sure of. If it's spread as far as the CIA then this is not a good situation."

I toyed with the phone in front of me, then opened the Facebook app and found a recent post on the bookshop page. I left a coded message, and it wasn't easy to do it on the fly. I needed Steph to work her charm and gain access to the supermarket surveillance video around the time I thought Luke was there.

If he went into the supermarket and was escorted out, then we might get a look at whoever took him. If it happened in the carpark, we could probably see something, depending where he parked. Even a partial plate would be helpful. I watched the screen and sure enough, a couple of minutes after my comment, there was one from Steph in reply. She'd do it. I knew she would. There's a reason Steph, Jenn, and I are in business together.

"The plan?" Ben asked.

The door opened and Crockett angled his way in carrying a take-out tray with three coffees in it.

"Smells good," I commented, as he pushed the door closed and joined us at the table.

"Anything happen while I was gone?" he asked, looking from me to Ben, as he gave us our coffees.

"Sort of," I replied. "Not to do with this *Exodus* situation, as far as I know. This is about the job I took this morning."

"You want to fill me in?"

Not really, but I will.

"I need to get into the city, to a restaurant in Newtown. I think the person I'm looking for is being held there. He was alive this morning but that could change at any point."

"How do you know where he is?" Crockett asked. A slow dawning occurred in his eyes. "Is this your woo-woo talking?"

"What if it is?" I snapped.

"Nothing!" He held his hands up in mock-surrender. "Just a question. That's all."

"Ronnie has special skills," Ben said, nudging me. "And very few people are trusted with that knowledge."

"That stays between us three," I reminded Crockett.

"Sorry, I didn't mean anything by it," Crockett said.

"I know, but it's my thing. I don't publicise it."

"Suppose that's wise. Not everyone would get it or accept it. Or maybe you just don't give people a chance?"

I shrugged. "I can't explain it, therefore I don't expect people to *get it*."

"Just us two then?" Crockett asked, looking at Ben.

"Sort of. There aren't many people I trust with sensitive information."

"I'm honoured."

"Don't be. It's all about who can survive enhanced interrogation."

"Serious?"

"Yes. I know enough about both of you and what you've lived through, to be on my list."

"You asked about me?"

"Of course. Do I look stupid?" I chuckled. "MacKinnon's last surprise was Ben. And I asked about him too."

Ben nodded. "She did. And she gave me a hard time when we first met."

"What about Steph, Jenn, and Donald?"

"They all know something about how I'm so successful at finding people but not enough to talk about it except for cousin Donald." And Emily knew everything, but that knowledge was trapped in her forever changed brain.

Crockett laughed. "Donald?"

"He's blood. Nothing is stronger when the chips are down." He wouldn't say anything to anyone even if they threatened his fancy diamond watch. The man magnet watch.

"I have seen him look fierce," Crockett said with a nod.

"See?"

"Enzo and Donald are solid, you know?"

"I know. He won't tell Enzo unless I give him permission." And I'm not ready to do that yet. Maybe when they've been married twenty-years and I'm sure it'll stick.

"It's not reservations over this wedding making you drag your feet?" Crockett asked. He was the most unlikely person to stand up for Enzo and be his best man.

The first time we met Enzo, I was aware of the history between him and Crockett, and I really thought Crockett might shoot him. Or that Enzo had popped up to harm Crockett. They moved in the same bad circles during Crockett's undercover assignment, but neither knew the other was undercover.

"I'm not dragging my feet." I sighed. "They're going to be great as an old married couple. You're the best man, right?"

"You know I am."

"Then have you seen the wedding colour scheme and the dress?"

"Magenta and tangerine," he said, like it was burned into his brain.

"Uh huh. Purple and orange. When is that ever good?"

"In the sixties?" Crockett replied. "I'm going to look like an idiot who stepped out of an Austin Powers movie. Specifically, *The Spy Who Shagged Me*. Couldn't they go with something from the actual sixties. *Easy Rider* would be the obvious choice?"

Ben laughed. "If the wedding really is sixties themed, that'd explain everything."

Crockett grimaced at Ben. "You're a lucky bastard. No magenta velvet suit and white ruffled shirt for you."

Ben roared with laughter. "I can't wait to see that. You, the bad-arsed biker, prancing about in a velvet suit."

Crockett shook his head. "There. Will. Be. No. Prancing."

"What possessed them to choose an Austin Powers theme?"

Crockett shook his head. "Insanity."

I thought gays had taste. Infallible fabulous taste, and those plonkers chose purple and orange and created a frock out of it. For a brief moment I wondered if I could switch with Crockett. I wouldn't mind the velvet suit.

"Okay, enough." I shook the images from my head. "Back to work."

"Is this a kidnapping for ransom?" Crockett asked, flipping his focus to the job at hand.

"Not so far. Abduction, but no demands were made before we dropped off the grid earlier."

"And how do we get to the city and rescue this person. Is it a sheila or a bloke?"

"Male," I said with a shake of my head at his use of 'sheila'. As if it makes a difference who the person is. "We can't exactly Uber or taxi."

And it's a bloody long walk.

I gave the Uber idea some more thought; supposed we could. It's not like they'd know if we used assumed names and with the mask mandate we'd have another level of security. Masks make it delightfully tricky to recognise people. No one checks ID's. Then there was the NZ COVID Tracer app, we'd have to scan in the Uber. Did we want to have a record of travel? No. We did not. What about the vaccine passes? Another reason to take the train. Less risk of having to show our passes, which we don't have, because they're in our real names and on our real phones. Probably wouldn't be asked these days anyway but I couldn't bank on it.

Train. The train worked before; it'll work again. We'll worry about the next step once we're in the city. We'd still be wearing masks and have to scan the QR code onboard the train, along with lots of other people. Safety in numbers.

"Finish our coffees and then we'll train into town," I said, with more authority than I felt. A plan emerged as I sipped the coffee. "We'll do the same thing as before. One of us goes to Ava, the other two use the Petone station. We get on the same train but sit separately. We make our way up to the war memorial on Taranaki Street. Walking will be fine, it's only about forty minutes from the station and there are several ways to get there."

"Then?" Ben said, placing his empty cup on the table.

"We could bus or walk to Newtown. It's not as if it's that far," I said. An evening walk to a restaurant. How nice.

"It's a plan," Crockett said. "Is it the best plan?"

"I never said it was the best or even particularly good, but it's a plan."

Ben smiled at me. "It's not a bad plan, Ronnie. Whenever you're ready."

I checked the train timetable on my phone. "Next train is in ten-minutes."

"We can't make that if one of us is going to Ava," Ben said.

He was right.

"One after that then," I said. "Crockett, you want to take Ava?"

"Sure, just give me directions."

I did. He stood, gathered the empty cups, and threw them in the bin by the door. He looked at us over his shoulder. "It'll be dark soon. That's got to be a help."

"That, and wearing masks," I said.

Ben nodded in agreement. "Be careful. We'll meet you in town."

"Bye," he said, and disappeared through the doorway. I watched him walk down the drive, only losing sight of him when he turned right onto Jackson Street.

Chapter Eight:
[Ronnie: Newtown]

I walked behind Ben and paused a few times to let him get further away. Sometimes it's hard walking slow. In the end, I crossed the road, so I could walk at my own pace and not obviously overtake him or look like I was awkwardly trying not to overtake someone.

I masked up and bought a ticket to Wellington at the station. Then found a seat and waited. From where I sat I could see Ben leaning on the station wall; he didn't look in my direction at all. Neither Ben nor Crockett would buy tickets. They'd get them on the train. Crockett had no option to buy tickets at Ava station so that made it easy.

The train arrived. I chose my carriage without glancing at anyone else who was waiting. Didn't take long before I was comfortably ensconced in a seat. I saw Ben enter the carriage and sit on the other side of the train. Crockett wasn't visible. I imagined he was in another carriage. Wasn't particularly bothered if he'd missed the train. There's always another. I glanced at the window beside me and saw it had a COVID tracer app QR code. I scanned it. Doing my duty as a good citizen.

The train pulled out. I watched the crew member make his way through the few new passengers, clicking tickets or handing out tickets and change. I'd heard that Snapper card readers were going to be added to all trains. That'd make this process easier. He reached me, clicked my ticket, and moved on. No conversation. I checked the Facebook page in case Steph had replied. She had. There was a short message that told me more than it told anyone else. I liked the comment then closed Facebook. When I say I liked it, it wasn't really me, it was the phone's alter ego. A man called Jonni W. Jonni W had a private Facebook account. I needed to use a secure message service and retrieve whatever it was that Steph found. Normally she'd save information as a draft in our email account, but I didn't want to log into that from this phone.

There was no one sitting near me and no chance anyone could look over my shoulder. Didn't take me long to log into the secure message service and open Steph's message. Two videos. The time stamp on the first one was just after I thought Luke would arrived at the supermarket and the second one, five minutes later. He wasn't there long.

I found AirPods in my jacket pocket, put them in, and then pressed play on the first video. As I watched I saw a man scan the QR code outside at approximately the right time for it to be Luke; I couldn't see his face. He entered the supermarket through the Geange Street carpark entrance. Several people entered within the next minute, one after the other. Two of the people were male, one walked with a familiar gait, and he scanned the code, but the other person didn't. It wasn't enough for me to identify him for certain, but my suspicions were aroused. Looked a bit like MacKinnon senior from the back, and he had a distinctive gait due to an old knee injury.

The next video was inside the supermarket. Three men, walking toward the exit camera together. I paused the video to get a better look at the faces. One was MacKinnon, the one in the middle looked like Luke O'Sullivan; I wished I'd brought his photo with me to confirm. The male on the other side of Luke was an unknown subject. Our UnSub and kidnapper? I pressed play. As the three of them neared the camera, MacKinnon looked directly at the lens and mouthed something.

One word.

I paused it and replayed it. Looked like he said, '*Exodus*'.

I replayed the moment four times and each time he looked to have mouthed the word *Exodus*. On the fifth replay I took careful note of the body language of the men on either side of him. MacKinnon walked next to O'Sullivan. One hand looked to be resting on O'Sullivan's elbow. Trying not to be obvious about it. Luke wasn't struggling. He didn't try and pull away at all. The other male had one hand inside his jacket and the other hanging by his side. There was no one else nearby as they exited. Did he know them? Maybe he did. Why would he let anyone escort him away? Why did MacKinnon have his hand on Luke's arm? Why did MacKinnon mouth '*Exodus*' except to alert me? Who else would be looking for a missing person? How did either of them find O'Sullivan at the supermarket, minutes after he arrived?

I played the video a few more times in case I missed

something. I didn't. The night deepened, making the warm yellow lights inside the carriage seems brighter than they were. The train bumped into the rail yard and past the *Cake Tin*. Before long, I disembarked at Wellington station and chose my route to Taranaki Street. I decided to go via Featherston Street, across Hunter Street to Willis Street, up Willis, down Manners to Cuba Mall, up Cuba Street to Ghuznee Street, down Ghuznee to Taranaki, then straight up to Pukeahu National War Memorial Park.

Shadows lengthened around corners of tall office buildings. Little pools of light spilled from bars and restaurants. They were inviting, and in other circumstances the lure would've pulled me right in, especially as I walked past *Rydges*. I love their wedges with truffle oil.

There weren't too many people walking around. Voices and delicious smells wafted as doors opened. I stuck to the shadows as much as possible.

At the Ghuznee Street intersection, I crossed Taranaki and headed for the war memorial park. It was much darker up there. Coloured lights lit the tree sculptures making them stand out against the night sky. The fountain glowed in the darkest area beneath the memorial. During daylight this was a good place to sit and watch youths and young adults skateboarding and playing hackie sack. At night, the homeless tucked themselves into the most sheltered corners hoping to go unnoticed. I chose the place I wanted to sit and waited. From my position I could see every approach. Time crawled in the smallest of increments while I waited for the familiar shapes of Ben and Crockett to emerge from the darkness.

They did. I saw Ben first. He waved when he got within three metres. Old friends greeting each other. Not that the homeless or huffers cared. Crockett ambled into view as Ben sat down next to me. He waved, but it would've been easy to miss. He sat on the other side of me. Perfect. I showed them both the video.

They agreed that the word mouthed was *Exodus*.

"So, why was MacKinnon escorting Luke and why did he mouth *Exodus* at the camera?" I said, pocketing my phone. "What the hell is going on here?"

It felt like we were the rescue team, and we were ill equipped for that mission.

"How did MacKinnon and the other bloke know where O'Sullivan would be?" Crockett said. "They got to him pretty quick judging by the time stamps."

Ben nudged me. "You were right about puzzle time."

Sometimes being right isn't that helpful.

Chapter Nine:
[Crockett: Manger]

Don't get me wrong, I enjoy working with Ronnie, but damn she attracts some shit. I found myself mumbling under my breath as we walked.

"Something bothering you?" Ben asked.

"Talking to myself."

"How about you share with the class," he said, his voice remaining low and quiet.

"I'm evaluating the situation and trying to understand MacKinnon's involvement. And how *they* got to O'Sullivan so quick."

"Any conclusions?"

I shrugged. "A tracker of some kind is my guess. I'd like to know who the other bloke is, and what he had his hand on under his jacket."

"The UnSub of the hour," Ronnie said. "We all want to know who the mystery man is. Wonder if he knows how popular he's become?"

"Can't we get someone … Jenn or Steph maybe … they could run facial recognition on him?"

Ronnie faced me; was hard to see her features in the night. "They can. The only problem with that is the program we need to use requires a login. If I give them my access to the main server over at Security Intelligence, someone will know I logged in and questions will follow."

"Chandler will find out, that's what you mean, isn't it?"

"I don't think we want him involved unless we have no choice."

She was right about that. He was one bad hombre and not someone I wanted to deal with again, unless forced. Couldn't guarantee I wouldn't smash him and that wouldn't be a good look.

The three of us walked together, heads on swivel. It was a walk, not a difficult one, just a walk. I could feel tension coming from Ronnie and Ben. Guess they could feel mine. We paused in a doorway, close to the intersection where Ronnie's woo-woo said the restaurant was supposed to be, and in it, the missing intelligence officer. Cars drove by. No one took any notice of us. Cars pulled in and parked on the other side of the road. There was the usual amount of traffic that I'd expect in this part of the city. Nothing to get worked up about.

"How close are we going to get?" Ben asked.

"No closer than here for the minute," Ronnie said. "We need to have a look-see. View what we're up against. Find the exits and entrances."

"I'll find a back way in," I said. "You two scope out the street and front entrance. Back here in five." I looked at the time on the phone I carried.

Ronnie swung her backpack off her shoulder and dug into it. When she straightened up she handed me a handgun in a paddle holster. "You're on your own so take my Glock."

"You sure?"

"Yes. We're together and look less threatening anyway. You look like someone people would challenge." She smiled. "I mean that in a good way."

"I'm sure you do. See you soon."

"Five," Ronnie said. "Don't be late."

Ben and Ronnie donned masks and crossed the road, hand-in-hand. I pushed the paddle holster clip over my belt, and checked the rig was hidden by my jacket.

With my mask on, I went down the block a little way until I found the alley we'd walked past a few minutes before. I used the torch on the phone to illuminate the area. It was wide enough to back a truck down. On one side there was a row of wheelie bins. The regular kind. I shone the beam near the bins. Five bins and five doorways.

Looking up I saw fire escapes and curtained windows. Good chance they were flats. If we were closer to the CBD I'd say apartments. Ahead of me to the right was where I thought the restaurant back door would be. I turned the torch off and moved on, sticking to the deep shadows provided by the buildings. A more industrial-sized rubbish bin, like a small skip bin on wheels with a lid. I lifted the lid. Not locked. It was full of food waste. I turned the torch back on to scan the sides for markings. A stencilled pig and the name *Manger*.

This was the right alley. Torch off. I hustled to the next biggish skip bin. Again, I used the torch and looked for markings. Stencilled words: Paper recycling and *Manger*.

I opened the lid of the next large bin and saw empty wine bottles. On the outside the name of the restaurant and the word 'glass'. On the other side of that bin was a wooden door with a small barred frosted glass window in the top third. I hung back using the bins as cover. Not that they were great, but they were bigger than the wheelie bins at the beginning of the alley. I checked the time and watched the door. Over the door was a dim light bulb. It tossed out enough light for someone to see their way to the first skip bin, but after that you'd need a torch, or to be very sure of the area.

Thirty seconds later the door opened. Cooking smells permeated the alley. A young male in black pants and a white shirt dropped wine bottles into the recycling bin. They clattered onto other bottles harshly interrupting the quiet night. I waited until he went back inside then cruised back to the main road and our meeting place. I learnt there was no security lighting in the alley. I didn't trigger any lights and nor did the guy dropping wine bottles in the bin.

Ronnie and Ben were waiting, unmasked. Ben was spinning his mask around his finger by the elastic. Ronnie had hers held firmly in her hand. I peeled mine off.

"And?" She asked.

"Found the back door. There's a food waste skip back there with a pig stencilled on it. They could have a pig farm."

"Or like many restaurants, that waste could be going to someone else's farm," Ronnie said. Sounded reasonable.

"I guess."

"Anything troubling down there?"

"Only the pig food."

"Don't like pigs?"

"I love bacon and there's nothing better than pulled pork belly. It's not the eating part that concerns me, it's what they eat."

Ben spoke, "If they farmed their own pork that'd be the ideal way to get rid of bodies."

"See, that, that's what I don't like."

"Don't worry about it Skippy, but now I'm hungry," Ronnie said with a wink. "We're going in the front door like customers. Looks like business as usual from what we could tell."

"You really think your guy and MacKinnon are here somewhere while the restaurant is open?"

"Yes. I do."

Ben's armed circled Ronnie's waist as he stole a kiss.

"Crikey, don't you two get out much? You're treating this like a date night."

"Table for two," said Ben giving me a good-natured nudge. "What kind of food?"

"Eastern European Mediterranean mix, I think," Ronnie said.

Not really my thing. If she'd said it was a steak house I might've fought them for it.

"Definitely a table for two." Ben laughed as he clocked my unimpressed expression.

I shook my head. "You're on your own with that unless there's steak." The pies we'd had earlier were all right, but I was starting to feel peckish. "Get your best bib and tucker on," I said. "We're going in."

Ronnie chuckled. "Or jeans and semi-tidy work clothes, that'll do."

Ben and Ronnie put their masks back on and continued on their way into *Manger,* posing as happy customers out for a meal. I kept an eye out until they reached the doorway then I skedaddled back to the wide service lane lined with wheelie bins. Mask on and torch off. I picked my path with care, remembering how many bins there were to pass. I didn't want to walk into anything and hoped to avoid the smallish dumpsters in the shadowy alley world. I moved past them to a lit area near the solitary tatty door, with one small barred frosted window. Definitely no security lighting. There was also no cover.

I scooted back to the bin area I'd used earlier, hoping to keep my largish frame out of sight. Aromatic spices and the unmistakable smell of pork cooking made my mouth water and stomach rumble. The door opened halfway then closed. No one exited. A flood of food smells filled the short alley. Saliva juices flowed causing me to swallow quickly. Part of me wished I was inside with Ronnie and Ben ordering whatever it was that smelled that good.

The door opened again, this time it stayed open, and a male in a chef uniform stepped outside and lit a cigarette. Nothing like cigarette smoke to ruin a nice smelling alley. The bloke had a couple of drags of his smoke then stubbed it out, pocketed the butt, and hurried back inside. I ran to the door as it was closing. He clearly expected it to close behind him just like every other night. I pressed a hand against the door to prevent it latching. Kitchen noises rose from beyond the door, then went quiet. I pushed the door open and found a hallway, with doors opening off both sides. I stepped inside and pulled the door shut quietly behind me. The sounds of people working came from the left side of the hall behind a closed door. Pots rattled. Boiling and bubbling noises mingled with the sound of a knife on a wooden surface. Probably the kitchen.

I moved quietly past that door. On the right were two doors. I listened outside the first one. All quiet so I eased it open. A storeroom. Nothing to see there. The second was a dimly lit stairwell. Promising. I stood still and listened but heard nothing. With care I closed the door and turned to face the unexplored part of the hallway. A few metres ahead of me was a curtain across the hallway. It looked to be a heavy velvet. Beyond were softer noises. I slipped my hand into the middle of the curtain where I saw light and pulled it to one side. It was velvet.

I stepped through and the soft noises became a hum of voices. Restaurant? I walked on and found the bathrooms and a door with the word 'exit' above an image of a green and white running man. A layered thrum came from beyond the exit door. I decided I was right about it being the restaurant. There was one more door to the right. A door opened down the hall behind me. Footsteps moved toward the curtain. I opened the nearest door and ducked inside. Standing on the top of a steep set of badly lit stairs, I waited. Not a good place to be if someone intended to open the stairwell door. Footsteps closed in.

The door handle moved.

Shit.

A muffled voice called out.

The handle pinged back, and the footsteps hurried away. I darted down the staircase, stepping as lightly as I could. Barely breathing. One wrong foot and I just knew the old stairs would let out a loud creak, or I'd misstep, and crash down them. Below me, a hallway stretched into darkness. Indistinct voices and sounds of life reached me. My heartbeat increased. There was nowhere to conceal myself if a door opened. I moved down, a step at a time. My hand reached for the Glock in my waistband. Good to know it was there if needed. A quieter more hands on approach would be better. Gunshots tend to upset people. No one wanted undue attention. I stepped off the last stair and moved along the hallway a few metres.

The voices were louder but not clearer.

An angry voice followed by a calmer quieter voice.

I still couldn't hear what was being said but I could make out tone.

Then I heard footsteps.

Fuck me.

A door opened somewhere, and a draught wafted an earthy musty smell toward me. Time to move. I bolted for the stairs. At the top of the stairs, I paused to listen. Below me a door closed. Then another opened. A small flash of light illuminated the hallway.

Someone left the room.

As long they didn't look up it'd be fine.

I breathed slowly and opened the door at the top of the stairs.

The coast was clear.

I shut the door behind me as a deep male voice said, "Who's there?"

The ghost of Christmas past.

I leaned on the closed door for a second then took a breath and went into the nearby men's bathroom, thanking my lucky stars no one was in there. My heart rate slowed to normal. Nearly got snapped. Going to have to be careful about the next part.

It was time to message Ronnie.

Me: There are two sets of stairs leading down from the main hallway. One from near the bathroom and one from down by the kitchen. If your bloke is here then he's probably down the stairs by the bathroom.

Phone 1/Ronnie: What makes you say that?

Me: Heard voices. Saw light. More than one person is down there.

Phone 1/Ronnie: Me or Ben? Where?

Me: You. Bathroom.

Phone 1/Ronnie: Great.

Chapter Ten:
[Ronnie: Men's Bathroom]

I glanced at the last text from Crockett and then smiled at Ben sitting opposite me.

"How long do you think our meal will be?"

"Fifteen minutes give or take," he replied. His fingers entwined mine across the table. "Was that our pal?"

I conjured up a seductive whisper, "Baby, he's found two staircases and wants me to meet him."

"Saucy minx. Where?"

"Men's loo."

A smile twisted the corner of Ben's mouth. "We're out for dinner and you're going to meet another man in a men's bathroom."

I laughed softly. "Nana always says my moral compass needs adjusting."

"Maybe she's right?"

"Next time you're feeling brave you should tell her that."

"Hard pass."

"Back shortly." I stood, bent toward him, and planted a kiss on his lips, then popped my mask on and hurried through the door with the male/female sign above it. Once through the door I chose the male bathroom. Figured I could always feign confusion and apologise if someone caught me.

Two stalls. One with a closed door and no sign of Crockett near the urinals.

"Crockett?" I kept my voice just above a whisper.

The closed stall door opened with a flourish. Crockett was wearing his mask. He winked at me. "Ready?"

"Did you notice any surveillance cameras?"

"No. They either trust their staff or the cameras are very well hidden," Crockett said. "Time to rock and roll?"

"Sure."

"The first stairs are close by," he said, opening the toilet door and looking around. "All clear."

We left the room. I followed Crockett through a doorway and into a poorly lit musty stairwell. Wooden stairs and a rickety banister.

With every groan and creak under our feet my heart lurched.

I struggled to keep my footsteps as quiet as possible while keeping my hand on Crockett's shoulder. One of us was armed and it wasn't me. Made more sense for him to take the lead. Crockett lifted his hand at the elbow and clenched his fist.

I froze behind him. He cupped his left hand around his ear.

He'd heard something. Perhaps it really was my heart thumping. It was loud and hard enough that it threatened to break through my rib cage.

In the stillness outside my body, a voice rose. No words. More like an expression of frustration or anger. Crockett dropped his arm and flicked his hand behind him. Okay fine, I'll stay behind. I'm not in a hurry to walk unarmed into nonsense.

I squeezed his shoulder to let him know I was ready to move with him. And move we did. Down the last six stairs and into the hallway at the bottom. I looked right. Nothing. No doorways. Dead end. We moved a few metres along the hall.

Crockett's arm rose again. I froze. He pointed left, then signalled two. He pointed left again and changed his mind. He cupped his ear and then flashed three fingers.

Okay. He heard three voices. Three people. He pointed to himself. Three males. I slipped my phone from my pocket, double checked it was on silent, texted Ben with our location and the bit about three males, then asked him to bring my backpack. I showed Crockett the text.

I pushed my phone deep into my pocket. Didn't want it falling out by accident. Crockett motioned that we'd wait for Ben.

Counting to four, I took a deep inward breath through my nose, counting to four again, I exhaled through my mouth. Warm air lingered under my mask. I repeated the process until I could no longer feel my heart punching through my chest wall.

Counting, breathing, waiting.

A flash of light in my periphery. My heart skipped a beat. Wood creaked. I swallowed hard. Quiet footsteps moving down the staircase between soft creaks.

Slow breaths.

Please be Ben.

I tapped Crockett's shoulder to get his attention. He rolled around me to face the stairs. I listened for noises from the room close to our position. A male voice rumbled on and on. I didn't like the tone. It was badgering.

Crockett nudged me. I glanced at him just as a hand reached around and grabbed my arm.

Ben. He slipped my backpack over my arm. I wriggled it onto my back.

Crockett switched places with me again. Hand signals flew among us all. The last one was Crockett's and he signed: On two.

We moved along the corridor to the door. Crockett tried the handle gently then nodded when it turned. Ben moved past us and stood on the other side of the doorway.

Entry order was decided. Crockett, Ben, then me. Left, right, then left. Crockett opened the door and spun left, Ben peeled right, leaving me to follow Crockett.

A man jumped back, his arms raised, mouth open. Ben smacked him hard. Elbow in the side of the head. The male stumbled. Ben hit him again. He lost his footing, tripped, and fell. A swift kick to the head and he lay motionless. Inert. Possibly dead. My eyes moved to the other occupants of the room. One was ruffled, crumpled, and stubbled. William MacKinnon. And the other, a younger less bedraggled, but not exactly put together, guy who looked like the photograph I'd seen of Luke O'Sullivan.

"Luke?"

"Ronnie? Man, I heard you were good," he spoke quietly. Dried blood on his busted lip, and bruising down the side of his face, suggested his day wasn't much fun.

I did nothing but tag along, but now's not the time for that conversation.

Crockett produced a knife and cut the ties holding their wrists to the arms of the chairs, then freed their feet. I presumed the man had knives hidden everywhere on his person. Seemed like a thing Crockett would have.

"You good to walk?" he asked MacKinnon.

"Yes."

"Then let's go."

MacKinnon looked around the room. "Our jackets," he said.

"I'll grab them," Luke said, stepping over the man on the floor, and covering the distance to a table at the back of the room in three strides. He handed MacKinnon his suit jacket. Then he put a brown leather jacket on.

"Thanks," MacKinnon said, plunging his right arm into a sleeve. He had the jacket on within seconds.

Ben watched the hallway. He whispered, "Let's haul ass."

"Same way we came down," Crockett said. "We're walking out the front door."

I pushed MacKinnon and Luke in front of me toward Ben. "Ben's got point."

Crockett closed the door behind us and fell into step beside me. "Hospital?"

"Yes. It's close and safe. We need transport back to the Hutt and a safe house would be helpful, don't suppose ..."

84

"I'll get that happening," he said.

I moved past Luke and MacKinnon to reach Ben at the bottom of the stairs. "Hold up."

"Problem?"

"No, but if we have to split up, Wellington Hospital is the destination."

"Okay, that's good." He linked his arms with mine. "Ready?"

"Yes."

"Up we go then."

I looked over my shoulder at Luke. Nothing else for it but to brazen our way back into the restaurant and out the front door. Unless? Three of us went out the front and two out the back. Divide and make it harder for the bad buggers to round us up. I waved at Crockett who hurried to me.

"Pick a mate and go out the way you came in?"

He smiled. "I see where you're going with this. I'll take Luke. You've got the old man. See you in the emergency department."

I motioned to MacKinnon to move closer. We finished the stair climb without looking back. Once down the hallway and into the restaurant I saw our meals were waiting on our table. They looked good. My stomach growled and mouth watered as we walked past. Such a shame. The lone server was occupied with another table on the other side of the room. I grabbed MacKinnon by the arm. "Come on Dad, let's go."

The door swung shut behind us. We kept moving. No

looking back. No slowing the pace. I don't think I took a proper breath until we walked into the emergency department entrance of Wellington Hospital. I glanced around and saw the COVID QR code, hand sanitiser, and a box of masks. I scanned in, used the sanitiser, and grabbed a couple of masks. Never hurts to have spares and MacKinnon didn't have one.

"Put this on," I said to MacKinnon, handing him a mask. I stuffed the other one in my pocket.

He did as I asked. Ben scanned the code.

In: one, two, three, four.

Out: one, two, three, four.

Repeat.

"You okay?" Ben asked, nudging me into a seat in the waiting area.

"Yes. Just breathing."

He smiled. "Good."

MacKinnon slumped into a chair on the other side of me.

"What's this all about?" I asked him. "What the hell is *Exodus*? Why did the Albanians grab you and Luke O'-Sullivan and, while I'm at it, why did he call me and not his unit? And are they even Albanian?"

Well, I'd figured some of that out, the reason was right in front of me, but still. He called me to get them out. Why?

"There's a problem in the unit."

"Are you sure there's a problem in the unit?"

He glared at me. "Are you questioning me?"

I smiled. "Yes. Because nothing makes sense here," I said, keeping my voice quiet and calm. "Has this got anything to do with anything I'm involved in?"

"I don't know what you are involved in," he said, his voice pancaking on the tiled floor.

I wanted to call bullshit, but he was technically a superior even though I worked for myself most of the time. "Why did they want you?"

"There is a problem in his unit."

"It's a bit early in the game to start spinning in circles, MacKinnon." I leaned forward and placed my elbows on my knees. "Why did the three of us get the *Exodus* message. I have a feeling that this is a bigger problem than one military unit. And a military problem doesn't explain why you were taken with O'Sullivan." I let that sink in for a bit. "Also, why did it look like you were helping the other guy take Luke?"

"Who else knows about the *Exodus*?"

"I have my suspicions that at least one person in the CIA knows something is up," Ben said quietly. "A contact of mine was bailing in a hurry."

MacKinnon shook his head slowly. "That shouldn't happen."

"So, we three were supposed to disappear for whatever reason, but no one else? You need to talk to us and make it snappy," I said. A nurse approached. Her eyes smiled above her mask. I hoped mine smiled back and readied a reason for our presence.

"Have you signed in?" she asked.

"We scanned the QR code at the door. We're just waiting for someone. Is that okay?"

"Absolutely. If we get busy though you might have to wait outside. Thank you for wearing masks and using the COVID tracer app."

"Let us know if you want us to go outside," I said, keeping my tone friendly and even. Nothing to see here.

She moved on to the next cluster on the far side of the waiting area.

My attention turned back to MacKinnon. "Why did you want us gone? What is it we know that endangers Luke's op or you?"

Considering he denied the *Exodus* was anything to do with operations I was involved in this was getting super interesting. Someone wasn't telling the truth. Big surprise. Not.

"You're not gone, Ronnie. You're right here."

"That's right." Bloody hell, he planned it; there was my confirmation. "We were your rescue mission. Just. Like. You. Wanted. So, what is all this about?"

Crockett and O'Sullivan walked through the double doors and straight toward us. Crockett's eyes crinkled as he closed the distance. The world was getting very good at picking smiles on masked faces.

"I got hold of Art. We've got a ride and somewhere to stay."

"Great. And the smile is about that or something else, because it's very creepy how much crinkled skin there is around your eyes." I waved a finger at his face. "Old before your time by the look of that."

"Enzo rang."

I groaned. "How is that even possible? No one has the numbers."

"Not me, he rang Art."

"Okay, yeah, that makes more sense. And?"

"Donald is in a flap about his best woman not being available for the dress fitting and Enzo couldn't find me, so he tried Art."

"And that made your eye skin scrunch up like crinkle fries?"

"You saying it doesn't amuse you at all, knowing they're running around like blue-arsed flies?"

I shrugged. It did. I'm a bad person. It shouldn't. I'm being a horrible best woman. Poor Donald is probably really worried, and I'm amused. "Anything about Nana?"

"I did ask. Art said all was quiet on the Western Front."

That was actually good of him to ask. Maybe Crockett's not a complete Australian tosser.

"All right. When can we expect our lift?"

"Half an hour."

That's a long time out in the open. I looked around the room. Okay, so not technically in the open. But, not exactly out of sight. Any bad bugger worth his salt would work out we'd gone to the hospital. It was the closest safe place and being here could put innocent people at risk. I took a slow inward breath and counted to four.

"There are two public entrances," Ben said. "If we have

to we can go through the actual emergency department and out the ambulance entrance."

"How easy will that be? There are security guards."

"They're not armed, Ronnie. We're in New Zealand."

"No, they're not but have you seen them? They look like rugby players."

"We'll have to play defensively."

"Pretty sure there is another way out that doesn't involve being tackled."

I stifled a laugh. Good luck playing a defensive game with the old man. He wasn't in the best shape of his life. I gave him another look. He didn't look good at all, grey around the gills.

"MacKinnon. You okay?"

Crockett knelt in front of him. "What's happening here, old man?"

Sweat beaded on MacKinnon's forehead. His skin took on a greyer pallor.

"I don't feel that good," MacKinnon mumbled. "My chest."

Ben shot over to the triage desk. He returned with two nurses and a gurney. A flurry of activity followed, and they left with MacKinnon, Ben in tow. I ran after him.

"Go with Crockett. I'll stay with the old man and catch up when I know what's going on. No one will be looking for me by myself."

"You've got the phone?"

"I do. I'll be in touch. Stay safe."

"You too." I wasn't sure if I should kiss him or just

wave. I waved and returned to Crockett and O'Sullivan. "We need to get out of here before the Albanians figure out where we are."

"Let's go," Crockett said, grabbing Luke by the arm and lifting him to his feet. "We'll go through that door." He pointed to a door on the far side. It wasn't where they took MacKinnon. I knew there was another way out and hoped that was it.

"And this leads us where?" I asked, as he pushed the door open.

"To a corridor that tracks to the rest of the hospital," Crockett said. "We can find our way to the front entrance. Art will text when he's near and tell us where to meet him."

"There are parking buildings?"

"Yeah."

We walked in silence, following lines on the floor, and keeping our eyes open for anyone who, like us, was out of place. The foyer was enormous and smelt of fresh flowers. They always did. I turned slowly and took in the area. There was a florist and a gift shop, now closed for the evening. ATM's. Reception. Several other office-type spaces that held services people might need. Everything was closed. No one lurked. The lighting was dim. A big signage board showed the direction of parking buildings and various wards and departments. We waited in the shadows, not near the windows. I had a feeling the main doors were locked at night and that the only way in was through the emergency department. Probably good that we weren't there anymore.

Although it wasn't that late, it was dark.

Covertly sneaking through town and breaking people out of basements takes time.

My stomach growled. Memories of the sumptuous meals we'd left sitting on our table drifted in my mind. It didn't help. Crockett nudged me. "You good?"

"Hungry."

Luke spoke, "There's some vending machines over there." He nodded his head to the wall behind us.

"Good spotting." I checked my pockets and found my wallet. "Anyone want anything?"

They nodded. "Anything works," Luke replied. "I haven't eaten since before I went to the supermarket."

"What he said," Crockett agreed. "Anything works."

"Okay. Trusting leaving it up to me. But, okay." I went to check the machines out. I don't know what I expected but not the junk I found. It's a hospital for goodness sake. Chips. Chocolate bars. Cheese and crackers. That would do, in a pinch. I got us cheese and crackers times three and chocolate bars times three. That should give us a bit of energy and something to do. Better than twiddling our thumbs and making ourselves dizzy constantly looking around. Now we'd eat snacks with our heads on swivel. Crockett ambled to the front of the foyer and checked the doors. He gave a thumbs up on his way back. They were locked.

That meant the corridors leading off the back of the foyer and maybe the stairs/escalator and lift, were the only ways in. We could be viewed from above via the mezzanine floor.

I pointed above us then to the escalator, stairwell door, and elevator. "We need to separate."

Crockett nodded. "Luke, move back toward the vending machines. From between them you have a view of anyone stepping off the escalator before they can see you. You will have time to hit that door on the right."

"If someone comes in through there?" Luke asked.

"Stay put, let one of us get you out."

I scanned the expansive room. There were elevators at the side near the florist shop. I pointed. "I'll be over there. That covered rack should give me enough shelter from anyone coming off the elevator. I'll hear the ping."

Luke hurried to his designated position, and I moved to mine. We were both safe from anyone looking down from above. From behind the stand, I munched on cheese and crackers. Wasn't too bad a vending machine snack. I could see Luke eating. Crockett was gone from my line of sight. Luke could probably see him and would be able to relay hand signals to me. Thoughts edged in as I ate the last of my snacks and waited for a sign that our ride was here. Did this really have anything to do with the Albanians or was this something else? Was this part of *Genesis*? The last information I saw regarding anything terror related was a series of attacks planned by ISIL after the Taliban took over Afghanistan. We had people trapped inside Afghanistan. It's always the case that not everyone gets out in the allocated time. Sometimes we have people stay inside hot spots on purpose when terrorism is involved. There was talk of WMD's, but I didn't see anything come through ... but then again, I don't see anything but Intel picked up by me and Ben, and we're not currently traveling to places where we'd pick up that sort of information. I do occasionally hear about it via other channels though. The last time I saw the *Genesis* Atlas, Crockett wasn't in it. Seeing that document meant I was one of the few people who knew who was part of the *Genesis* group. That knowledge made me valuable. Or would if anyone knew what I knew.

Just because Crockett wasn't on the list before, didn't mean he hadn't been added by MacKinnon's son over the last few months. I'm sure people are added all the time. Keep it fresh and all that. My eyes flicked around the area I could see, then back to Luke. Constantly moving, reassessing, watching for the smallest movement.

I thought about Albania. Apart from this situation I hadn't seen or heard anything recent that spoke of any confirmed threats from The Balkans. Something must've changed.

Hurry up, Art.

Chapter Eleven:
[Crockett: Out of town]

The phone in my pocket buzzed. I checked and it was Art. Good on Art. He came through for me again. This is why I have that bloke on my team. He's not just good at making people vanish. I moved from my location to Ronnie, and beckoned Luke to join us.

"We're moving. Art is in the carpark waiting. I have the floor number. He's driving a black Mercedes," I said. "Let's go." I pointed toward the corridor. "Left," I said. "Stay sharp."

We moved fast with Luke between us. The corridors were wide and without many people around we could walk three abreast. Every now and then a nurse came toward us. Ronnie and Luke fell behind in those instances.

A small amount of relief let loose when we made it to the badly lit parking building. A black Mercedes crawled towards us and flashed its lights twice. I grabbed the front passenger door handle and swung the door open. Art leaned across the console toward me.

"Getting in, or standing there looking stupid?" He said with a grin.

I opened the back door. "Ronnie," I said, watching as she slid across the seat to the other side of the car and fastened her seat belt. She dropped her bag at her feet. Luke climbed in. I pressed the door closed and jumped in the front. Masks came off.

"Buckle up," Art said, while watching the rearview mirror. "We don't want a reason for us to be stopped by police."

Don't need to be told twice. I clicked my seatbelt and found myself glancing in the wing mirror. There was no one around. Not a soul. For a regional hospital it was very quiet. Maybe it wasn't a high traffic night.

Art pulled out of the parking building and onto the street. I was watching people on the footpaths, and I knew Ronnie was doing the same. I took a sneaky look at the restaurant when Art drove past.

"Quiet, isn't it?" Ronnie said from the backseat.

"Yeah. Don't know what I expected though. Wouldn't look too good if men with guns were running all over the city," I said.

"Speaking of," she replied. "Something you want to give back?"

I wrestled the holster and handgun from the inside of my waistband. "I'm glad you store the Glock in a holster." I passed the gun behind me, and let it go when I felt Ronnie take it.

"Next time bring your own," she said with a small laugh. "We got lucky this time around. But two weapons are better than one."

"Where are we going?" Luke asked.

The inner city fell away as we hit the motorway north.

"Somewhere safe. It's need to know. And you don't," Art said, flicking the indicator. "Crockett and Ronnie have been there before."

"If it's where I think it is, then we'll be very comfortable," I said. "Settle back. You may as well get some rest."

"Do you think MacKinnon is going to be all right?" Luke asked. Judging by the quietness in his voice he was talking to Ronnie not me. I checked the wing mirror again. And listened without listening.

"I don't know. He didn't look that good," she replied. "Get some rest. We're going to want to talk to you when we get to where we're going."

The conversation halted. I checked the wing mirror again. Nothing had changed.

"No one followed us," Art said with a half-smile in my direction. "Did you clock the plates before you jumped in?"

"No."

"I borrowed this car from a friend. It's got D.C. plates."

"Diplomatic Corp?" Didn't think it would be District of Columbia.

I could tell he was smiling even though he was looking straight ahead. "I've done a few jobs for this bloke, and he owes me. He's a handy friend."

"What did you say you were doing with his car, and does he have a driver?"

"Told him I wanted to impress a lady I had a first date with tonight. And his driver got the night off."

"Nice."

"He often leaves town about this time to go his residence so this car, on the road now, isn't out of the ordinary. I was lucky that he went home early for his son's birthday party."

"I knew I kept you around for a reason, bud," I said, looking at the traffic on the road. It was still fairly busy, but mostly going north, and not south into the city.

"Anything I need to know?" Art asked, as he changed lanes.

"MacKinnon looked like he was having a heart attack. Reynolds is with him. He'll make his way to us later. Apart from that, I don't think so."

"How long do you need to be off the main grid?"

"No idea at this point. First we need to work out what's going on, and then make a plan."

"The house is yours as long as you need it. I ordered groceries for tomorrow morning. Contactless delivery."

"Thanks."

"No worries."

"Did you install the cameras in the bookshop?"

"Yes. Two; one above the door pointed inward and one down the back. The only blind spot is right by the interior door to the utility rooms." He changed lanes again. "But even then, it's not actually a blind spot; no one can get there without being snapped by camera one at the door."

"Thanks for that. Is there an app I need to download?"

Ronnie coughed. "Excuse me. If there's an app then I should also have access."

"Of course," I said, glancing over my shoulder at her. "Of course."

"The app is called CrystalClear," Art said. "You'll find it

98

in the App Store."

I woke my phone and typed the app name into the App Store search. Within seconds it downloaded, and I opened it. "I need a code," I said to Art.

"One-seven-nine-six-eight," he said without skipping a beat. "Do I need to repeat it for you, Ronnie?"

"No, ta, got it," she said. "I'm in."

So was I. I checked each camera view. All quiet. As it should be. The shop was closed. Emily would've gone home hours ago. I was supposed to pick her up. Not a good feeling knowing I'd let her down. Especially after Toby the dickhead and his disgusting bullshit. I was pretty sure he'd slung his hook, but it didn't ease my concern for Emily. I flexed the knuckles on my right hand. They were stiff, bruised, and roughed up. It was worth the discomfort knowing that Toby wouldn't be able to chew for a week. I clocked him pretty good on his jaw, a couple of times. That wasn't the best. I should've handled it better and not lost my cool. Done is done. I hope the arsehole learnt a lesson. I closed the app and plunged the phone screen into darkness. There was nothing to see and that was a good thing.

We passed the Upper Hutt boundary. Art crossed the bridge leaving River Road to the ribbon of cars behind us. It was a little quieter as we drove under the underpass and into Silverstream. Pinehaven was quieter still. Instead of going up Blue Mountains Road, he veered right and went all the way through Pinehaven, up Forrest Road, joined Blue Mountains, and turned right at Chichester and left into Fendalton. Moments later we were driving up the long right-of-way to Art's secluded safe house on a section that backed onto Witako Reserve.

"We're here," Art said, looking over his shoulder into the back seat. "Everyone good?"

"Yep," Ronnie replied.

I heard her seat belt release, then Luke's.

"Where are we?" Luke asked, opening his door.

"My home away from home," Art replied. "Come on."

We trudged behind Art to the massive front door with a central doorknob. He pressed a code into a small panel situated just above the doorknob. He then turned the handle. Lights came on as the door opened.

"Code?" I asked.

"One-seven-nine-six-eight," he replied.

I made a note on my phone. The note said: Art uses the same code for everything, and what the code was. Wouldn't be great to get ourselves locked out if my memory failed me. Once we were all in the foyer, Art closed the door. It locked automatically. He motioned for us to follow him up the wide staircase.

"Looks okay here," Ronnie said from behind me.

I knew what she meant. Last time we were here we made a bit of a mess. Wasn't our fault but still, there was a shambles. Broken glass, chunks of masonry missing. High-calibre rifle rounds aren't good for houses. I'd be hard pushed to tell anything untoward had happened here now. Art did a great job of restoring everything.

Art reached the landing first and opened the double

doors into the lounge; a light flicked on. "Come on in and get yourselves settled. I've got a car to return, so I won't hang around." He nodded at me. "There are enough supplies to get you through the night and morning. Don't draw attention to yourselves."

"No promises," I replied, and shook his hand. "Thanks for the rescue."

"All good. Catch ya."

Art ran down the stairs and out the front door. Ronnie watched him leave from the lounge window and then pulled the curtains shut. I went around the rest of the room, and then the dining room and the laundry, closing curtains. Shutting out the night and any prying eyes, from neighbouring properties. Bedrooms could wait until later.

"Do we have computing power?" Ronnie asked.

"Yes. In the study, there are laptops," I replied. The study was through a door at the end of the lounge.

"When did you find that out?"

"Last time we were here. Art's a creature of habit. I imagine everything is still where it belongs."

Chapter Twelve:
[Ronnie: Here we go again]

I took a laptop and went back to the dining room. The chairs were comfortable, and the table was huge. Because something didn't feel right, I fished a flash drive out of my bag, checked the laptop wasn't connected to the internet, and then plugged the flash drive into a USB port.

The drive contained what I thought were backup files, and it was given to me weeks ago by MacKinnon. Now having something from MacKinnon seemed important. He asked me to always carry it. That also seemed important. The drive was securely password protected by fingerprint. My thumbprint activated the drive and I imagined MacKinnon's did as well. As soon as I plugged it into the laptop, it let me open the device and access the information. On the screen were thirteen folders. Each was named. Almost all of the names were operations. Except one. That was the starting point. I began digging in a folder called 'Bible Studies'. A huge part of me thought this current situation was somehow connected to *Genesis,* but I didn't have the Atlas. Or as far as the world was concerned, I didn't have the Atlas. I still had it hidden on a flash drive, but it was deeply encrypted, and I'd lost my key.

What I could access though was whatever MacKinnon put on this drive. Despite the folder I chose having the name 'Bible Studies,' it looked like many of the enclosed subfolders contained information that pertained to now closed operations. My curiosity grew. Some of them were operations I'd heard of before. I recognised a few because I'd written the reports. Then I found some files that were shared with me *accidentally,* a long time ago, by my former boss. She was selling secrets, and until we caught her she had no clue we were following her trail. It was an awful situation and good people died before we managed to plug the leak and stop her in her tracks.

My bones told me this flash drive from MacKinnon was a good place to start looking for answers to what was going on now. If I could find a link to something I knew to be within the *Genesis* wheelhouse, then I'd know if I was right or wrong about this whole mess being a *Genesis* thing. Maybe.

"What are you doing?" Crockett asked. I looked up and saw him lounging against the kitchen doorway.

"Looking for a connection. Trying to find some sense in all this," I said. "I'll tell you if I find something."

I ran the cursor over each subfolder within the main 'Bible Studies' folder, hoping something would scream 'click me'. Nothing was jumping out. I changed my approach. What if I tried to use the cursor as a pendulum? What if I employed my special skills in a different way? It was worth a shot. I took a deep breath and slowly let it out. Placing my feet flat on the floor, I centred myself. I called the corners internally and asked for help. Carefully I moved the cursor over each folder, holding it for a second before moving on. Over a folder marked 'Expenditure' the cursor felt different, it jerked and stuck. It didn't want to move. I double clicked to open the folder and reveal the contents. Spreadsheets. That made sense since the name of the folder suggested spreadsheets. Boring, long winded, detailed spreadsheets that accounted for every paperclip and pencil used during operations. I moved across the many files, looking at the names. Everything was higgledy-piggledy. At the top of the folder, I sorted the files by name. It didn't much help. Most of the file names were dates. Nothing stood out. I tried something else and sorted the files by size. My magical cursor powers didn't seem to want to pick a file for me to explore.

I opened the first file and scrolled through its many pages. They were definitely expenditure with columns of numbers. The spreadsheet was big. I closed it again. Nothing of interest popped up. That was when I decided to start searching for words pertaining to the situation.

I wanted to dig up anything and everything that could've had any significance to *Exodus,* especially a biblical reference, given what I already knew about *Genesis,* and my part in it. Chances were high that *Exodus* was developed in a similar vein and that the keys were biblical. It made sense, or it did to me. I busied myself feeding searches into the folder. The last search netted a spreadsheet. Why would a spreadsheet that actually did contain expenditure on an old operation, have the words *'Burning Bush'* right smack in the middle of a column? And why would a file containing just a bunch of numbers be enormous? I grabbed my bag and fossicked through it until I pulled out a flash drive. I inserted the drive into the second USB port. I found the answer to why the file was so large, and extracted the reason, using a nifty little piece of software on my flash drive. My old mate Justin gave it to me years ago. *Just in case.* Buggery bollocks. Never mind ghost chips, I found a ghost file.

An easter egg hidden inside a spreadsheet that contained nothing but dollar amounts for an operation long over and of no interest to anyone except me, now. Why was it hidden and who hid it? Was it MacKinnon? It's his drive, odds were good then.

"Crockett?"

"Listening," he said, moving in his chair and looking up from the other end of the large dining room table. "Speak."

"Woof." I rolled my eyes at him then growled.

"Sorry," he said. "What did you want to tell me?"

"I found something."

"Carry on." He put the pen he had in his hand on the table surface and looked at me.

"It's an old file, we're talking Windows '98. Ancient. The creator is Michaela Kennedy-Carlisse. It seems to be a story and I have no idea why it would be a hidden file. And absolutely no idea why biblical search words would uncover it." I scrolled through the file that I'd extracted. "It's a book. It's a flipping book, Crockett. Since when do books get hidden in expenditure spreadsheets?"

His chair pushed back as he stood. "You're shitting me," Crockett muttered, approaching my end of the table like the floor was lava. "You used *Genesis* search words?"

"I did. And I am not shitting you," I replied. "Who is Michaela Kennedy-Carlisse?" The first and last part felt slightly familiar, but I couldn't place it, and then I did. Oh no. That was the woman Nana and the *Cronies of Doom* asked me to do an internet search for, and I didn't find. I also didn't look too hard. But they were going to carry on their enquiries by themselves. Hairs prickled on the back of my neck.

"I'm surprised you don't know," Crockett said.

"Surprised I don't know what?" Surely Nana hadn't talked to him?

"Focus, Ronnie. What do you think I'm talking about?" He leaned a hip against the edge of the table next to me and turned my laptop to face him without asking permission. "She was a kiwi who married Peter Carlisse, and briefly became the First Lady."

I could feel frown lines deepening. "Surely not." Famous, Nana said. That would qualify as famous in her eyes.

"Scouts honour."

"How briefly?"

"I think he was president for just over a year." Cogs turned. It appeared painful. "Do you mind?"

"Yes. This is not connected to the internet. Get another one," I said, and turned the laptop back toward me.

Crockett pushed himself away from the table and went

to the study. He was only gone a few seconds. He walked toward me with a laptop open, perched on his left hand and arm, while he typed with his right hand.

"Look what I netted." He spun the laptop so I could see the screen. Then sat in a chair close to me.

"Looks like a family photograph."

"It is."

"Okay. Who are they?"

"Former FBI Director Caitlin O'Hare-James, Ethan James, Quinn James. Quinn is their son. He's a doctor now. Next to Quinn, the tall bloke is Sean O'Hare; he was Cait's twin."

"Okay, and ..."

"Next to him, is his wife, Libby or Elizabeth Collins; she's a kiwi."

"You know a lot about this family."

"The internet knows a lot about everything. Now, back to the photograph. In front of Sean is a blonde, curly haired woman, who is Michaela Falacco. They call her Mikki. She's better known as Mikki Kennedy, a thriller author. She married a movie producer years ago. No kids. Once upon a time she was hot property, and her face was in every gossip mag there was. She was a kiwi-born First Lady. She was Michaela Kennedy-Carlisse."

You'd think I'd remember that. Can't believe the bloody Aussies didn't try and claim her as their own like they did every other Kiwi who made good. Focus. It's not a competition.

"How long ago?"

"Twenty-five years give or take." He frowned. "Might be nearer thirty."

That explains it. My biggest concern back then was trying to work out how *CatDog* pooped. "Who in this picture is still alive?"

"Mikki and Ethan maybe. Quinn, I'm pretty sure. Don't know about Libby. Longevity doesn't appear to be a thing in the O'Hare family," Crockett replied.

"Who can we talk to about why this book was hidden inside a spreadsheet?"

"I'd say Mikki. Wouldn't it be best to go to the source?"

"Is she still a Kiwi?"

"As far as I know, but then again, how would I know?"

"And what the actual fuck has this got to do with *Genesis,* and possibly *Exodus,* and how did a bloody book get hidden in a file in New Zealand?"

"I've got no more knowledge regarding that than you."

"What'd that short-term president do?"

"Fuck knows, probably not much." He spun the laptop and typed. "Holy smoke, I think this might be why he didn't last long. He managed to get a comprehensive gun-control law change, through the house."

"What happened to it?" Clearly, it died somewhere. It was a sticky subject throughout our lives to date that's for sure. I doubted it mattered or had anything to do with us or now.

"I don't know." His typing filled the silence left by his lack of words. "Here we go; it was overturned." His fingers pounded the keyboard. "He died suddenly." He typed some more. Then stopped and stared at the screen, then over it at me. "Elizabeth Collins is in New Zealand."

I'm pretty sure my face went into place saver mode and my mind went blank, just for a second. Crockett frowned at me, then gave me a catch-up look.

"The Libby woman?"

"Yes."

"Where? What does she do?"

"Not why does she use Collins, and not O'Hare?"

"That too, but what does she do? She must be getting on a bit by now. Is she a link to this fucktastophe?"

Crockett held up one finger on his right hand. "She's not that old but is retired and lives in Upper Hutt."

"That's handy." The bottom fell out of my stomach. Unless she lives in a bloody retirement home and knows Nana. "How old is she?"

"Mid-to late sixties I'd say. Younger than MacKinnon I think. I don't honestly know." He must've seen the look on my face. "Not Nana old." He paused and frowned. "How old is June?"

I shrugged. "She says ninety-four, but she's been saying that most of my life."

"A Sheila who won't tell her real age," he said, grinning.

"I think she's forgotten, and did you just call Nana a Sheila?" I shook my head. "At least it wasn't old Boiler, I suppose."

"Either way, mid-sixties isn't Nana old."

"Nana has young friends. That lady we met at the

movie theatre café. Remember, Pat?"

"I do, she was a very helpful ..."

"Do *not* say old boiler!"

"Sheila," he said with a smile.

"That's right, and she is nowhere near Nana *old,* and she knows Nana. I don't think we can discount it." I flapped a hand at Crockett. "Go make us coffee or something and let me do my thing." He closed the lid on the laptop he'd been using and slid it across the table to the seat he had before.

The cell phone in front of me rang. I saw the words 'cell phone two' on the lock screen. Ben. I swiped right and answered the call.

"How is he?"

"Dead."

"MacKinnon died?"

"Yes."

"Did he say anything?"

"No. They said he had a massive heart attack and he never regained consciousness. They tried."

"You confirmed he's actually dead. No signs of life. One hundred percent. Dead."

"Yes. I accompanied him to the morgue and waited. I've checked for vital signs twice in the last half hour. He's gone."

"Exfil."

"To?"

"One second caller." I jumped up, whipped around the table to Crockett's laptop and opened an internet browser. I navigated to the What3words website and typed our current address into the search bar. "Specialists full stop Pinstripes full stop Overheating." As soon as I had the coordinates I closed the browser and the laptop and popped back to my seat.

"Coming to you," Ben said.

The screen on my phone went blank. Crockett poked his head around the kitchen doorway. "Was that Ben?"

"MacKinnon died."

I heard movement in the other room. Luke jumped up from the couch in the lounge and hurried into the dining room. "What did you say?" He asked.

"MacKinnon died."

"Oh, man," Luke replied.

"Want a coffee, Luke?" Crockett asked. "Didn't ask before, I thought you were asleep."

"Yes," he replied, and pulled a chair out from the table. He lowered himself into it. "Did they kill him?"

I shrugged. "He was no spring chicken. Ben said it was a massive heart attack."

"I heard you say something before. You found something?" Luke said to me.

"Maybe. It might take a bit of reading. What was it MacKinnon wanted from you?"

"I don't know. We talked when we were alone. He asked why I met with one of his people in the Balkans. So, I told him. There was nothing to it. She gave me a gift to bring home for her mother. She wasn't coming back for several months, and mail is slow."

I nodded. Slow was an understatement. It wasn't unusual to ask people to bring things home. We did it all the time, but usually we knew the person.

"Did you know her?"

"Yes. We'd worked in the same theatre for a few years. Jobs cross over."

They do.

"What was it?"

"A present. It was a small flowery rug and a card."

"Where is it?"

"At my father's house," he said.

"Why?"

Crockett put our coffees on the table and joined us.

"I had the rug in my bag and went straight to dad's. It's a doormat, or something, you'd put it inside rather than the outside. Maybe nine-hundred by six-hundred millimetres.

"Was there anything else? Did she give you any information?"

"No. No shop talk at all. We had coffee a few times over several weeks. She asked if I'd take a present to her mum. She'd given my dad a present when I couldn't get home a couple of years ago."

Crockett nudged me under the table. I caught his eye.

Certainly, seemed innocent enough. Then again, innocent doesn't get two men snatched from Countdown. And it doesn't spin up a weird file from back in the day, but searching for biblical terms, I could've found that file at any point. The kicker is, I wouldn't have if it hadn't been for *Exodus* and my curiosity. Furthermore, innocent doesn't have ties to Albanians. That felt a bit racist, to be honest. I backpedaled my own thoughts. We needed that rug.

"What was the intelligence officer's name?"

"Zillah."

And if this has nothing to do with the *Genesis* program, I'll eat my hat.

Crockett nudged me under the table again. When I made eye contact, his eyes were almost popping out of his head. "I need to see you in the kitchen for a moment. Please?"

I rose to excuse myself, then said to Luke, "Do you need anything?"

Luke shook his head.

Crockett and I conferred by the backdoor.

"That *Genesis* Atlas we saw had Zillah on it?" he whispered. "I'm right, aren't I?"

How on earth would he remember that? I made sure he barely caught a glimpse of the names on the list. Even I didn't know if Zillah was on the list. But there was a good chance it was.

"It is a name I recognise from *The Book of Genesis*. So, there's a good chance it was someone's alias or used in some form in the *Genesis* program." I leaned against the glass door. "There's also a chance that it's just her name."

Crockett rolled his eyes. "It's fishy as fuck."

"Probably."

"Fishy enough that it's got something to do with that

rug and the story?"

"Puzzle time! Seriously, who knows?"

"What is it with you and puzzle time?"

I grinned and shrugged. "Meh. You had to be there. It's a Kiwi thing, goes with ghost chips." Or in this case, a ghost file.

"You Kiwis are a strange bunch. Must be the isolation."

"And Australians are normal? Your country is either burning or flooding, and everything wants to kill you." I smiled at him. "I'd sooner eat ghost chips."

Crockett inclined his head toward the dining room. "You buying his story so far?"

"Let's say I'd like to know more before I commit."

"Fair enough. Something is out of whack."

"That's a no brainer."

Chapter Thirteen:
[Crockett: How did he die?]

I spent time trying to reel in information from the short gander I got at the *Genesis* Atlas a while back. I was certain Zillah was a name on the list. I knew Ronnie and Ben were too, but I wasn't about to tell either of them I knew that. Had a feeling that knowledge would make me a liability. Liabilities don't last long in our world. One of those 'less you know the longer you live' deals.

The other thing occupying my mind was Libby Collins, or more accurately, why I didn't tell Ronnie that it was Collins who de-briefed me after the drone strike that killed Delta A and SAC Ellie Iverson. I never questioned why she did the de-brief; figured she was Johnny-on-the-spot. Now it looks like she stayed in New Zealand. That shouldn't be a problem. Or shouldn't be our problem? Who did she used to work for? She was a US marshal once upon a time. Her ex-husband was CIA. Collins made the move to FBI. There was a good chance she'd made another move to CIA.

A noise on the driveway interrupted my thought train. I eased out of the chair and made tracks for the front door.

Over my shoulder, I said, "Stay put. Someone is outside."

"Probably Ben," Ronnie replied. She didn't move. "Do

you want the Glock?"

"Yeah," I said, loud enough for her to hear me from the top of the stairs.

She caught up to me and handed me the paddle holster containing the gun. I shoved it into my waistband, checking it was properly seated. I was pleased she kept the Glock in a holster. Nothing worse than shoving a gun down your waistband without a holster.

"Be careful. Don't shoot Ben."

"Go back to the dining room," I said, and ran down the stairs as a knock echoed in the entrance way. I drew the weapon and from the stair-side of the door, I said, "Identify yourself."

"Reynolds, Ben. You kangaroo fornicating freak."

A grin spread across my face as I entered the code into the keypad above the handle. The door unlocked. I swung it open.

"Nice to see you, bro." I holstered the Glock.

"Tell me there's coffee," Ben replied. "This is a cluster fuck."

"We got coffee, and you're dead right about the cluster fuck." I closed the door, gave the handle a wriggle to check it had locked, and motioned to Ben to go up the stairs. "Ronnie is in the dining room."

He walked up the stairs ahead of me and vanished through the kitchen door. I detoured down the hallway to check the bedrooms were habitable. Not that I imagined they wouldn't be. Didn't take me long to close all the curtains and have a quick look to make sure the beds had sheets and bedding. All good and ready to rock. I checked the bathroom for towels and toiletries. All good there too. Art was a considerate host. I had no plans to screw this up and make him regret helping us. Again.

Back in the kitchen, Ben motioned to the full French press, and asked if I wanted a cup.

"Yeah, hold on, I left the cup I was using in the dining room."

Ronnie called out, "It's in the sink now."

"Cheers."

I picked the cup out of the sink and rinsed it before setting it on the bench. It was just me and Ben for coffee.

We each took our fresh cups into the dining room.

I scanned the people at the table. "Bedrooms are habitable, if anyone wants to get some shut-eye."

Wouldn't hurt any of us to close our eyes for an hour or so.

"I'll nap when I know what this hidden file is all about," Ronnie said.

Luke yawned behind his hand. "I had a few minutes on the couch. I'm good."

"Entirely up to you. I just wanted you to know the rooms were ready," I said, and sipped my coffee. Ronnie was reading from the screen in front of her. "How you doing with that research?"

She didn't reply.

"You see anyone dodgy on your way out of town?" I asked Ben.

"Bit of activity near the restaurant, but apart from that,

nothing."

"Activity?"

"I found a spot to watch for a few minutes. Saw two sets of two men. It looked like they were patrolling the immediate area."

"That's interesting. Not looking for us then. Cameras would've shown you three moving away from the front entrance." I sipped the hot dark coffee. "No doubt Luke and I were on at least one camera as we high-tailed it out the back."

"You sure there were cameras?" Ben said.

"Nope, but if it were my joint, there would be." Just because I hadn't seen any did not mean they weren't there.

"Fair call. We should work on the assumption that they had CCTV and saw us."

"What's your take on this situation?" The coffee was going down easily. Ben made a half-decent brew.

Ben placed his cup on the table. "I'm not willing to voice my thoughts just yet. If there were cameras, then we were on camera. Good chance they know who they are looking for."

I shot him a half-arsed smile. "They'd have to be exceptionally high definition before they could even attempt facial recognition. My considerable experience is that surveillance cameras aren't that good, unless the subject walks up to the camera face on, and even then, they're good, but not great."

"Are you sure we didn't do just that, at any point?"

"No. But I think we would've noticed if we were directly in front of a camera." I'd like to think the three of us
were aware of our surroundings at all times. "Worst case
scenario, they pulled images and printed them to hand to
the goons patrolling in the hopes that we were still in the
immediate vicinity."

Ben nodded slowly, but didn't look convinced.

Ronnie spoke, "We aren't on any accessible databases,
Ben."

"Doesn't mean someone can't identify us," he replied.

"All right, I'll play," I said. "They have photos, not the
best quality. They pass them around and someone recog-
nises one of us. They still can't get to us here right now.
So, identifying us gets them nowhere, fast."

Ben stood and headed for the kitchen with his cup. At
the doorway he turned. "Refill?" He tipped his head.
Guess he wanted me to join him.

"Don't mind if I do," I said, with a glance in Ronnie's
direction. She didn't look up. She was too engrossed in
whatever she was reading.

I grabbed my cup and followed Ben into the kitchen.

"What?" I said, putting the cup next to his on the
bench.

He pointed at his face. "I'm not invisible. All it takes is
for one of them to have seen my face on television, right
there in their living room."

Got it. He's concerned about his face leading someone
to Ronnie.

"I forget people know who you are," I said. "You worried about Ronnie?"

He shook his head. "She can look after herself. I'm worried about Nana. I'm concerned about Steph, Jenn, and Emily."

"Not Donald?"

Ben grinned. "You think Enzo would let anything happen to his precious Donald?"

Nope. Not at all. I shook my head. Enzo is not someone to mess with. He sure as hell doesn't *look* like someone you'd mess with. No worries there.

I cleared my throat as quietly as possible. "We need to mitigate any backlash to the family."

"I don't want to raise my concerns with Ronnie."

"Not surprised. No one likes being offered a problem. It's much better to come at this with a solution."

"Right now, I have no idea how to handle it. I need to do some thinking."

"Between us I'm sure we'll come up with a strategy."

Ronnie called out from the dining room, "What are you two dreaming up now?"

"Just making coffee," I replied.

Backlash that could lead to *Wherefore Art Thou* could also lead to the bookshop and Emily. That would not do. There must be a way to prevent Ben's face from causing chaos. I had an urge to go grab Emily from her bed and bring her here. I could guarantee her safety that way. How could I do that without alerting Ronnie to a problem? Ben's face was bound to cause trouble at some point. He was high-profile.

Chapter Fourteen:
[Ronnie: About MacKinnon]

"Ben, are we certain it was a heart attack and not some kind of toxin?" I asked, tapping my fingernails on the table.

"Don't think we can be one hundred percent sure of that without an autopsy," Ben replied. "There will be one. As soon as the authorities are notified of his death."

"You didn't do it?"

Ben shook his head. "No. The hospital know who he is. They can do the notifying."

Even though he didn't tell him, I felt we were only minutes off Chandler finding out about MacKinnon's death and wanting to know more. Everyone will be on high alert. Chandler hates being woken at night, but I wouldn't want to make the decision to not tell him until morning. That's a tantrum situation that no one would enjoy. I gave it a little more thought. He'd send flunkies to the hospital, and someone would remember us all being there. Then those flunkies would grab the security footage. I did not want to deal with his questions tonight and I'm pretty sure no one else wanted to either. He's a vile creature. Then I remembered we were off the beaten path. Even if he tried, he couldn't reach us. Small mercies. No doubt when he identified us all, he'd have a monumental fit. I wouldn't put it past him to put out an alert and try to get us scooped up.

I carried on scrolling through the document, or book, or whatever it was, that I'd found. I was skim reading to get the gist. If it didn't feel like a clock was ticking before, it sure as hell did now. Someone hid this for a reason. And to hide a book made me think the reason was bad. It read like a novel but didn't feel like one. I scrolled past pages of text hoping something would jump out and scream 'this is it, read this part'. Five chapters in, I saw a chemical formula. $Hg(CNO)_2$. I knew it was mercury something or other.

"Hey, Ben, what's $Hg(CNO)_2$?"

"Fulminate of mercury."

"It's a primary explosive," Crockett said. "Used in percussion caps."

"Why?" Ben asked.

"To set off a bigger charge," Crockett said, with a shake of his head.

"You're pretty funny for an Aussie," Ben said with a small chuckle. "I was talking to Ronnie, you wallaby aficionado."

Crockett laughed.

"Are you listening?" I asked.

They nodded, still grinning like idiots.

"Continue," Crockett said.

"I found the formula in this document and it's the first interesting thing I've come across."

"Is it in context?" he asked.

"No, it's scrawled on a page. Looks like parts of this

document were scanned in."

"If you find anything else, let us know."

I continued reading and six pages later I saw another formula. $C_5H_8N_4O_{12}$. And I thought I recognised it. "Am I right in thinking that $C_5H_8N_4O_{12}$ is pentaerythritol tetranitrate?"

Ben's eyebrows rose. "PETN. Yes, you are correct."

"Right, so, I imagine that $C_3H_6N_6O_6$ is the chemical formula for RDX?" I said, as another formula popped up in the margin of some text.

Crockett moved closer to me and peered at the screen. "Combine them and you have Semtex. That story is getting interesting. What's it about?"

"It's about President Carlisse, his wife, Michaela, and the O'Hare family. Looks like Michaela wrote a book about Cait O'Hare before she knew she was Cait and Sean's younger sister. She wrote it here in New Zealand. It was almost published but when the editor was running some checks on the research involved, he discovered it was creative non-fiction and not fiction. After that, the O'Hare family were alerted to Michaela's existence, and she was spirited away to the US and became part of history."

"The O'Hare family ..." Ben said slowly. "I heard they were eccentric in some interesting ways. Believed in things most rational people discount."

I made eye contact with Ben. "That sounds like insider information."

"I know the stories, that's all," he said with a smile.

"Cait had quite the sixth sense, so the stories go." His eyes met mine, holding my gaze for a few seconds.

"Great. Well, we've got explosives in this story. I'll keep reading." It's not eccentric to use your entire skill set. It's smart.

I skimmed a few more chapters after discovering the explosive references. It looked like there was an attempt on the First Lady's life. Explosives were used. Cait took Mikki's place.

"Hey, Crockett, that photo of the family. Would you say that Cait and Mikki were similar to look at?"

He nodded. "Yes. Why?"

"Cait took her place for a few days. I wonder if this is real. Did this happen just like it says in this story?"

"I don't know, and we weren't working when this file was hidden."

That was true.

"I'll sing out if I find anything interesting."

Four chapters later I found Peter Carlisse's death and slowed down to read. According to the document I read, Peter Carlisse was physically fit, had a clean bill of health, and yet died suddenly from a heart attack. Two paragraphs later the name Natalia Sokolov appeared, followed by a bio.

"Okay I've got something that probably doesn't belong. Just after a mention of the President's death, there is a bio for a Natalia Sokolov. She is a Russian scientist who developed a chemical that causes a massive heart attack. It's clear and tasteless with no smell, and it can be administered in food or drink. She took her research to the US and asked for asylum. Takes a mere two mils to kill someone and it doesn't work immediately. She worked out a way of making it a slow-release liquid to allow escape time, some sort of nano technology. Sounds as though each nano thingy carried a load and they all worked together. There's forty minutes to an hour before death occurs. If this is real, then it was super advanced tech when this was hidden." Futuristic Star Trek stuff.

"What happened to the research?" Crockett asked.

I read another few pages. "Says it was destroyed."

Judging by the noises of disbelief, none of us thought that happened. The CIA would've snaffled that up and locked it away for their own use, or the military would've stuck their hands up for it.

"How did President Carlisse die?" Ben asked.

"Suddenly," I replied. "Heart attack."

"And he was healthy beforehand?"

"Yes," I said. "According to this."

"Someone murdered the President?" Ben's incredulousness resounded.

"If that's the case, then why hide this story, why not sing it from the rooftops?" It didn't make sense. Sokolov arrives in the US seeking asylum, with her research. The President dies within weeks of her arrival. No one connected the dots? Unless it was an inside job. CIA. "I need to read more. This is plain weird."

"What happened with the explosives?" Ben asked.

"Someone set off explosives at the President's private

residence, Andrews Airforce Base, and then blew up a new building at George Washington University ..." I looked back over those chapters really quickly. "They were attempts on the life of the First Lady. Our Michaela Kennedy-Carlisse."

Crockett was running an internet search on the laptop he used earlier. "None of that was made public," he said. "Could it all be an actual story, proper fiction?"

"It could. But this Sokolov thing is interesting. I'd like to think she was fictional."

"You think someone killed MacKinnon, don't you?" Crockett queried. "He wasn't in the best shape, and he wasn't young."

"I've found a few references to this particular chemical weapon, so, I wonder ... is it a possibility? What if this Sokolov woman didn't destroy her research, and went on to live a quiet life tending roses and sipping tea?"

Crockett walked into the lounge and returned with a bleary-eyed Luke. "Ask him," he said.

I looked up at Luke. "Is it possible that something was given or administered to MacKinnon while you were held by the Albanians?"

Frown lines deepened on Luke's brow. He started to speak, then stopped and started again. "I was going to say we weren't given food or drink but, ... I wasn't." He shifted his weight from foot to foot. "MacKinnon was given water just before you rescued us."

"Anything else?"

"No, just a glass of water."

"And nothing for you?"

He shook his head. "Nothing. I asked, but they wouldn't give me anything."

I looked at Crockett. He nodded. One glance at Ben told me he really wanted that autopsy done. I had a feeling nothing would show in the autopsy except a heart attack.

"Any chance we can get hold of Zillah?" I asked.

"I don't know where she is and I have no way to contact her," Luke said. "MacKinnon was the person to ask about Zillah."

"Hmmm. And it's probably not a good idea to reach out to the son, James MacKinnon, right now. He wasn't answering his phone earlier." I had to wonder if his sudden dropping off the grid was related to the current situation. My money is on it being very much related.

Ben grumbled, then said, "He could be gone."

"Gone as in grabbed?" Crockett asked.

"Yes," Ben said. "James is involved in *Genesis* and this mess appears to link back to that program."

Or someone wants it to look like it links back to *Genesis*. That didn't make sense. What would the motive be to fudge a *Genesis* connection? I couldn't think of one.

Chapter Fifteen:
[Crockett: This isn't good]

"Okay. Someone - the Albanians - poisoned the old man and made James vanish? They took Luke along with the old man, why?" I sank into a chair leaving Luke standing on his own. "Were they after MacKinnon, and Luke here was collateral damage?"

"That begs the question, why did MacKinnon go to the supermarket Luke was in at that particular time?" Ronnie said. Her fingers moved on the mousepad. It looked like she was scrolling through more text before she looked up again. "Did you get a call from MacKinnon?" She looked at Luke.

His eyes stayed focused on me.

"I've had no contact with him. Was surprised to see him at the supermarket."

"Also, how did the Albanians know where MacKinnon was?" I asked. "It's starting to look like some heavy-duty surveillance."

"Someone is wearing a tracker?" Ben queried, looking at Luke and leaning back in the chair he sat in. "That would explain why no one was running around the city looking for us after we freed Luke and MacKinnon. They don't need to if they're tracking one or both of them."

Bloody hell. I don't want another shootout at this property. Art won't let us use it if we keep smashing it up.

At this rate we'll be in a tent in the bush instead of comfortably in a big house with bathrooms and food. Ronnie made eye contact with me.

"Do you still have your wallet, Luke?"

He shook his head slowly. "They took our wallets and phones."

So, if there's a tracker, it's in his clothing.

"Did they take anything else?"

"Our jackets were searched," he said.

"Did they do it in front of you?"

"No," Luke replied.

"How do you know they were searched?"

"I could hear them behind us. They were talking. I know they had my wallet because it was in my jacket pocket."

Couldn't help wondering what else he heard or what else they did.

"Where's your jacket?"

"On the couch." He indicated to the lounge by tipping his left thumb toward the door. I rose to my feet and retrieved the jacket and started with the obvious. The pockets. Nothing. Then I moved to the inside seams, running my fingers around the bottom of the jacket then around the edges of the sleeves. Nothing. So much for that idea. Unless ...

"If they had a tracker on you, Luke, I'm sure they would be on us by now. This has to be HUMINT. Someone had you under surveillance from the moment you got off that plane." Probably MacKinnon's people and then the Albanians watching MacKinnon.

Ronnie's head shook slowly. "What about MacKinnon's presence?"

"Maybe the old man was leverage over James," Luke said, his voice faded away. "And that's why they grabbed us."

Hang on a cotton-picking minute. My eyes bored into Luke's. "The old man was leverage?"

"Why?" Ronnie asked. "We thought this was about intelligence. Why take you both, and why kill their leverage, if that's what happened?"

I held up my right hand. "Hold it. How did MacKinnon know you were at the supermarket?"

Luke shrugged. "No idea. He appeared next to me."

"Poof, and there he was," I grumbled. "Not likely. He wasn't a fucking magician. He had someone watching you as well, I'd bet on it."

Ben leaned closer across the table. "Luke, what is it you have that's so damn interesting and worth killing for?"

"Everything I gathered had already been passed up the line before I set foot back in New Zealand."

"That doesn't work for me. Want to take another run at it?"

"I passed all my Intel up the line before I got on the plane."

"Yeah, you just rephrased your answer." I shook my head. "All right. Let's run with that. You were debriefed and all was well. Then for no fucking reason, MacKinnon appears at the supermarket, and you are both grabbed by thugs. At some stage you use some magic powers to get free long enough to make a phone call." I looked at him. "How does that sound so far?"

"Not good."

"Can you see why we're bothered?" Ronnie asked Luke. He nodded.

"Why did you call Ronnie and not your boss?" I asked.

"MacKinnon told me to call her. If I could get to a phone, he said, call Ronnie Tracey. No one else. He told me to memorise your number, Ronnie." A little bit of desperation crept into his voice.

"How exactly *did* you get to a phone?" I knew my words rang with suspicion. "Think about that for a second," I said, when I saw Ronnie stand and motion to me from the lounge doorway.

We excused ourselves. Luke sat down across from Ben. Ronnie and I went into the lounge. I slid the door closed before we walked to the large windows down the far end. The curtains were shut.

"What the fuck is going on?" I muttered.

She shook her head. "Nothing good. MacKinnon didn't want military intelligence involved. Luke magically found a phone. Whatever he has, it's big."

"And he's denying having anything usable. Does he know he has something worth killing for or does he not?"

She shrugged. "Your guess is as good as mine. If he does know, then he's having a jolly fine time playing the victim." Her uncharacteristic hardness surprised me.

"That came across callous."

"It is what it is. Maybe I'm not buying his 'I don't know anything' line, as much as he'd like," she replied.

"Or maybe he's being set up," I said. The expression on Ronnie's face told me that was possible. "Let's go back in there and find out how he got to a phone?"

"I'm getting a little curious as to the whereabouts of James MacKinnon ..."

"You want to try reaching out again?"

"No," Ronnie replied. "I do not think that's wise."

I slid the heavy door open and nodded at Ben, before sitting at the table. Ronnie sat in front of the open laptop screen. I could see that the screen saver had kicked in. She touched the trackpad to clear it.

She smiled at Luke. "How did you get to a phone?"

"We weren't in that room where you found us for the whole time," he said.

"They had you in a room with a phone?" It didn't seem very clever, and it was difficult to keep the disbelief from my voice. Perhaps Ronnie was onto something with her opinion of Luke O'Sullivan. Perhaps they allowed him to 'escape' to a phone.

"No. We were in another part of the restaurant. A storeroom with shelves of dry goods and cans. I broke the tape around my wrists, MacKinnon stood guard, and I found an office with a phone."

The first door I opened in that place was a storeroom. It was upstairs, within cooey of the backdoor. If it were me, I would've taken the opportunity to get out of there with the old man.

"Why not just make a break for it?"

"I didn't know where we were."

"You're in New Zealand. You must've had an idea how long you were in the car or van or whatever the mode of transport was. That would be your first clue." He was starting to piss me off.

"And your first response was to ring me not your boss," Ronnie said.

"MacKinnon insisted."

"You could've said that when you rang instead of saying you remembered my number."

I was getting the feeling that Ronnie didn't much like Luke.

His head moved in the slightest of nods.

"Not telling me you were with MacKinnon when you rang has made me suspicious of you and your story," Ronnie said quietly. "You better hope you're telling the truth."

"I didn't have much time. MacKinnon told me to ring you." He looked at me. "He said Ronnie would find us."

She damn near spat words at Luke, "So we were the bloody rescue team for MacKinnon. What do you know about *Exodus*?"

He shook his head. "Nothing. What should I know?"

"That a little while after you rang me, the three of us received a single word message. That led to us disappearing from the grid. Somebody planned this and used an *Exodus* message, to get us to free you and MacKinnon. Or

MacKinnon, and you, were along for the ride." Ronnie barely contained her annoyance.

Ben tapped her elbow to get her attention. "Somebody who knew that you had a new case." He tipped his head toward Luke. "And that you wouldn't walk away from it. Feels more like the *Exodus* order was to save them both."

How much surveillance was needed to know that? Had to be an electronic component.

"I was hired by Luke's father this morning," Ronnie said.

"Hang on Ronnie," I said, making eye contact with her. "Luke, does your father have a landline?"

Luke nodded. "Yes."

"How did the old bloke contact you, Ronnie?"

"He rang the on-call number on our machine last night and got through to Steph."

"That could be the answer to how they knew you had a new case, and that O'Sullivan was part of it."

"A phone tap," Ronnie said. "I wouldn't stop with that, would you Crockett?"

"Nope."

"Good chance the house is bugged then," Ben replied.

The three of us sighed. Of course. That made sense.

"What'd you do after the call from Luke, Ronnie?"

"Well, Crockett, I reached out to someone who I thought might know what was what. Bill ..."

Luke interrupted, "You spoke to Bill Bailey, my boss?"

"Yes, I met with him. I also told him to clean house because the whole situation reeked."

"Why clean house?" Luke asked.

"You have to ask that, in light of current events?" Ronnie said, staring at him.

Her instincts are good. This whole thing smells fishy as fuck.

"You didn't know much then," he said quietly.

"I knew you didn't call your boss or anyone from your unit, Luke. That's a fucking red flag, right there," she said. "At that point I considered the problem might have been within the unit; now I'm not so sure."

Luke leaned back in the chair. "Now you think it's me, right?"

"Tell me it isn't."

"You won't believe me if I do."

"That's not denial is it?" Ronnie said. "We now think your father's home is bugged, and his phone tapped, and it has everything to do with you."

Time for a change of direction. "How many people did you talk to when you landed?" I asked.

"I went through customs in Auckland and then caught a flight to Wellington. I spoke to customs agents, flight attendants, and the passenger next to me on the Auckland to Wellington flight."

"And you talked about what on that flight?"

"The coffee and the weather in Wellington." He looked right at me. "I did not tell anyone I was an intelligence officer coming home."

"Chit-chat then?"

"Yes."

"And when you arrived, how did you get to Upper Hutt?"

"Taxi."

Ronnie took over, "At what point did Bill give you leave to go home?"

"There was no conversation about leave. I debriefed overseas. I wasn't expected in either Trentham, or the Wellington office, for seven days, and that's when my resignation becomes formal."

"All right. What if I told you that Bill said you were on compassionate leave, and were supposed to check in at various times while on leave?" She drummed her fingers on the table.

"Perhaps you misheard."

"I did not. He told me you were on compassionate leave, and you were supposed to check in regularly."

"That's not true. I came back early because my father has cancer. My resignation was already pending. I've been offered a civilian job. I completed my last tour. I'm out of the army in seven days."

This was becoming a crapfest.

"How did Bill know you were missing?" Ronnie asked.

"I don't know," Luke said. "Maybe Dad called him."

Maybe, I looked at Ronnie and gave her a nudge under the table. "Did the old bloke ring Army Intelligence?"

"He did. He also said no one rang him back. And I know he rang Luke's phone several times during the evening. Whoever bugged the house, and I fully believe someone or multiple someone's bugged the house, they would know that too."

Regardless of the phone call to Bill, anyone with active surveillance in the house knew he was gone, because of the old bloke's repeated calls that weren't picked up. File that away for later.

My turn. "You took a taxi from the airport to your dad's?"

"Yes."

"Bet that cost a bit." About a hundred and eighty dollars, last time I did that, not something I'll do again.

"It did."

"You arrived at your father's house, then what?"

"I dropped my duffle in my old bedroom. And spent time talking to dad."

Ronnie jumped in, "Did your father know you were moving on from the army?"

"Yes. I told him I'd accepted a civilian job," Luke said.

"When?"

"Weeks ago. I emailed home when I accepted the job and gave my resignation."

"Did you contact Zillah's mother from your father's house?"

"No. I was going to give her a ring in the morning."

I interrupted the questioning for a brief moment. "Is there anything else you were supposed to deliver?"

"No, just the rug and birthday card."

"And where is it?" Ronnie asked.

"In my duffle."

"Did your father know about it?"

"No."

"You're certain you did not mention the present, or Zillah, or anything, to your father when you got home?"

Luke shook his head slowly. "I would've once I'd dropped it off, but we were talking about Dad's treatment options and how it'd be better for him having me home."

He was an unhappy bloke, but I still wasn't sure if it was about his dad or that we'd stomped on some truths, and he knew it was going to fall down around him.

Surveillance meant other people knew what we didn't know. Other factions had better Intel and Luke knew something that was worth all the effort. MacKinnon, as per usual, dropped us in the middle of his bullshit, half-cocked.

"Stay put for a minute." Ronnie stood and left the room with her phone in hand.

Chapter Sixteen:
[Ronnie: Roping in the gang]

I touched the Facebook icon and checked out the book-shop page. No more comments from Steph. It was late. I had a feeling we needed that rug ASAP. I left a message on the site. I carefully coded it, so she knew to go to a secure message server. While I waited, I paced up and down the lounge room. Three minutes later my message got a like from Steph. She must've turned alerts on instead of having her phone in sleep mode for the night. Another twenty seconds went by before my phone buzzed again. A comment in the same code. I opened the Signal app, added Steph's phone number, and initiated a text conversation, quietly pleased that I could still retain phone numbers in my head.

Me: Go into my new case file. Find the address. And retrieve the duffle bag belonging to Luke O'Sullivan from his bedroom.

Steph: What do I need to know?

Me: Other people want what we think he has.

Steph: I'll take Enzo and Jenn

Me: I need to speak with Enzo prior to the extraction of the duffle.

Steph: Do you need his number?

Me: Please.

Steph rattled off Enzo's mobile number.

Me: Thank you. I'll tell him to reach out to you and Jenn.

I closed the app and considered what I'd asked of Steph and Jenn. I opened the app again and added Enzo's number while I walked back into the dining room. Then made a voice call.

He answered quickly. "Who is this?"

"Your favourite soon-to-be cousin-in-law," I said, pushing a smile into my voice.

"Ah, the AWOL best woman. What's up?"

"I need you to do a black bag job, tonight."

"What am I looking for?"

"A duffle from my client's home. The man who lives in the house cannot know about this. We're pretty sure the place is bugged, so act accordingly. Use your toys, but disrupt, don't disable. We don't want whoever is doing this to know we know. I'm putting you on speaker."

"Okay."

"Steph and Jenn have the address. They're going with you, but you are going in alone."

"Where is this duffle or do I have to search the entire house?"

Luke spoke, "It's my father's home. The duffle bag should be on the floor beside my bed. Go in the back. The room you want is second on the right down the hallway. Dad's room is the third room. You don't have to go near it."

"And the hallway?"

"Back door opens into a laundry. Door on the right is the kitchen. Door opposite the backdoor is the hallway."

"Any animals or alarms?"

"No."

"How soundly does your old man sleep?"

"He hasn't mentioned any sleeping trouble. Maybe gets up a few times to pee."

"Got it."

Luke gave me a slow smile. "He's my dad, he's elderly and ill, be careful with him."

"Got it."

The rumbling noise in the background stopped. There was a quiet click. "Where are you, Enzo?"

"Walking to Steph's front door."

"You were on the Harley?"

"I was. Donald bought me a fancy new headset for my helmet. You are my first hands-free caller. I was on my way home and now I'm about to knock on Steph and Jenn's front door. And I'm no longer hands-free."

"Put Steph on when she answers."

I heard him knock, then the door hinge squeak as the door opened, and Steph greet Enzo. Next thing I heard was Steph in my ear. "Ronnie?" Her voice was crisp and clear.

"You okay being Enzo's wing woman?"

"Of course. Jenn and I will keep an eye out while he does his thing."

"Take one of the company cars. I suspect external surveillance as well as electronic. But don't know. Also, don't know who could be involved, or who else they're watching."

Company cars live out of the way in a Naenae garage owned by a shell company, that's also owned by a shell company, and then buried. It's like the shell game gone mad. All the regos point to various companies, but none point to 'Wherefore Art Thou' or any of us.

"I have the SUV out back. New plates arrived today."

"New plates?"

"Four sets arrived this arvo. I'll change the SUV's plates before we go."

"Thanks, be safe."

"Donald's on the war path, by the way."

"What's his problem?"

"You and your frock."

I smiled. That damn dress will be the death of me. "I'll sort the great big man-baby out when this mess is tidied away."

"Surprised Enzo didn't tell you."

"He knows better, I guess. Send a message when the job is completed. Stay cool."

I ended the call. I'd managed to walk into the lounge while speaking with Steph. The only thing about the job they were on that pleased me was Enzo doing the breaking and entering.

A cough from behind startled me. I turned and saw Ben grinning.

"Sorry," he said. "Everything all right?"

"I asked the team to retrieve Luke's bag from his father's home."

"Was that wise?"

I shrugged. "We need to know what he has, and if this whole thing is about a bloody piece of carpet, then we need to know what's so special about it. I have a horrible feeling that's what got MacKinnon killed."

"You're not happy with the heart attack scenario?"

"No."

"What was supposed to happen to the carpet or rug or whatever it is?" Ben asked.

"Luke was asked to deliver it to Zillah's mother."

"And then what?"

"I don't know. I think we need to talk to Zillah's mum." I hurried across the lounge room and entered the dining room. "Luke, do you have the address for Zillah's mother?"

He frowned. "Yes, I do. But not on me. It's written in a notebook in my bag."

"Okay, thanks." I placed my phone on the table and sat back down by the laptop. There was nothing to do but wait.

A small sigh escaped. Babysitting. That's what it felt like. I'm not at all sure that being a bodyguard for a wayward intelligence operative was the best use of my skills. Skills. I wondered if I could find James MacKinnon the way I found Luke. Worth a shot. All I needed was a map and a pendulum.

Chapter Seventeen:
[Crockett: Enzo comes through]

Coffee without food wasn't the best late at night. I hated to admit it, even to myself, but I might be too old to pull this all-night shit. I opened the fridge and spied a few cold beers. Tempting. Instead of beer I took out a carton of eggs, a block of tasty cheese, some butter, and a bottle of full-cream milk. Once I'd put them on the bench, I poked my head around the dining room doorway.

"I'm making scrambled eggs, who's in?"

A chorus of yeses returned. Ben stood up and walked toward me. "I'll give you a hand and make the toast."

We spent the next twenty minutes making much needed food. And the following ten eating in silence. Eating filled in time and improved the collective mood.

Ronnie's phone buzzed. She grabbed it and looked at the screen for a second.

"They have the bag," she said, and typed a response. "I asked Steph to call me via Signal."

Her phone rang. She put it on speaker.

"What do you want done with this stuff?" Steph asked.

Ronnie looked at me. I knew what she was going to say.

"Is Enzo there?"

"Yes, here he is."

Enzo's voice filled the dining room. "Yo. It's Enzo."

"Bring us the bag, please," Ronnie said.

"Going to need an address," he replied.

Ronnie looked at me and I spoke, "Bro. You know, Art, right?"

"Yeah." I could hear him breathing and hoped he was thinking. "He ended up in prison, if I'm not mistaken."

I had to think to find the meaning in that comment. The bush behind the house was Witako Reserve and it went all the way over the hill to a prison that used to be Witako Prison and was now Rimutaka Prison. Donald must've given Enzo some Upper Hutt history lessons.

"Yeah, that's the one."

Ronnie smiled at me, then spoke, "Give me back to Steph."

"It's me," Steph said. "What now?"

"You and Jenn go home, take the long way, lots of lefts. Be evasive."

"Got it. I'll run an SDR. No sign of surveillance so far."

"Doesn't mean it's not there. Someone's watching."

"Stay loose," Steph said, then the line fell silent.

The phone screen dimmed then went black.

"Dishes?" I said, standing and stacking the plates in a pile, with the cutlery perched on top.

"Luke and I will do them, you two cooked," Ronnie said. "Keep an eye out for our mate."

Ronnie and Luke took plates and mugs into the kitchen. I paced the living room. Ben joined me when I went into the study. I could see the driveway from there. No curtains. Ben shut the door which blocked the light and made the driveway easier to see. We stood in the dark watching, even though I knew it would take Enzo a minute or two to get the bag to us. I'm sure Ben knew that too. The silence became deafening. I cleared my throat.

"What do you think we'll find?" I asked, leaning on the wall, and watching the dark driveway.

"I don't want to speculate," Ben replied. "Whatever it is, it isn't good."

He was right. Something so sensitive it wasn't delivered in a usual manner, straight up meant it was bad.

"What's your take on O'Sullivan? Does he know what this is about?"

"Honestly, I don't know. Leaning toward - he probably knows something."

"Do you think MacKinnon was murdered?"

Ben's head swivelled so he was looking at me. "Yes."

"Makes a person wonder who could be next."

"I'm more interested in who or what killed him."

I caught a glimpse of car headlights between houses and trees. Too soon for it to be Enzo. The car turned off the road. I spotted taillights going up the adjacent hill. Someone going home after a night out. The silence resumed. Ten minutes ticked by, then a ruru called from the bush on our right, 'more-pork'. Another ruru answered. Easy to see why the little brown owls were colloquially called *moreporks*.

A low rumble gathered momentum as it neared. I listened and recognised the familiar sound of Enzo's

Harley. A single headlight shone before disappearing behind houses. The noise grew. Tires on gravel combined with the rumble of the engine. A bright light illuminated the driveway below. I didn't expect Enzo to be on his bike. There are more subtle modes of transport.

"That Enzo?" Ben asked, peering out the window.

"Nah, it's a wombat with a cold." I gave him a gentle shove.

"Dick," Ben replied with a grin. "What's the deal with Enzo anyway?"

"He's about to marry your girlfriend's cousin. Isn't that something you should've worked out by now?"

"Girlfriend is a strong word."

"Didn't take you as the type for a commitment phobia."

"Not a phobia. This life isn't conducive to longevity in relationships."

"Not a phobia, just a cynical prick. Got it."

"You always have to be an asshole?"

I shrugged one shoulder. "Shall we?" I asked. I motioned to the lounge as a knock resounded from the front door of the house. I moved first. Ben wasn't behind me when I reached the bottom of the stairs.

"Identify yourself," I said to the shadowy figure I could see through the frosted glass next to the door.

"Enzo."

I opened the door. Enzo stepped in with a large duffle over his shoulder, and his helmet in his hand.

"All good?"

"Yeah, the old man never stirred."

"Come on up."

Chapter Eighteen:
[Ronnie: Enzo and a secret]

"Hey, gang," Enzo said, as he strode into the dining room. "I come bearing gifts." He set the duffle bag on the table, and his helmet on a vacant chair.

"Anything we need to know?"

"No. Quiet and easy."

"Did you see evidence of electronic surveillance?"

He wiggled his eyebrows. "The second I walked through the back door lights went off on my RF detector. Couldn't tell if anyone saw me enter, but I can say they saw and heard nothing else while I was in there."

"Good work," Ben said with a smile. "You get all the fun."

"Tell me you were careful and weren't followed here," I said, smiling at Enzo.

He threw a lazy salute my way. "I wasn't followed." His voice dropped to a low whisper, but I still heard him. "I'm not an idiot."

"I know. This is a situation. I suspect surveillance and counter surveillance, and more than likely, counter-counter surveillance. The thing is, we're not a hundred percent sure who is surveilling whom."

He nodded. "What's so exciting about this duffle. It's not light, by the way."

Luke stood up and unzipped the bag. He quickly unpacked everything onto the table. The last thing out was the rug. "I lined my bag with it. Easier than trying to fit it in last."

Smart. Also, that wouldn't have creased it, if that was even possible. He freed the rug and it flipped itself open. It looked like it wouldn't crease in a hurry. I moved the laptop to make extra room. The rug was beautiful. It had an intricate floral design with everything from tiny violets to white roses. It was richly coloured too, with orange, yellow, red, white, pink, several shades of purple, and many greens.

"Stunning. I don't think I could bring myself to let people stand on it," I said, rubbing my hand over the lush surface. "You said there was a card?"

Luke passed me a white envelope. I turned it over in my hands. It was sealed and addressed to mum. That was it, just mum. I opened the envelope. Inside there was another, slightly smaller envelope. This time it was addressed to William MacKinnon. Now we were getting somewhere.

"That's interesting," Crockett said. "Let's see what's inside."

I peeled the flap up without tearing it. It was stuck, but not with anything stronger than the glue that came on the envelope. With care I pulled a card out. It looked as if it was made from a photograph. A single violet amidst a green leafy backdrop.

Upon opening the card, I saw a handwritten message. 'Dear Uncle Bill, a violet to remind you of me.' I passed it to Ben, who had appeared next to me. "What do you make of that?"

"Violet and Zillah have the same number of letters," he said, reaching for my pen and the notebook next to me. If violet means Zillah, then we might have a starting point for a code."

"How many of each flower are in the rug," Crockett mused aloud. "And are the flowers a code, or could it be the number of letters in each flower that helps form the message?"

"The colours could also be significant," I said.

Ben was writing as we talked.

"What if it's more than just flowers and colours?" Ben said. "A combination that gives a numerical code."

Potentially. I studied the flowers on the rug.

"You ever heard of the language of flowers?" I asked the men at the table. "It's a thing, look it up."

Ben wrote on the page in front of him without looking up at me.

Crockett nudged me. "Language of flowers. Okay. I'll bite. What do these flowers tell you?"

I ran my hand over the image, taking note of the flowers and bringing back all the times Nana had told me about flowers and their meanings.

"None of these flowers mean anything good. Including these delicate blue violets."

"How do you know what flowers mean?" Ben asked, a note of incredulousness in his voice.

"Something Nana taught me as a kid, it was fun. It

stuck." I replied. "But it would be handy to hear her take on this."

"Let's not bring June in ..." Crockett muttered. "She's probably fleecing the cronies out of their chocolate. Isn't it their poker night?"

My turn for a touch of surprise. "You remember what night they play?" He shrugged and looked way too innocent. "Oh my God, you play with them, don't you?"

One shoulder shrugged and he grinned. "Might've had a few games with the old boilers."

Ben's eyebrows shot up. "Sneaky bastard."

"They're not bad," Crockett said with approval.

I shook my head in disbelief and went back to thinking about the flowers on the rug, pulling in memories of Nana telling me about the language of flowers. "The blue violets say to be watchful. White roses are secrecy. Tansy, which is an odd flower to have really, it's more weed these days than flower. Well, that means hostility or even a declaration of war." I moved my hand to touch a bunch of snapdragons. "This is deception." I touched an orange rhododendron bloom. "Danger, beware."

"Surely the lavender is something nice?" Ben asked.

"Nope. That means ..."

Crockett interrupted, "distrust." He showed me a page on the phone in his hand. He'd done an internet search for flower meanings. "Flowers were how Victorian ladies and gentlemen sent messages. Clever."

"I'm not sure about this one," I said, touching what I believed was cyclamen.

"What is it?" Crockett asked.

"I'm going to say cyclamen."

There was a silent moment while he scrolled. "Resignation or goodbye."

"And the bittersweet berries?"

"They're poisonous and it means truth."

"There's only two more. I think the pale pink is a begonia," I said.

"If it is, it means beware."

"And this is a dahlia, a black dahlia." I knew what that was. "Evil."

"Imagine getting a bunch of flowers like that?" Luke said. "It'd probably come wrapped in poison-soaked paper."

"I guess a handmade rug is the next best thing." I rubbed my hands on the thighs of my jeans. The words *poison-soaked paper* stuck in my head. "Something bad is happening in the world," I mumbled, and turned the rug over. On the back was a sticker with the name of the person who made the rug. One corner of the sticker was missing. "Do you think Art has nitrile gloves handy?"

"I'd say so," Crockett said. "Hang on. I'll find some." He left the room. The sound of cupboards opening and closing followed.

"How about tweezers?" I raised my voice toward the kitchen. "And a knife?"

"Got gloves. Hang on," Crockett said.

He appeared with disposable tweezers the type seen in first-aid kits. In his other hand he carried a box of nitrile gloves and balanced on top a vegetable knife. "Medium," he said pushing the box across the table to me. The knife clattered to the table surface.

"Thanks."

I pulled a pair of the black gloves out of the box and put them on. They were a bit loose, but not annoyingly so. My attention returned to the sticker on the back of the rug. I felt a bit better about poisoned paper now I wore the gloves. The piece missing from the corner was about a five-millimetre section, and it exposed another glimpse of white paper underneath. I scratched at the edge with the point of the knife until the top paper began to lift. Using the plastic tweezers, I peeled the paper back with care. Underneath the sticker, I saw what looked like eight barcodes. They weren't exactly barcodes, but close enough. "Look at this."

"Strange place to find eight barcodes," Ben said.

I took his pen and the paper and wrote the numbers as I saw them: 2121631, 1353634, 2163212, 3232515, 6123612361, 232252, 2212231, 1555256. As soon as I'd finished writing the numbers I knew what it was. "Zillah and Violet are both six letters. This is a six number code." I wrote the alphabet across the paper, then starting with *A,* I wrote numbers from one to six, then repeated the numbers from one to six until I reached the end of the alphabet.

I handed the paper back to Ben. "Work out all possible letter combinations. I want to check something in the manuscript I found."

Did MacKinnon know I'd start digging into old files? Did he want me to dig around? Was there something he knew, but couldn't say? Did he know I'd use *Genesis* buzz words?

Of course, he did. I peeled the gloves off and dropped them on the table.

Crockett took a pen from his pocket and began helping Ben. Luke watched. I went back to the story and scrolled through the pages hoping that something would pop up and provide more of a link to present day. There didn't seem to be a connection. The final page came up fast. And I was none the wiser. What is it I need to find, Mac-Kinnon?

I looked up to find Crockett watching me. "Can I help you?"

"Do you want coffee?"

"Tea, please."

"Find anything?"

"No."

Crockett took my cup and disappeared through the kitchen door. My attention landed on Ben.

"How's the code breaking coming?"

He shoved the paper toward me. "Look for yourself."

There on the page was the name Natalia Sokolov.

And just like that there was a link to the hidden story.

"Natalia Sokolov, she was a Russian scientist who created a slow-release chemical that used nano technology to deliver it to the programmed location. Her creation mimicked heart attacks and the nano tech meant the heart attack was designed to kill well after the assassin was clear and gone."

"What the hell?" Enzo replied.

"It was in the story hidden inside a file. She defected and was given a new life. The technology was supposedly destroyed."

"MacKinnon had a massive heart attack," Ben said. "This was from the story?"

"He did and it was," I said. And he's not the only heart attack that might have a link here.

"How's that even possible?"

"I don't know. Unless the person wrote the story with insider knowledge, but couldn't prove what had happened, so it was buried. She wrote a tell-all story in the guise of fiction and then the thing was quashed and hidden."

"I think we need to find the author then, don't you?"

"I guess so."

Crockett placed a steaming cup of tea in front of me. Just the right shade of brown. I like my tea dark.

"Let's finish decoding these numbers before we go charging into the night to locate anyone," Crockett said.

Sensible.

"You heard?"

He nodded. "We've got a couple of people to locate, and that's your thing. So, let us finish this job and find out what this is about, then, you do your thing ..."

"Deal."

Enzo frowned at me from the other end of the table.

"Do you still need me?"

"No. Go home. Tell Donald I'm away working a case. I'll be in touch when I get back."

"Great, not even married, and already lying," Enzo said.

"It's not a lie. I'm definitely not home, therefore, I'm away. And this is very much a case."

Enzo's frown eased. "You could justify anything couldn't you?"

"Probably. Ride safe." But I can't justify the horrendous purple and orange frock Donald decided was perfect for me to wear to the wedding. I've tried, but it's not happening.

He stood, picked his helmet up, and headed for the door with Crockett following. Luke wandered back to the lounge leaving Ben and I alone to work on the code.

By the time Crockett returned we had two more words: Chinese and Taliban.

It was shaping up to be a disaster. A disaster hidden inside a pretty rug, because unless you knew what the flowers meant, it was just a pretty rug. It was far too pretty to sit inside an external door and have muddy shoes stomped all over it.

I drank my tea and stared at the unfolding message on the paper in front of Ben. Crockett worked on the next set of numbers. An ethereal knife twisted in my stomach. Nothing good would come of this rug, code, and Sokolov. Absolutely nothing good would come of Chinese working with Taliban. And there was the word, laboratory. Just what we wanted to see. Not.

"That can't be good," Crockett said, tapping the page under the word laboratory. A scientist, Chinese, Taliban, and now a laboratory. Is she re-creating her nano particle assassination tool funded by those two? And if so, to what end?"

"Is this for surgical type assassinations or something on a larger scale?" I added. "If it's what killed MacKinnon then she's not making it, she's made it. We need to find the target before people start dropping."

"If they took MacKinnon with Luke to find out what he knew, then there's a chance the target information is here somewhere," Ben said, waving his pen in the direction of the rug and Luke's duffle.

The next three numerical codes were worked out over two cups of tea and a snack. Sleep became a distant fleeting thought.

"What could bonnet, phantom, sweeter, mean?" Ben asked. "Maybe I got it wrong?"

I held my hand out for the other laptop. Crockett gave it to me. I checked it was connected to the Wi-Fi, pulled up a web browser, and navigated to What3Words. Then I typed the three words into the search bar using full stops between them.

"Bonnet-full-stop-Phantom-full-stop-Sweeter," I said. "Coordinates for the University of Tirana."

"Albania," Luke said quietly. "Does that mean the lab is in the University?"

"Would make sense. They'd already have labs there

and they could be hiding in plain sight," I said. "So, this is the intelligence that MacKinnon was supposed to get. Coordinates for a laboratory and Natalia Sokolov."

"There wasn't anything saying what she was, or is, working on there, or what she's doing with the Chinese and Taliban. Once upon a time I would've thought they were strange bedfellows, but not since Taliban came out, once they re-took Afghanistan, saying the Chinese were their trade partner and allies," Crockett said.

I stared at the screen in front of me. I knew where in the university building the lab was, but we were in New Zealand. MacKinnon was killed in New Zealand. How did the nano tech chemical get into New Zealand and why? It probably walked across the border with someone. It wouldn't trigger any alarms. Especially if the liquid was inside luggage and therefore in the hold, not carried on-board, and if it was concealed in something that usually carries a small amount of liquid. A woman could have a small bottle of skin toner or Micellar water in a toilet bag, and no one would check.

"What do we need?" I muttered, more to myself than anyone at the table.

"A target," Ben replied. "If we think this nano tech killed MacKinnon then it's in the country and we need to know why?" He gave me a look.

"What?"

"What big event is coming up that's bringing world leaders to Wellington?"

There was only one that I knew of. "The wedding," I

said, slumping in my chair.

Luke's eyes widened. "I didn't know your cousin was so influential."

"Not that wedding. The *other* wedding."

Luke smiled. "That makes more sense. Security will be tight. A year's worth of planning tight."

"Exactly. Any chatter would have caused even more security, or postponement, or even cause the whole event to be taken online," Crockett said. "Likewise, zero chatter would cause concern, because we've seen chatter dry up before an attack."

"Attacks don't materialise from thin air. There is planning, months of planning, and if this is an attack on New Zealand soil, and we have zero chatter, then we are very close to the execution of said attack," Luke said shaking his head. "I was boots on the ground and I heard nothing."

"Put on your waders," Crockett said. "This is going to get muddy and deep."

"Nothing came through the usual channels, and no one is talking except in person, so, our intel is it?" Ben asked. "Ironic isn't it? They're using high-tech nano particles, but going old school on the information channels."

"Could Sokolov be here?" I wondered.

"I doubt she'd need to be. What would be the purpose of getting Sokolov into New Zealand?" Crockett replied.

Good point. "Imagine for a moment that they used Sokolov to bring the nano thingamajigs into the country."

Crockett and Ben stared at me for a beat. I could see

my words sinking into their brains.

"If someone is intent on killing world leaders, or particular leaders, and they use something pretty well invisible, how do we stop it?" Crockett said.

"We get back into the restaurant. That's the crime scene. That's the link," I said.

"And look for what?" Ben asked. "A bottle marked with a skull and cross bones?"

A smile radiated from Crockett's face. "Aren't we lucky that bad guys always wear black."

Luke laughed and the mood in the room lightened.

"For starters if we go back, Luke here could ID the person who gave MacKinnon the drink," I said.

Crockett held his hand out and indicated he wanted the laptop back. I passed it to him. A few moments of silence punctuated by the soft click of keyboard keys followed.

He looked at Luke. "Albanian?"

"I think so," Luke replied.

Crockett spun the laptop around. "Take this, use the arrow keys to scroll."

Luke lifted the laptop from Crockett's hands. He sat quietly moving through images.

I kicked Crockett's foot under the table. "What did you access?"

"ASIO watch list." He smiled. "I used a VPN before using my login."

"Good."

"It routed me through Russia."

"Fitting."

We smiled at each other. "It's time," Crockett said to me. "There are maps in the study. You need anything else?"

"No." Candles are nice but not necessary. Everything can happen in my head if I need it too, as long as I have a map. My fingers sought the gold chain and quartz crystal pendant around my neck. I had everything I needed. "Carry on here. I'll be back." If the gods are in my favour, we'll have answers, or locations. Who am I kidding? I don't know how this works.

I walked into the study while taking the necklace off and refastening it. I closed the door behind me. With the necklace encased in my right hand, I looked for the maps while thinking about my intentions, and who I was looking for. A knock resounded on the study door.

"Come in," I called, spreading a map of Wellington on the desk.

The door opened and Crockett ambled in with his phone in his hand. "Thought a picture of Sokolov might help." He showed me a picture on the phone screen.

"Thanks." It was James MacKinnon I really wanted to find. "She doesn't look like a murderer. She kind of looks like a grandmother. Nana would be friends with her."

"Babushka," he said, as he turned to leave.

"No, you are."

"That doesn't even make sense," he said, shaking his head while grinning.

"Hey, Crockett." He stopped walking and looked over

his shoulder at me. "I'm going to call the *Exodus* over and done. MacKinnon is dead and we need to get back to the land of resources. I'm confident we can keep Luke, and the Intel safe, and work out what is actually going on here."

"You want me on babysitting duty," he said.

"I heard you weren't half-bad as a bodyguard."

"Stories, just stories." He gave me a fast smile and left the room.

I grounded myself and held my necklace over the map. The image of Sokolov stayed in my mind, despite me wanting to find James MacKinnon. Looked very much like the universe had other ideas. The map I'd opened was a map of the Wellington Region not a world map. I couldn't think of a reason for Sokolov to be in New Zealand.

I cleared my mind and focused on my intent. Slowly, I moved the pendulum across the map from right to left. Starting in the southernmost part of the region. My hand was pulled toward the restaurant. *Manger.* I moved on despite the reluctance of the pendulum. I re-focused on my intended target. James MacKinnon. The pendulum swung in slow lazy circles across the map. At Ngaio it tightened its circles, spinning into a small area and then stopping over an address. That was MacKinnon senior's home. Or more accurately, a New Zealand residence provided by the agency he worked for. I thanked spirit and put the pendulum on the map so I could write down the address. There was a pen and a notepad on a bookshelf

163

under the window that overlooked the stair well.

We didn't try the phone number at MacKinnon's residence. We tried James' cell and his home number. I picked the pendulum up again.

"Okay, show me Sokolov, if that's what you want to do."

The wide circles began. I watched as my hand was pulled across the map. Pendulum work never ceased to amaze me. It was proof that there are more things on earth that we still don't understand. Again, the pendulum drew my hand to MacKinnon's residence. What the hell? Then it moved away. She was there? I stopped the pendulum.

"Was she at MacKinnon's?" The pendulum spun in wide circles anti-clockwise.

There was no debating the yes for that question.

"Thank you."

I repositioned my hand and the pendulum over the map and let the pendulum dictate the direction. Eventually the circles tightened over Birchville, in north Upper Hutt. Seriously?

"Is she really here?"

The pendulum switched its spin from clockwise to anti-clockwise. The circles shrank until they were barely circles at all, then the pendulum stopped dead. The point was over an address in Gillespies Road.

"Thank you," I said, and gently laid the pendulum down. It rolled until the point was on the address. I wrote it on the note pad and Sokolov next to it.

It didn't feel like I was done yet. There was someone else the pendulum wanted to find. The family photo of the O'Hare's came into focus. A spotlight highlighted Elizabeth Collins.

"Okay, I'll play. Show me Elizabeth Collins."

I let the necklace chain run through my fingers, closing them at the last second. Immediately the pendulum began to swing, anti-clockwise. I let it take me wherever it wanted. I was along for the ride. When the pulling stopped it was over Nana's retirement home. The spin changed from anti-clockwise to clockwise. What were the odds? I knew she'd be somewhere near Nana. The circles tightened and spun faster and faster. Then stopped abruptly over the new apartments.

"Can you narrow it down?" I said, lifting my eyes to the ceiling before looking back at the map. The pendulum swung in a straight line, pointing to the west wing. "Thank you."

I lowered the chain until the pendulum touched the map, and let it go. It tumbled until the point was directly over part of the retirement home. The part it had already indicated on the west side of the new apartment complex. Those apartments didn't have garden access like Nana's. They were fully contained, one-and-two bedroom, modern apartments, but only the ones at ground level had external access and there weren't many of those. It was a three-storey high building and meant Elizabeth Collins could be anywhere on the west side.

"Thank you spirit," I said, quietly.

I wrote down the address on the pad, under the address for Sokolov.

I fastened my necklace around my neck and left the room with the paper in hand. What the hell was Sokolov doing at MacKinnon's?

A feeling of foreboding crawled up my spine.

Chapter Nineteen:
[Crockett: Nana]

Ronnie didn't look happy when she joined us in the dining room.

"What's going on?" I asked. "You seem annoyed?"

"Let's call it annoyance, that'll do." She beckoned to Ben and me. "Back in a minute, Luke," she said with a small smile.

Ronnie led the way up the hall and into the master bedroom.

"Tell me again how Elizabeth Collins isn't Nana old," she said, staring into my eyes.

"What's happened?"

"Looks like Collins is living in the retirement village."

"Didn't see that coming," Ben said.

"Doesn't mean June knows her," I replied, hoping I sounded convincing. "It's a big place, especially with all those new apartments."

"The indication is that Collins is in one of those new apartments."

"See, that's not near June at all. June has a garden apartment and no need to go near the new building."

"You are underestimating the nosiness of the *Cronies of Doom*." Ronnie sat on the edge of the bed. "This is a disaster. Elizabeth Collins is a wildcard as far as I'm concerned. From what I've gleaned so far from that story, she had dealings with Sokolov back in the day."

"What else, because that look in your eye isn't just about Collins and Nana," Ben said.

"Sokolov is in Birchville, and James MacKinnon is at William MacKinnon's residence in Ngaio."

"Sokolov. Is. Here. In. New Zealand." The words refused to make a proper sentence as they formed. My thoughts caught up. "Why would she be here? Was it to bring her tech bugs into the country?"

Ronnie shook her head. "I don't know, but that makes sense to me. We think the lab she used is in Albania and yet she's here. Another what the fuck moment brought to us by the buzz words *Exodus* and *Genesis*."

"You got us locations, Ronnie. That's what we needed."

"We can expect surveillance on Sokolov. Whoever she's working for is not going to want her running around getting spotted," Ben said. "What's the deal with James MacKinnon?"

Ronnie shook her head slowly. "We didn't try MacKinnon senior's residential phone line. I would've expected James to be monitoring his own messages though. He certainly didn't ring me back when I reached out. Maybe he can't."

I narrowed my eyes. "You don't think he's breathing anymore, do you?"

She shrugged. "If William was leverage and they killed him ... he might've given them James. We don't know that he didn't."

"Luke would?" I queried.

"Perhaps. They could've separated them. Or he might not be the wholesome wee spy we think he is."

There it was again, her suspicion of Luke. I can't say I blamed her, and I even thought she might be onto something.

"Could be something else though. If the Albanians didn't know exactly what Luke had, but suspected the intel was something tangible that he didn't know about, that'd explain why they kept him alive and let us escape," I said. "What if we were supposed to break them out and lead them to the prize?"

"Does Bill Bailey know about the prize?" Ronnie said. "Why were/are Army Intelligence so worried about O'-Sullivan when he was retiring and, according to Luke, didn't need to check in ... if he didn't need to check in, how did Bill know he was missing?"

Ben sat next to Ronnie. "We're pretty sure he has the house rigged with some cool tech; that's how he knew."

"Someone, or many someone's, are not telling the truth," Ronnie mumbled. "What if we send Luke home, without the rug, and wait to see what happens next?"

"You serious?" I asked. I had to ask because I couldn't tell.

"Yes. I've done what my client wanted. I've found his son. Let's send him home to his father. Job done."

"What about the nano-bot whatchamacallits?"

"Not part of my brief," Ronnie replied. "My job was to locate Luke O'Sullivan. I did my job."

"And the *Exodus*?"

"MacKinnon is dead. He was the only person who could've had that message sent. Must've been automated somehow. If he didn't log into something by a certain time we got a message?"

I nodded. "Seems logical." Similar things have been done before. Not unheard of for someone like MacKinnon to have an automated delivery system that sends an alert out. Files were probably destroyed at the same time. I took a beat and let that sink in. Ronnie has a flash drive belonging to MacKinnon. That could contain the only surviving files. "Did James get the same message?"

Ronnie frowned. "Possibly. We don't know who else was involved or who else was on his contact list."

"You said James is at MacKinnon's residence, his official residence?"

"Yes."

"Maybe when he got the message he knew to go there and do something …" I paused, mostly because it sounded stupid saying it out loud. Suck it up. "Maybe he went there to destroy something."

"*Genesis*," Ben whispered, his voice growing slightly louder as he continued, "We thought the old man didn't know who was involved, but we never knew for certain. If you stop and think about it for a minute, it makes sense that they would run it together."

"Why destroy *Genesis*?" Ronnie asked.

"What if … what if, the targets are worldwide. What if it's a two-fold plan?" I wondered out loud.

"Expand on that," Ronnie said.

"We think they're after heads of State at the Prime Minister's wedding, and that makes sense. But what if this is multi-pronged. As well as the heads of State, they go after the officers, agents, analysts, collectors who provide intelligence to the *Genesis* program?"

Ben and Ronnie looked at each other briefly. Maybe it was time I told them that I knew, but I didn't.

"Without access to the files we can't warn anyone," Ronnie said. "And if James did go to destroy those files, then we can't even use his key to unlock the files I have."

"The key would still be there, on the computer," I said. "There's no need to destroy that if it no longer unlocks anything."

Ronnie smiled. "It would be destroyed, everything would be. Leave nothing behind."

Ben stood up and walked across the room, stretching his arms above his head a few times. "We have a lot of what ifs, and not enough actualities."

I could see flickers in Ronnie's eyes. She was thinking, and so was I.

"Zillah, can we reach out to her?"

Ronnie's eyes flicked up to meet mine. "Maybe. Her mum's address is on that envelope. Luke was going to deliver it. She might have a way of contacting her while she's working overseas."

"Okay. You want to turn Luke loose and see what happens. We really should go find out what the story is with James MacKinnon. Zillah's mum is a possible way of contacting Zillah. Sokolov is in a northern Upper Hutt suburb, and Elizabeth Collins is in June's retirement home. We don't have enough boots on the ground to cover four targets, and surveil Luke."

"I can get Steph and Jenn onto the surveillance. We have another couple of surveillance people on the books. I can get them involved, it's no problem. They're good. That'd give us two teams watching Luke."

"I'll get Art and Enzo," I said.

"Discounting Luke's surveillance," Ronnie said, "We have four locations of interest. The retirement home, MacKinnon's Ngaio residence, Birchville, and Zillah's mother's. And five people. Would be better if we had three teams of two."

"Surveillance really needs four people." Hard to build a box around the target without four sets of eyes. "We're going to let Jenn and Steph, and the other two you spoke of, run without any backup?" I asked.

"We don't have a choice." Something switched. Ronnie gave me a wicked grin then did the best impersonation of Chandler I'd ever seen. "I've got four really good surveillant operatives and that's it. I need my best surveillants surveilling with surveillance." She completed the impersonation with a well-placed hand gesture, implying he was a wanker. We all chuckled. She had him down pat.

Ronnie was herself again, and serious, when she said, "We need Emily in on this to make up our numbers."

I held my hand up, palm out. Stop right there. "No."

Ronnie nodded. "Yes, we do. What you don't know about Emily would fill a library. She can do this; she just doesn't remember she can do this."

I cast my mind back to the night I saw her grab a Glock from midair, perform a press check and settle it in her right hand, like it had always lived there.

"This isn't muscle memory, Ronnie."

"It sort of is. You put her in a situation she's been in before and she'll rise to the occasion. She knows so much, but she doesn't know she knows." Ronnie was sure. "The knowledge didn't vanish, it's there, but it's trapped behind a shield of some sort."

"Pretty dangerous to drop her in it like that."

"Take her with you, she'll be fine," Ronnie said, sounding like she meant it. She also sounded like she'd argue until the cows came home. Having seen her go down that road, I knew I should shut up and accept that I'm taking Emily with me.

"All right. I'll take her with me."

"I'll make the calls to my people. You call Art and Enzo."

Chapter Twenty:
[Ronnie: Mistakes were made]

Steph's phone rang and rang. Eventually a sleepy voice answered, "I hope this is life or death."

"It is."

"Ronnie, why are you ringing again? You should be asleep."

"We can't all sleep all the time," I said. "I need you and Jenn on deck for a surveillance job."

"Right, send me the deets, and we'll get to it first thing."

"Not so fast, it's a now thing."

Steph groaned then sighed. "I guess it's pretty important if you're calling me like a real person, and not all secret squirrel."

"Time to play this out in the open or pretend we're in the open. That's where you come in. I'm turning Luke loose. And I suspect his father's house is under surveillance. Don't lose him and see if you can find out who is watching him and the house."

"Righto."

She sounded more awake.

"We'll put him in a cab from Heretaunga in an hour. You have an hour to wake up and get into position. Four cars. I'm calling in Jo and Brie."

"They'll love that." Even half-asleep, her sarcasm

shone.

"Triple time."

"We'll see about that once they turn their time sheets in. Don't go making promises."

Nothing woke Steph up faster than mentioning money.

"You're in charge of the team."

"Right, got it."

"Be safe."

"Will do." Steph hung up.

Ben and Crockett were looking at me.

"Problem?"

Ben frowned. "Just a logistics query, how are we getting Luke to Heretaunga?"

I smiled and Crockett shook his head.

"You're joking," he said.

"Apparently not."

"What?" Ben said. "What is she not joking about?"

A wry smile formed on Crockett's lips. "She's going to send him over the hill, through the bush."

"That'll take longer than an hour," Ben said. "He'll get lost. That's a nuts thing to do."

I chuckled. "Of course, he'll get lost."

"Then why?" Ben asked.

"Because if he's lost in the bush he can't cause trouble, and no one can get to him." I took in the horrified looks of the two men in the room and winked. Their senses of humour failed them. "You idiots. I was kidding."

"That's okay then," Ben replied with a smile.

"Yeah, come on, let's get on with it. We can't exactly

call a taxi from here, so we'll walk to Heretaunga, and call him one then. It's not far."

"We need wheels," Crockett said.

"Where's your car, Crockett?"

"Near Heretaunga railway station."

"Great, then you can take Luke, and call him a cab while you pick up your car."

"Where are you two going?"

"We're going to train to Naenae, and I'll grab one of my cars from the garage."

"Then what?" Crockett said.

"We'll carry on south and go see what's up with James MacKinnon. If the key still works I'll use it to find and warn the *Genesis* list." I was certain that anyone on the Atlas was now in grave danger.

"I'll pick up Emily, and take her with me to watch Sokolov," Crockett said. "Do you want us to drop by Zillah's mother's place too?"

"We'll see how we get on at MacKinnon's place first. I'd rather not drag another elderly person into something. Bad enough Luke's dad is in the midst now. As far as we know, they don't know about Zillah's mother, yet."

"I'd like to know exactly who 'they' are," Ben said, half under his breath.

"Us all," Crockett said.

"Brie and Jo will join up with Steph and Jenn," I told him. "That gives us a four-person surveillance team."

Crockett pushed off the wall he leant on. "The mother concerns me. We don't know that Luke kept his mouth shut. We don't know what questions he was asked."

"Fair call." I gave Zillah's mother more thought. I had Art and Enzo to deploy.

"Okay, you're right, we don't know. Let's put Art and Enzo on the mother."

Ben smiled. "Sounds like a good plan." He stuffed his hands into his pockets. "What about Collins?"

"She's not going anywhere tonight. We'll call in first thing and make sure she's nowhere near Nana," I said. I glanced at my watch. "Even Nana isn't awake at three. Is that everyone covered for now?"

"Yes," Crockett said. "So, we're back on the grid?"

"May as well be. We can liberate our own phones as soon as we get to the office. I don't imagine that will be until morning."

"Stay frosty," Crockett said, throwing a grin over his shoulder as he left the bedroom.

Ben grabbed my hands and pulled me to my feet. "Let's go find ourselves some wheels."

"It's over one and a half kilometres to the train station. The next train isn't until five," I said.

"What do you want to do?"

"Go to the office and get our real phones. We can train from Upper Hutt." On the face of it, it wasn't a bad idea. To keep it like that, we'd have to walk back streets and alleyways rather than the easiest route up Fergusson Drive.

"That'll be a nice walk."

"Nothing like a relaxing five-kilometre stroll at three

a.m." It'd be a lot longer than that with the twists and turns we would be making.

"And the rug?"

"I think we should leave that here. There's a safe?"

"Don't know, ask Crockett."

"In my bag near the dining room table are four Air-Tags. Can you slip one into Luke's bag and one into something else of his, while I talk to Crockett?"

"Consider it done."

We left the bedroom and found Crockett in the dining room with Luke. I beckoned to Crockett and went into the hallway. Ben stayed with Luke.

"Is there a safe?"

"Yeah. In the dining room."

"Okay, weird place for a safe." I expected him to say in the master bedroom wardrobe, or in the garage.

"Go to the end of the breakfast bar, where the house telephone is. Bend down and push on the left side of the wood panelling, directly under the telephone nook. It'll open a type of priest's hole." He tipped his head to the side and looked at me. "Inside that you'll find a built-in wall safe. It's set about three hundred mil back from the door. Pretty sure the code is the same as the door entry code. It's Art, he likes to keep things simple."

"Right, got it. Luke can take his duffle, but the rug and card stay here. Memorise the address on the envelope meant for Zillah's mother."

"Already given it to Enzo and Art. They should be in place within the next fifteen minutes."

"Great."

Crockett nodded. "We'll get going. I'll drop him home. Trains aren't running yet."

"Don't go right to the house. Be evasive. Someone is watching, or multiple someone's are watching, the house. They'd be idiots if they weren't."

He wiggled his eyebrows. "This is going to be fun."

"I don't see the fun." Tiredness and too much coffee fought a duel in my body. "I'd very much like some answers," I replied. "Be careful. It might be a good idea ..."

"... to swing home and grab something from my gun safe?"

"Yes, and ..."

"... And my real phone from the faraday cage at your office." He finished my sentence again.

We smiled at each other. We were starting to think like a team. Crockett vanished from my sight, only to reappear with Luke, ready to leave.

"Go well," I said. "Stay in touch."

They went down the stairs and out the front door. Once the door closed, I gathered the rug, card, our scrawled notes, and the laptop I'd used, into a pile on the table. The flash drive was still in the laptop. Oops. I lifted the laptop lid. On the screen was the story, or book, or whatever it was. I'd got just over half-way. A quick glance at my watch told me I had plenty of time to skim some more.

Ben walked in. "Are we going?"

"Soon. I just want to have a quick look at some more of

this strange story." I moved the laptop to a more comfortable position. Sat at the table and began.

Ben sat next to me. Not quite reading over my shoulder, but close.

"What are we looking for?" Ben asked, as I scrolled through another four pages.

"Anything that stands out."

"How about doing a search?"

"That's not a silly idea." I chewed my lip as I typed Sokolov into the 'find' function. Twenty instances. I'd seen six. I navigated to the next mention of Sokolov.

Ben and I read the paragraph.

"She wasn't just working on nano tech. She designed an early Directed Energy Weapon."

"This woman is a menace to the world," Ben muttered.

I skipped to the next mention of Sokolov. Again, we read the paragraph. "She wasn't easy to manage. They had round-the-clock surveillance and she was in a safe house."

Ben pointed to the bottom of the page. "She escaped multiple times."

I bounced my way through the remaining mentions, pausing long enough to get the gist.

"Everyone liked her, but no one trusted her. Her DE weapon failed to produce the desired results. She stopped working on it, after the fifth failure. Sokolov put her energy into nano technology and was working on a way to combine molecular biology and artificial intelligence."

"Sokolov is brilliant and was ahead of her time. In

2020, the first living robots were developed from frog stem cells." Ben leaned back in the chair and shook his head. "Her research and work paved the way for some crazy shit."

"I think I heard something about that. Xenobots?"

"Yes. They're less than a millimetre wide and can move and work together in groups; they can also self-heal." He sighed. "And then it gets creepy. They reproduce by themselves. They're Pac Man shaped and they scoot about cramming tiny stem cells together in their mouths. A few days after that, they spit out a new xenobot created from the mouthful of stem cells."

"They decided to be little bio-Pac Men by themselves?"

"No, researchers used AI to test billions of body shapes to make the xenobots more efficient at replication, and they ended up with Pac Man."

"That sounds like something the Defense Advanced Research Projects Agency would fund. One of their special projects."

Ben nodded. "Partially at least." He touched the screen lightly. "Let's see if Sokolov was working on DARPA funded projects."

I added DARPA and Sokolov to the search.

Nothing.

I changed the search to Defence Advanced Research Projects Agency. And there it was, along with a note from someone. I tapped the cursor on the purple line. The note popped up.

'We need to be very careful with this. E. Collins.'

"Careful with what, I wonder?" I said, "The DARPA mention, or the research with stem cells, or the Directed Energy Weapon trials, or the whole thing?"

"Probably the whole thing," Ben said. "Also, we know Collins is here, so, we can ask."

Curiosity rampaged, so I put O'Hare into the search. Two comments from Cait O'Hare.

I read the first comment out loud, "'How can we prove Sokolov's nanobots were involved in Peter's death?'"

My eyes widened. Ben moved my hand to reveal the second comment from O'Hare.

He read the comment out loud, "'Are we positive that the nanobot technology is secured?'"

"I think the answer is no, to that one."

I scanned the surrounding text looking for something that answered her question. How can you prove nanobots were used to kill? Nothing. No one had an answer.

"It says nanobots are so tiny that the body probably doesn't know they're there, so even if they were injected to a particular site and stayed or were immobile, there wouldn't be any scar tissue created."

"And if they deployed some in a glass of water and the thing was programmed to go do damage in the heart, all we'd see would be the new damage, but not the cause?" Ben didn't sound pleased.

"How much of a chance do you think anyone would have at finding the xenobots when they're biological?"

"If they can't locate a tiny machine ... it doesn't look good, does it?"

"And if she's created something that kills, like we suspect, then we have no way of proving it."

"Disaster."

"Yes."

"Let's put this away and get going," I said, disconnecting the flash drive, and putting it in my bag that was on the table. "Hey, Ben, that story?"

"Yeah what about it?"

"They were using it to share knowledge. Multiple people must've had access to the story."

"We saw comments from Collins and O'Hare. Shit, you're right."

I added the laptop to the pile of stuff to put in the safe, then looked at the breakfast bar. It definitely had wood panelling underneath.

I stood up, walked to the end of the breakfast bar, then crouched by the recessed telephone nook, I pushed on the tongue and groove panelling. A door popped open. Shuffling back, I opened it properly. Sure enough, there was a safe with a digital lock. It looked to be a fairly big safe. Holding my breath and wishing for luck, I pressed in the door code. Lights flashed. There was a quiet clunk. I twisted the handle next to the keypad and pulled. The safe opened.

It was too dark to see inside.

I wrestled my iPhone from my back pocket and turned the torch on. It was a big safe. Right at the back was a shotgun and boxes of ammo. Good to know.

"Ben, can you pass me the pile of stuff on the table?"

He appeared next to me with the stack I'd asked for. I pushed it all the way in and closed the safe door. A red light flashed. I tried the handle. It was locked. Good. I closed the outer panelled secret door. Satisfied I stood up and smoothed my shirt.

Ben waited with my backpack slung over one shoulder and his messenger bag over the other.

"Loo first," I said.

I joined him by the front door a few minutes later. All the house lights were off.

The night deepened as we stepped out the front door. The night was darkest before dawn. The darkness in my mind mimicked the night.

Chapter Twenty-one:
[Crockett: Here we go again]

Luke didn't have a lot to say as we walked up Chatsworth Road. It was a slow slog. My boots were better suited to riding around on the Harley than climbing a dark hill footpath. The street lights weren't that good either. I imagine that the people who live up Chatsworth don't walk much. Luke breathed hard next to me.

"Slow down, Crockett," Luke said, between tired puffs. "How far does this road go up?"

"No idea. I think we're turning off soon." The ground flattened out a little under my feet. "Not so bad now. It's a bastard of a hill."

Nothing else came from Luke until we made a down-hill, left turn and he stumbled on a curb.

"You right?" I said, grabbing for his arm in the dark.

"Yeah. Are we there yet?"

"What are you, five?"

Luke laughed lightly. "Well, are we?"

"Cross the road," I said. "We're not far away."

A dog barked as we walked down yet another poorly lit suburban street. We rounded another corner to the right, then curved left, but were on the same road. A cat shot across in front of us. My stomach leapt.

"Jesus!" The animal population is set give me a heart attack.

"You right?" Luke said, amusement ringing his words.

"Fine. The cat startled me a bit." A small chuckle escaped. "Glad Ronnie didn't see me jump."

"How far now?"

"Not far at all. My car is up ahead about a hundred metres." Can't say I wasn't relieved at the prospect of finally getting to my car and getting off the streets.

No noise, but our footsteps, as we approached the car. From ten metres I pressed the unlock button on my key fob. The indicator lights flashed once. In the dark I saw a faint tiny red glow under the car. Fuck!

I grabbed Luke's arm and spun him around. He dropped his duffle bag as I dove over a low wall, dragging him with me. I shoved him to the ground. "Stay down."

"Get off me," he said, with a groan. "You're heavy."

A deafening explosion shattered windows, and rained metal chunks and debris over the area, and us. Something hot hit my back. Stung a bit.

From under my arm came a muffled voice, "What was that?"

"My car," I replied, wondering how loud my voice was. My ears rang. "My fucking car!" I poked my head over the wall. Flames, smoke, disaster. People were moving. Lights flicked on. Curtains twitched.

"We've got to move before the cops arrive."

Luke clambered to his feet and dusted himself off. I gave him a visual once over. "You okay, not hurt?"

"I'm fine," he replied.

I wasn't convinced, and the left side of my lower back

smarted.

"Come on," I tapped his arm to get his attention. We stepped over the wall. A few bricks were missing now. Luke grabbed his bag from the ground and slung it over his shoulder. "Stick to the shadows. We need to get across the train tracks."

"There's an over-bridge?"

"There is but going up makes us a little too visible. We'll cross at Trentham, down by the racecourse."

"The new subway?"

"Yes. Can't be seen in there from any of the roads."

Stepping over pieces of my car, we walked away from the mess behind us and the people gawking out their curtains. We moved as fast as we could in the deepest shadows. By the time we were approaching the racecourse, sirens filled the air from all directions. The station itself was well lit and so was the underpass. We walked down the steps into the tunnel.

I pulled my phone from my pocket and woke it. Ronnie needed to know what just happened. I texted her phone.

Me: My car exploded.

I watched the three dots that told me Ronnie was typing. Then she paused and started again.

Ronnie: Are you two all right?

Me: Mostly.

Ronnie: So, someone had *you* under surveillance. Take Luke to his house then go get Emily.

Me: Need wheels first. I know where to get some.

I added a smiley face and pocketed my phone.

Luke leaned on the wall, his bag hanging from his right hand. I could see him much better in the subway lighting. He looked shaken but otherwise okay. Didn't see any blood. Sirens wound on and on as emergency services converged on the explosion site. We needed wheels. Emily had a car in her garage. It was hers even though she no longer drove. I took it out once a week to keep it running. It wasn't the car she had the accident in, that car belonged to Ronnie.

Emily's place was in Wallaceville, but closer to Trentham than Upper Hutt. If we kept off Fergusson Drive it'd be better.

"Come on, let's go," I said, leading the way to the ramp at the other end of the subway. It made more sense to take the ramp; we weren't going toward the platform; we were going in the opposite direction.

Just before I stepped out of the tunnel, Luke spoke, "You're hurt."

"Nah, something hit my back that's all," I replied, and moved my shoulder and back muscles. Something pinched in my lower back. I'd probably have a nasty bruise.

"Yes, something did hit your back," Luke said. "It's sticking out about fifteen centimetres."

Sticking out. That explains the pinching then.

"Can't do much about it out here. I'll sort it when we get where we're going."

"Doesn't look good," Luke said.

"I guess as long as there's more sticking out than sticking in, it'll be fine." I walked up the ramp with Luke following behind. "Looking at it won't help."

He caught up and walked next to me.

"Where are we going?"

"To a see a friend about a car." I didn't feel like talking and conveyed that with my tone.

Footfalls rang on the concrete. I moved to the grass verge. Luke followed my lead. Dogs barked. Cats congregated in pools of yellow light under the lampposts. Some stayed their ground and others took off under hedges and fences.

And we walked.

At the end of Emily's driveway, I stopped.

"We're here," I said.

I glanced at my watch as I walked up the driveway, the hands glowing green. Security lights came on. Two-second delay. Not bad. The cameras would've activated as soon as we started up the driveway. I'd installed night vision cameras for Emily three weeks earlier.

I knocked at her front door and waited.

The hall light came on a few seconds later, and then Emily said, "Who is there?"

"Crockett," I replied, as quietly as I could while still being heard through the solid-core door. Another of my installations.

The bolt on the inside moved, followed by the deadbolt. Emily opened the door with the internal safety chain still on. She sleepily peered at me through the twelve-centimetre gap.

"Crockett?"

"Yes. It is me."

The door closed while she turned the safety off. When I said, internal, I meant it. The safety chain is hidden inside the door and can't be released without first closing the door completely. It's pretty-well cut-proof too.

The door opened fully. "Why are you here?"

"I need to borrow your car, and I also need you to help me with a surveillance job."

Emily nodded, like it was an everyday occurrence.

"Who is that?" She pointed to Luke, who stood to the side of the doorway.

"This is Luke," I replied with a smile.

"Hello, Luke." Her attention turned to me again. "I am not dressed in going outside clothes."

"You have time to get dressed. Can we come in?"

She nodded and moved away from the door. I indicated for Luke to shut the door behind him and then follow me up the hallway into Emily's lounge.

Emily smiled at me, yawned, then went to her bedroom.

"Have a seat, Luke," I said, sitting on the couch gingerly. I didn't want to lean back. Luke sat in an armchair across from me. "Emily won't be long. Then we'll take you home."

"Who put the explosive device in your car?" Luke said, quietly.

"Friends of yours I presume," I replied, studying him for a moment.

"You're not as funny as you think you are." Luke half smiled. "Let me take a look at your back. You're not going to be able to drive very comfortably, with that metal sticking out of it."

Up until that point I didn't know for sure it was metal. Now was not the best time to refuse help, so I conceded. "Go ahead."

"Stand up and turn around, I'll assess the damage."

I did as he asked, and called out at the same time, "Hey, Emily, can you bring me a first aid kit when you are dressed?"

I felt Luke touch the metal. This was going to be bad.

"Go easy there."

"It's pinned your jacket to you. I don't think there is any way for me to get that jacket off you without cutting into it."

A voice from the doorway said, "There is, let me."

Emily moved forward carrying a first aid kit.

"Luke can handle it. I can get a new jacket," I said, quietly.

"You have a hole in this one. A new jacket is a good idea," Emily said from behind me. "It does not need to be any worse."

"How are you going to do it?" I tried to fill my voice with confidence despite not feeling very comfortable with Emily trying out a plan.

"Stabilise the piece of metal. It is this long on the outside." She held her thumb and forefinger fifteen-centime-tres apart in front of my face. "Take your jacket off, and then cut into your shirt to have a look at the damage."

As much as I wanted to tell her to cut my jacket, I didn't. I shut up and let her do whatever she thought she could do. Last thing I wanted to do was undermine her confidence, or make her overthink, and unable to act.

"Can you get your arm out of the left sleeve?"

"Not without moving that metal," I said.

Emily spoke to Luke. "Hold the metal still. I will go underneath Crockett's jacket and tee shirt and secure it with wads of gauze and long pieces of tape.

"All right," Luke said. I got the feeling he was relieved that someone else took control. Don't think he would be if he knew Emily like I knew her. I had to admit though, that I was not seeing amnesia Emily tonight. That alone was unnerving.

I breathed slowly. The metal moved a tiny amount and stung like a motherfucker. Another slow breath. Scissors cut away the back of my shirt under my jacket. The metal was low, just above my hip. Any lower and it would've speared my arse, embarrassing, but easier to sort. My mind wandered around that thought to stop myself thinking about the pain. Better to have no shirt, than no jeans.

"Crockett, I'm going to help you take your jacket off," Emily said. "Luke is going to keep hold of the metal to make sure it doesn't move."

"Okay," I said.

She lifted my jacket by the shoulders and eased it slowly down my arms. So far so good. Slow deep breaths.

Emily took the weight of the jacket in her hands. "Take your right arm out."

I did and exhaled slowly.

She repositioned the jacket; I felt a slight pull on my lower back. "I'm going to cut the slit made by this metal bigger."

Luke must've taken most of the jacket weight while she did that. I didn't really feel it too much.

"Lift your left arm out," Emily said.

Gingerly, I did as she said.

"Luke hold the jacket up a bit."

I could feel her sliding my heavy jacket backwards, even though there was no real weight to it with Luke holding the jacket up. I held my breath.

As I exhaled, Emily said, "It's free."

Luke chucked my jacket past me and onto the couch.

"Great, thank you."

"Hold still, Crockett. I don't think you've pierced anything important, but I need to check."

This was not the Emily I knew. I expected my Emily to turn up at any second. She moved the tape and wadding. Then she spoke to Luke. "Get me the antiseptic liquid from the kit, clean gauze, and tape."

"What are you going to do?"

"Take this out," she replied, tucking gauze into my waistband. "On three. One, two ..."

"Jesus," I muttered between clenched teeth. "That was

two, not three."

"It is out," Emily replied. I felt cool liquid run down my back. She pressed on the wound. "There is a packet of butterfly wound closures in the first aid kit. Get me the big ones."

I could feel Emily's fingers squeeze the skin on my back. She dried the area with more gauze then stuck the butterflies over, holding the edges together. She placed more gauze over the wound and stuck the edges down.

"Is it good?" I asked.

"Yes. You will need a doctor." Emily gathered bloodied gauze from the floor and dropped it into a plastic bag. "I do not have suture kits in my first aid box. The good news is that the cut is not as deep as it looked."

I turned to see Luke looking pale. "You all right?"

He nodded.

Emily smiled at me. "You are all right," she said. "Why are you here?"

There she was. The Emily I knew.

"I came to see you because, I need to borrow your car, and I need your help."

Luke took the rubbish bag and dropped the piece of metal into it, but not before showing me. "Where is your rubbish bin, Emily?"

She pointed to the kitchen, then turned her attention to me again. "Did I help?"

"Yes. But I need your help on something else as well."

"Okay." Emily looked at her hands. "They have blood."

"Go clean up, Emily. Thank you for helping me."

Emily smiled and went to the bathroom.

Luke reappeared from the kitchen doorway.

"Have to say I'm glad Emily took over," he said, wiping his wet hands down his jeans. "She's great."

"Yeah, she is."

I picked my jacket up and stuck a finger through the hole. It wasn't too bad. I could still wear it. In a couple of days, I wouldn't even notice the hole. I was lucky it wasn't a more serious injury. Very lucky. "As soon as Emily is ready, we'll take you home, Luke."

"Thanks, I appreciate it."

"Probably not going to take you all the way though. I'll drop you a couple of streets over."

"Fair enough."

It dawned on me that neither of us noticed the cold on our night-time walk. Or if Luke did, he didn't mention it. I didn't even notice the wintery chill in the air. Adrenaline has benefits.

Chapter Twenty-two:
[Ronnie: Now what?]

I felt trepidation as I approached the garage in Naenae. My heart beat faster, the closer my feet carried me to the roller door.

Ben touched my arm. I jumped. "Whoa," he said. "It's just me."

"I know." I shrugged. "They knew about Crockett and where he left his car."

"Does anyone know about your garage?"

"Only Steph and Jenn."

"Okay, have either of them been here since Luke was grabbed?"

"I don't think so." We walked around the building to the side door. The outside light came on, dousing us in a watery-yellow glow. "I don't know. Steph got new plates for the cars, but I don't know if she came down here and put them on."

"We haven't been gone long and she's been fairly busy." He smiled at me. "Open the door Ronnie. It'll be fine."

"Look at you, being all manly and taking charge," I said with a small laugh. I fiddled with my keys, putting the garage key between my thumb and forefinger. Ready.

"I don't think we're dying tonight." There it was again, the take-charge, no-nonsense Ben I'd grown to like, a lot.

"I'm holding you to that," I said. I plunged the key into the deadlock and turned, while pushing the door open. Once it was open, I ducked to the left and disarmed the alarm. Ben took the key from the lock and closed the door behind us.

"Alarm was still set, so I doubt if anyone has tampered with the cars," he said. "Which one do you want to take?"

"I thought we'd take one each. That way we can cover more ground and do a better job of the surveillance."

"I have a different thought around that. Hear me out," he said, as I started to complain.

"Okay."

"We take one car into the city to see if we can find James MacKinnon, then swing back here and pick up the other car. Use two cars for Upper Hutt."

That wasn't a silly idea.

"Good idea."

I took a black key fob from the hooks by the door and pressed the disarm button. The Mustang's indicator lights flashed. Ben slipped the key fob from my hand.

"Do you mind?"

"Not really."

Three minutes later we were out of the garage, the alarm was on, and the roller door closed.

"Might stay on the Western Hutt Road until Petone and go along the Esplanade."

"Sounds good." There was no avoiding the main road between the valley and Wellington, but at least we could stay out of the way until we got to it. Dawn began to creep over the hills. It'd be light before we got to Ngaio.

A yawn evaded capture. It'd been a long night.

"I'm too old for this shit," I said, watching the sky lighten in increments.

"What shit in particular?"

"The zero sleep, bad guys blowing stuff up, not knowing what's going on, shit."

"Maybe drinking coffee all night doesn't help either."

"Yeah, that's the problem, too much caffeine."

"That's not what I said."

"It's what it sounded like," I snapped.

"You are great at gathering HUMINT and finding people, but boy, do you need sleep."

"And you like to live dangerously. Hasn't your job provided enough excitement?"

"Of course. And hanging out with you is never dull. Doesn't change the fact that you need sleep."

"I can't decide if you're stupid or brave." I leaned my head on the cold car window, hoping it would keep me awake. "You're a Yank, so I'm really leaning toward the former."

Ben laughed. "Glad you still have your sense of humour, despite the over caffeination and lack of shut-eye."

Laughter welled up, threatened to choke me, then leap-frogged from my mouth, jumping any retort I might have had. It took a lot of effort to rein it in and compose myself. He wasn't wrong about needing sleep, and too much caffeine.

"Feel better?" Amusement was obvious in Ben's voice.

I swallowed hard a few times and tested my voice. "Yes." Another bout of laughter ensued. Control was beyond me. Tears trickled down my face. It took several minutes before I could force the laughter down and resume normality. Whatever that is.

My phone rang. It was Crockett.

I answered, then turned the speaker on. "You okay?" I asked.

"Yeah. Emily patched me up."

That was one of the many skills that we thought she'd lost, but more and more I believed it was all still there, but inaccessible for the most part.

"Where are you now?"

"Dropped Luke off a couple of streets north of his father's house. We swung around and did a big circuit of the block. No obvious signs of surveillance."

"And our counter-surveillance?"

"Only saw Jenn."

"Good."

The other three would be there, up driveways, or parked in other roads. They would've set up a surveillance box making sure all the exits were covered.

"Art and Enzo reported in, they're in position to watch Zillah's mum's place."

"Sokolov?"

"Emily and I are watching. How are you doing?"

I looked out the car window. "Almost at Mackinnon's. I'm not looking forward to the walk up those steps, but at least it's not raining and it's nearly light enough to see."

"Be careful," Crockett said. "You're armed?"

"Yes."

"Stay in touch."

I hung up. Opened the Find My app on the phone and touched the 'items' icon. The AirTags popped up on the map on the screen. Luke's bag was moving toward his home. Seemed a smart idea to keep track of the bag in case anyone tried to grab it. I added an alert, so I'd be notified if the tagged bag left his father's property. I now didn't need to keep checking because my phone would do it for me. We were following a narrow winding road in Ngaio. Most of the road was still in darkness. The bush and trees kept it shadowy for a decent part of the day even in the summer. A kilometre later, Ben announced we'd reached our destination. There were no cars parked in the designated parking spaces for household residents. If James was there, his car was not. Perhaps he Ubered.

Together we climbed the many steps cut into the bush-clad hill. Birds twittered and sang in the treetops. A piwakawaka flittered across our path. My eyes tracked its movements as it caught a tiny bug in mid-air. It flew around us and disappeared. Piwakawaka are harbingers of death according to Donald. It's worse if they are inside a house, but not great flitting about a person outside either.

Trepidation tingled in streaks down my spine the closer we came to the house. I paused before stepping onto the wide asphalt path that led to the entrance way and looked up at the house towering above us in the cloudy dawn sky. A large balcony stretched out from the second storey and overhung the front entrance, providing shelter from rain and sun alike. I couldn't see any lights glowing in windows. The front door was closed. Windows that I could see on the ground floor were all closed and curtains open. Nothing appeared untoward or out of place in any way.

Ben nudged me. "We knocking?"

I nodded. Together we walked to the large front door, the sort of door that belonged on a castle. Arched, aged wood, with wrought iron fittings. A brass bell with a chain pull was mounted on the wall next to the door. On the other side of the door was an electronic panel that contained a speaker and a call button.

I rang the bell. It reminded me of an old school bell. Loud.

Ben pressed the call button on the panel.

We waited in silence for the longest two minutes ever. No one came. I rang the bell again. Ben pressed the call button a moment later. Once the residual clanging from the bell died away, the silence continued. Even the birds were quiet. No doubt the bell ringing disturbed them.

"Do we find a way in?" Ben asked, peering in a long narrow window about half a metre from the door.

"We came all this way. I'm concerned about MacKinnon's welfare."

"Not the dead one I presume," Ben said, with a wry grin plastered across his face. "Welfare check it is." Ben hammered on the solid door with the side of his closed fist, three times. Then called out, "MacKinnon!"

Nothing.

I walked around the left side of the porch to the corner of the house where it met the hill and bush. It was a walk. This was not a small house, but a three-storey mansion built into a bush-covered hill. The bottom storey, which included the massive entrance way, was set into the hill, with two more stories rising above the land and native bush.

A piwakawaka darted left and right across my path. There was no way in at the lowest level except through the entrance way at the front. I doubted we'd get that door open easily. The piwakawaka continued darting and flitting beside the path I walked. The black asphalt led up to the second storey and balcony stairs accessible from the path. I climbed the stairs and walked along the wooden deck. I could see that it led to the front of the house. I checked windows as I moved. Nothing unlatched. No curtains drawn. No signs of life.

Ben's voice floated up to meet me, "Find anything?"

"I'm up on the balcony," I called back. "Nothing so far."

As I walked around to the front of the house, I saw Ben coming to meet me from the other side.

"I haven't been here in a while," he said.

"Stairs on both sides. That makes sense." I stood in front of two sets of French doors and tried the doorhandles. Locked. "I've only been here in the dark." A memory of dinner with Ben on the balcony surfaced. It felt like a long time ago now. He was staying here then. The house was owned by the American Embassy. "Do the Yanks still own this place?"

"I suppose so," Ben replied, cupping his hands on the glass of one door and peering inside. "I thought MacKinnon was working for the Australians now," I said.

"Everyone works for everyone else sooner or later," Ben replied. "I think I see something."

I joined him and cupped my hands against the glass before peering inside. "A foot," I said. "I think it's a foot or a shoe."

Ben banged on the door. I watched for movement.

"No reaction." I tried to see the door lock on the inside of the door. "The key is in the lock on this door."

Ben glanced around the expansive deck. He hurried across the decking to an outdoor umbrella stand that contained a closed umbrella. He removed the umbrella and returned.

"That's going to make a mess," I said.

"I won't tell if you don't."

Ben shoved the umbrella top-first through one of the French doors, smashing the pane of glass in line with the lock. Glass crashed to the tiled floor. He wiggled the umbrella around knocking as much glass out as possible, then he put it back where he found it. Ben tugged his sleeve down to cover his hand and carefully put his arm through the broken pane and turned the key. With a satisfying clunk the door unlocked. He pulled his arm out, made sure his hand was still covered, and pressed the handle down, swinging the door inward. I made a mental note to wipe down the shaft of the umbrella, and the windows where we pressed our cupped hands.

"Watch your step," Ben said, and led the way into the house. Glass crunched underfoot. Ben called into the house, "James! It's Ben and Ronnie."

"I think if anyone is here then they heard that window smashing all over the tiled floor." I pointed to the shoe on the far side of the room. "The shoe didn't move. Wonder if it has a foot attached."

Something flickered in my peripheral vision. I spun around to see the piwakawaka flitter around the room. Death.

"Ronnie?"

I looked at Ben. "Yes."

"What's the matter? You gasped."

Did I?

"There's a piwakawaka in here. Fantails inside are bad. Really bad."

"We can chase it out, it'll be okay."

"You don't understand. Piwakawaka are harbingers of death. In the house they mean someone will die."

"Superstition. Nothing more." He knelt on one knee by the shoe. "Or not."

"Or not?" I moved closer so he wasn't blocking my line of vision anymore. "Shit. That's James MacKinnon."

Ben fished into his pocket and produced disposable gloves. He pulled them on and examined the corpse. "There are no signs of a struggle. No bruising or obvious injury."

"Then how did he die?"

"From death," Ben replied, standing. "Sudden cardiac arrest? An aneurysm? Blood clot?"

"That's not suspicious at all."

"There are hidden security cameras. We need to look at the footage before we call this in. Once the authorities are involved we won't get a chance."

True.

Chandler would be notified once police were called, and he'd take interim control until various embassy officials swooped down and plucked control out from under him.

We'd be shut out while he tried to find a way to make this mess stick to us. Did I really believe that's what he'd do? Yes. Wow. Knowing that was my truth meant I'd do everything in my power to keep away from Chandler's grubby mitts.

"Where are the cameras? I didn't see any outside." I followed Ben, carefully avoiding the body of James Mac-Kinnon.

"They're outside and inside the house, quite well disguised. You've seen those nature programs where they use trail cameras hidden in logs of wood and rocks?"

"Yes."

"They're disguised like that, but more sophisticated."

"I'll be on the lookout for rocks and branches lurking in hallways," I replied with a small chuckle. "Where are we going?"

"Control room."

Chapter Twenty-three:
[Ronnie: Who the hell are they?]

The control room was in the bowels of the mansion. I had no idea that there was a fully underground floor. Ben led the way down a bright and airy hallway. We walked past several closed doors. About halfway along the hall, he stopped and opened a small black panel. He pressed his thumb on a scanner. The panel sprang to life. A robotic voice said, "Access granted, Ben Reynolds."

The door unlocked with a clunk.

Ben pushed it wide and ushered me over the threshold.

"Won't Chandler know you were here, if you needed to use your thumb print to get in?"

"Chandler has no access to this room. Doesn't matter how much he bitches and complains. This is owned by the embassy. He will have some access because of James' death, maybe. But not to this part of the building."

"We should still clean any fingerprints on anything we touched, just in case."

"We will."

He closed the door behind us. Lights flicked on, filling the room with harsh whiteness. On the wall to the left I saw a bank of screens. Eight. On the opposite wall were another eight screens. Ben sat down at a computer desk in front of the wall directly across from the doorway.

"Grab a seat," he said, and entered a passcode into the

lock screen.

I moved a chair and sat down so I could see what he was doing. Ben was typing and checking the screen in front of him as he typed.

"And you're?"

"Rolling the tapes back to before William MacKinnon died."

"It's not actually tape is it?" I didn't think it would be, but then again.

"No, it's digital, and stored in the cloud." Ben spun his chair to face the left side of the room. "Join me."

I did as he asked. He had a remote in his hand.

The time and date on all the screens showed the night before last, the approximate time that Luke O'Sullivan and William MacKinnon were escorted out of Countdown Supermarket in Upper Hutt. "This is going to take some time," I said. "Should've brought snacks."

"Popcorn." Ben mumbled. "The cameras will roll at ten times speed until they come to a trigger point, then they'll slow to normal playback speed."

"And a trigger point is?"

"Where motion is detected."

"Right." Popcorn would've been fabulous, and a bag of Clinkers, all washed down with a malted vanilla milkshake. Movie night. Movie morning? I concentrated on the screens, my eyes moving across them all as video rolled. Hours raced by and finally camera one slowed, which caused the other cameras to also slow. Ben paused the other seven cameras so we could watch camera one at normal speed.

A man walked up the steps from the road toward the house. I didn't recognise him, but then the image wasn't the clearest.

"Do you know who that is?" I asked Ben.

"No. Let's see if there's a better picture when he gets to the front door."

The cameras changed. The next one picked him up and played. I thought it played by itself until I saw the remote control in Ben's hand. The male was closer to the door, but not there yet. When he arrived, the camera above the door had a clear image of his face. Ben took a screen shot and saved the image. Neither of us recognised the man. Could've been the person who took Luke and MacKinnon from the supermarket; the images from that footage weren't the clearest and he kept his face down most of the time. Only MacKinnon looked directly at the camera in the supermarket surveillance footage.

The UnSub knocked on the door. James MacKinnon opened it and appeared to invite him in. He certainly did not look under any duress. Ben cued the next camera. They walked into a ground floor room.

"A library?"

"Yes. It's the room MacKinnon senior used most often for receiving guests. Less formal than the main rooms on this floor."

The men sat in armchairs with a small table between them and talked. Just talked. The time stamp told us the man stayed an hour. He didn't go anywhere else in the house and then he left.

The next trigger point was four hours later. Another person walked slowly up the steps from the road and approached the front door.

"That's a woman," I said, "Look at how she's walking. She's older than us. Maybe MacKinnon senior's age, or a few years younger."

Ben waited for her to be directly in front of the camera and took a screen shot. "I know who she is," he said. "That's Libby Collins."

"How do you know her?"

"She worked, and potentially works, for us."

"By us, you mean?"

"America."

That's what I thought. "Have you met her?"

"Yes, several times. She's fascinating. Lived a very interesting life."

"I'm led to believe that is so. She came up earlier. When I was going through old files."

Ben paused the cameras and turned to me. "In what context?"

"The file I found mentioned her, and others in the O'Hare family." I sighed. "And Nana had me do a quick search of another O'Hare family member."

"That can't be good." Ben shook his head slowly. "Not good at all."

"I know, right? Also, I think Ms Collins is living in the same retirement village as Nana. Remember?" I took a breath. "Collins has something to do with Sokolov."

"Who was the family member Nana wanted to know about?"

"Michaela Kennedy-Carlisse."

"And why? Remind me."

"Nana and the *Cronies of Doom* think she's living in Upper Hutt. I don't think she is, as far as I can tell she's over the hill in the Wairarapa with her movie producer husband."

"What's Kennedy-Carlisse's link to the file you found?"

"I think she wrote it, the book, or whatever it is. Some sort of prophecy or something very odd. It's not just a story. If it were, why hide it?"

"Especially with Sokolov mentioned in it," Ben said. "Let's see how long Collins stays talking to James MacKinnon."

He rolled the footage on. We watched them also sit in the same chairs in the library. This time however, the conversation was quite animated, and ended with Collins standing abruptly, and leaving. James did not see her out.

"I don't feel like that was a happy visitation," I said, as the next trigger point appeared on the first camera. "It's like Wellington railway station, this house. People are coming and going in quick succession."

"Quick enough that Collins and this individual passed each other on the bush steps."

I watched the new person approach the door. The time stamp confirmed what we saw, they did pass each other. This time it was a male. Chandler.

"What the hell is Chandler doing?" I said, leaning forward for a better look. When the door opened, James stood in the doorway, blocking Chandler's entrance. Interesting. He sure did not want to invite him in. Can't say I blamed him. I wouldn't either. They stood in the doorway talking for several minutes before Chandler spun on his theatric heels and stormed away.

"It gets more interesting with each visitor," Ben muttered. "Who the hell is going to show up next?"

"The killer?"

If we're lucky.

Time marched on, nothing came and went. Eventually there was another trigger point on the first camera. The figure wore dark clothes and a hooded sweatshirt. The hood was pulled up and they kept to the side of the path that afforded the least amount of camera exposure. This time the person avoided the front door and went left, like I did. Unlike me, they seemed to know where they were going.

"Male or female?" Ben asked, as we watched the person get closer to the first camera on the second-floor balcony.

"Male?" I queried, not at all sure but noting the swagger. "And a dick. He's got a walk that suggests he's all that, and a hot dinner. I doubt very much that he is in fact all *that*."

The face came into view. We looked from the screen to each other. Not male at all.

"Did not expect that," I said. "Why is she back here?"

"For no good reason," Ben replied. "She was clearly seen leaving when Chandler arrived. That means he became her alibi."

"Of all people to be an alibi, but, also, hard to refute the head of the New Zealand Security Intelligence Service when he gives someone an alibi."

"I don't imagine he'd get too closely interrogated by police anyway."

"James' death is a police matter as soon as we call it in," I said, more for my own benefit than Ben's. I was getting things straight in my head.

We watched the screens as Libby Collins moved from camera to camera. We knew his body was upstairs, but he was nowhere in any of the upstairs cameras. Ben pointed to the eighth camera. "There's James. In his father's study."

He was rifling through his desk.

I looked at the time stamp. O'Sullivan and MacKinnon senior were being held in the restaurant at that time. My eyes sought Libby Collins; she was making her way down some stairs. Then there was another trigger alert. This time, the person walked straight up the steps, and to the front door. It was another woman.

James answered the door. Over his shoulder I saw light, then it disappeared. It could have been Collins opening something, or perhaps closing a door. James invited the woman inside and showed her to the library. She held the back of a chair before sitting.

"See that?"

Ben smiled. "We'll dust for prints when we're finished here."

Collins searched other rooms while James was busy.

"What is she looking for?"

"Something small by the look of her search."

In a bedroom, she opened books, hanging them upside down and letting the pages open. Then she scrabbled through trinket boxes and bedside drawers. Everything she touched was put back the way it was. She didn't want anyone knowing someone had been there. The fossicking continued until James suddenly stood. Collins hid.

"She must've made a noise," I said with a laugh.

James didn't leave the room; he went to the door and then a few seconds later returned to his guest.

"She almost got caught," Ben commented. "That'd be awkward."

"So, who is the second woman?"

"Don't know. But she's not young. I'm picking Collins' age or older."

"Are we looking at Sokolov?" Didn't look much like the image Crockett had shown me back at the house but people change. Who would know how old the photo he found was?

"Shit. Yes, we could be." He grabbed a screen shot and added it to the others. "We have one unidentified male and one unidentified female."

"Time to run those through facial recognition but be careful. If that's Sokolov then any ID on her is going to send up fireworks, never mind a red flag."

The most dangerous traitor is the enemy within. The pendulum told me Sokolov was at MacKinnon's at some stage. Seeing a woman on the screen fitted.

"Let's try and get an ID on the male first." Ben paused the video playback and opened a cupboard under the desk below the bank of screens. He took a laptop from a shelf, checked it was charged, then sent the images to it via Bluetooth. "Male first."

He dragged the image of the male into a program that ran facial identification software and linked to images stored in several databases, including the GCSG and Interpol.

I watched the screen as the program compared thousands of images. It would take a little while.

"Let's continue with the video surveillance. It'll alert when it's done," Ben said.

"Okay."

He partially shut the lid of the laptop, and set it down on the desk, before hitting play. James and the woman stayed in the room talking for nearly an hour. Then he went to the kitchen and made tea. While he was busily making tea, Collins was searching more rooms. James took a tray containing a teapot, two mugs, a sugar bowl and milk jug, into the library. We watched him set the tray on the small table then the woman spoke, and he left the room.

An alert chimed from the laptop. Ben paused the video. There was no match for the man's image. Ben added the screen grab of the female to his program and we continued watching the video footage.

James was picked up in the kitchen again, this time pouring a glass of water from the sink. In the library, the woman took something small from her pocket. It stayed hidden in her hand. Collins left the house, sneaking down the stairs on the other side of the building and creeping along to the path that led to the road. With her gone, we concentrated on what was happening in the library. James returned and handed the woman the glass of water. She drank half immediately then placed the glass on the table. James poured the tea. The woman knocked the glass over. Water splashed everywhere. James hurried away.

This time when he left, she held her hand over the cup nearest his seat. She tipped something from a small vial into James' cup. She pocketed the vial again. James returned with a dishcloth to mop up the water.

We watched the whole process.

They both drank their tea. James added milk and sugar to his.

"Guess that's the last thing he really did," I said. "I think we've found the killer, but how do we prove he and his father were killed by nanobots, or xenobots, or whatever the hell caused sudden cardiac arrest?"

"We get to Sokolov, if that's who that woman is."

"What are we even looking for? More importantly, what was Collins looking for when she searched the house?"

"Now that's a very good question. What was she looking for? And another question, does she know about William MacKinnon and James MacKinnon's deaths?"

"Someone else we need to have a conversation with."

"What now?" I leaned back in the chair and watched the movement on the screens. The woman left. She took nothing obvious with her. James removed the tray of tea things and deposited them in the kitchen. "Hey, he didn't do the dishes or tip the dregs out."

Ben smiled. "Then maybe we can have his dregs analysed."

"Right, let's go the kitchen and see if there is something useful there."

The laptop pinged. Ben pulled it closer and opened the lid. On the screen was a photo of Natalia Sokolov next to the photo he'd taken from the screens in front of us. The words 'ninety-five percent match' were in red across the top of the screen.

"That's what we needed to implicate Sokolov. Positive ID. She was in the house. We saw her tip something in James' tea."

"What's the time frame between her doing that and his death?"

Ben found the relevant CCTV footage and played it.

We watched the time stamp from when Sokolov left the house until James ended up on the floor, dead. Forty-eight minutes. Forty-eight. That's not long.

"That fits," I said. "So now we know she did something that killed him, and that she is here."

"We should get a sample from that cup in the kitchen,

prints off that chair she held and leave," Ben said. "We need to get back to Upper Hutt."

Chapter Twenty-four
[Crockett: Here's Emily]

Emily sat quietly as we watched the road. Every now and then, she glanced into the wing mirror, checking on anything behind us. I did the same and used the rear vision mirror as well. House doors opened and closed. Car alarms chirped as owners disarmed them. Car doors opened and closed. Engines started. Typical morning sounds as people left for work. Cars drove past our position. No one looked into our car or even glanced in our direction. Focus was on the drive to work.

A woman walking a white and black collie came around the bend in the road. She wore headphones and moved quickly with the dog right next to her. Neither looked at us.

My phone buzzed. I glanced at it in the console between the front seats. Cell phone one. Ronnie. Picking the phone up, I tapped the green icon.

"How's it going?" I said, keeping my eyes on the street.

"Positive ID on Sokolov. Definitely in the area."

"I never doubted you, you know that, right?" The phone buzzed in my hand. I looked at the screen. iMessage from phone one. A photo. I opened the message with a tap.

"I've sent you a photo of Sokolov, she looks a bit different to the earlier image you found," Ronnie said, while I scrutinised the woman in the picture.

I showed Emily. "This is who we are looking for."

She nodded.

Ronnie spoke from my hand. "We need to know who visits her. If she leaves, follow her. We're on our way to you."

"Got it, Ronnie. See you when we see you."

I hung up and placed the phone back in the console. Emily watched me.

"Are you all right?"

"Yes," she said, "It is quiet on the street now."

"I suppose the people who start work early are gone."

She adjusted her line of sight from me to outside the windscreen. "What did the person we are watching do?"

"We think she killed a man."

"I see. Are the police going to arrest her?"

"No, Emily, they are not."

"Why not?"

"Because Ronnie, Ben, and I will." That was partly true. There would be no arrest.

"You do not arrest people, Crockett. You make them go away."

I used my peripheral vision to check her expression. A smile. There was a definite change in Emily lately. She remembered things, not everything, but more than before. I got flashes of the Emily Ronnie had told me about. The Emily before the accident. The competent investigator, the surveillant operator, the woman who was confident with a weapon. When her hair moved and the scar that ran down the side of her head, face, and neck was obvious, I always wondered what she was like before. Who Emily Jones really was, and what she did. What was she like before she needed lists in every room to remind her to do simple tasks? What was Emily like before she needed her name above the bathroom mirror in case she forgot again?

"Emily, I'm glad you're helping me today," I said, smiling at her.

"I am glad too," she said, with a return smile. "I like being with you."

Doors opened and closed somewhere nearby. I scanned the street. "Might be time to move," I said, starting the engine. "Buckle up." I pulled my belt across myself and clicked it into place.

There was another gentle click as she fastened her seatbelt. I eased the car away from the curb and drove up the street past the house where we believed Sokolov was staying. I turned right into Edmund Lomas Grove, drove a little way down, then U-turned and cruised left down Gillespies Road. We passed by the house. No signs of life. I turned into Whangakoko Grove, did a U-turn, and parked far enough back from the intersection to be legal. We were just a little too far back to see the target house. The only problem with being so far out of town, was the risk of people becoming curious, as I manoeuvred for a better position. I waited until I heard car engines start again and then I headed straight for the target house. There was a white van parked one house back. I pulled in behind it and shut the engine down.

We couldn't see through the van.

"Can you see the target property?" I asked Emily.

"Yes. I can see part of the driveway."

"Okay. Tell me if you see a car or a person."

I watched as a car drove past us toward Akatarawa Road. Another came from that direction and headed up Gillespies. They could be going as far as Fairview Drive, or home after dropping someone to work, or the bus stop. Half an hour meandered by with no sightings of Sokolov.

Emily tapped my arm and said, "Nosebag?"

My eyes met hers, she smiled. Who were you Emily Jones before you lost yourself? I thought only 'Mericans used the term nosebag.

I reached into the back of the car and grabbed my bag. I lifted it through the gap in the seats carefully avoiding Emily. Then unzipped the bag and rummaged around until I found a packet of protein bars. I dropped one into Emily's lap and took one myself.

"It's the best I can do. Hope you're not too hungry."

"Thank you."

"You're welcome."

I tore into the packet and scoffed the bar. It barely touched the sides on the way to my stomach. I took another one from the packet and ate it slower. Emily was still eating her first one. By the time I finished the second, she was halfway through. I dropped the wrappers into my bag and found a water bottle. I offered the water to Emily.

"Thank you." She took a long drink, handed it back, and carried on eating the bar.

"Ronnie and Ben should be here soon," I said, and held my hand out for the wrapper she had in her hand.

"Okay." She frowned as she looked out the windscreen. "There is a person."

"Describe the person." I dropped the bag over the back of the seat and nestled the water bottle into the cup holders between the seats.

"Female, long dark hair, wearing a red jacket."

"On foot?"

"Yes."

We waited.

The white van blocked my line of sight almost completely until the woman appeared by the driver's door. She glanced in my direction, then opened the van door and climbed in. It wasn't Sokolov. The woman had long dark hair, she was olive skinned and fine featured, thirty, thirty-five tops, and approximately one-hundred and seventy centimetres tall. I committed her to memory, along with the rego of the van.

The van pulled away and drove toward Fairview Drive. We waited to see if she'd turn back, but the van did not appear again.

I made a note on my phone with a description of the woman and the van. Toyota Hiace. I wasn't sure of the year, but the plates could tell us. HWZ 5555.

I opened a browser window and looked up plates issued by year. HWZ was issued in 2015. Good chance the van was a 2015 model then.

"Who was the woman?" Emily asked.

"I don't know. I haven't seen her before."

I shifted in the seat. My lower back wasn't comfortable. Hardly surprising.

"Do you need to walk around?" Emily asked.

"Yes. But it's not a good idea here."

"When will Ronnie arrive?"

"Soon, I hope."

A car approached from the direction of Fairview Drive and kept going. At least with the van gone I could see the target house clearly. Any closer and we'd be in the driveway. Maybe that wasn't a bad thing. A high fence shielded us from anyone looking out the side of the house. If someone looked out the front windows though, they'd see us. See us, and do what? Not much. We now knew Sokolov wasn't alone earlier. There were no other vehicles around the immediate area. If she still had company they weren't going far. I'd had a look down her driveway when we drove past earlier. No cars. Into the bush via the backyard was a possibility but she, or they, would be on foot. It wouldn't be a fun time for them. I turned the key in the ignition and cracked the window a couple of centimetres to let some fresh air in and humidity out.

An hour vanished.

Emily touched my arm and pointed to the rear vision mirror. We both heard a car behind us. I watched it approach, pull in behind us, and Ronnie climb out of the passenger side.

"Ronnie," Emily said, unlocking her door.

"Don't get out yet, Emily." I smiled, and Ronnie knocked on my window. I rolled it all the way down. "Hey."

Ronnie leaned in and looked past me to Emily then back to me.

"You both all right?"

Emily nodded. I threw her a half-smile. "Mostly."

"Someone left, it wasn't Sokolov. It was a woman though. She was quite attractive, olive skinned, long dark hair, about your height, and she drove away in a white Toyota Hiace."

"Rego?" Ronnie pulled a phone from her pocket.

"HWZ 5555."

She wrote it in her phone. That's when I noticed it wasn't the spare, but her own phone.

"You went into the office, don't suppose you ..." She produced my phone from her back pocket. "Yes, thanks."

I transferred the notes I'd made on the spare phone to my own phone and switched the spare off, then handed it to Ronnie.

Ben opened Emily's door and spoke to her. I wasn't listening. I just heard his voice. Ronnie commanded my attention.

"Have you heard from Steph?"

"Yes. She checked in about an hour ago. They're all in good positions. No one has shown up yet."

"Luke?"

"Apart from Luke. They saw him walk up to the house

and go inside."

Good to know he walked, I only dropped him three streets away, so I expected him to walk and not try to call a taxi or an Uber. But people often don't do what you expect. It's the nature of the beast.

"Good."

"I think we should go knock on the door," Ronnie said, tipping her thumb toward the target house. "Let's get in there and see what this woman is really all about."

I nodded. Ben said, "Word of warning, no one accept anything to eat or drink from her. Nothing at all. Do not touch your face after touching anything in that house."

"Jesus. You think she'd deploy her bugs?" I asked.

"We watched her put something in James MacKinnon's tea, and an hour later he was dead."

"Righto then, touch nothing, accept nothing."

Ben scooted around to my side of the car. I got out, he got in.

"Ben's staying with Emily, they're on watch," Ronnie said. "You and I are going to meet Natalia Sokolov."

Chapter Twenty-five:
[Ronnie: Sokolov]

Crockett walked on my right. We walked straight up the driveway to the main door, which was situated on the side of the house. Further down the driveway, I saw a farm-type gate, and beyond that a garage.

Weeds grew in cracks on the concrete drive. There were no obvious security cameras. Crockett stepped up one of the four steps leading to the entrance and knocked firmly on the wooden frame of the frosted glass-paned door.

He stepped back next to me. No noises inside the house suggesting anyone was coming to answer the door. He stepped up and knocked again.

We waited. A shadow appeared behind the frosted glass.

"Who is there?" The accent was lighter than I expected, but then she'd been in the United States for a number of years before she vanished. She could have worked to make her Russian accent deliberately lighter in an effort to disguise herself. If I was her, I would have.

"I come from down the road." I shrugged at Crockett. "I wanted to welcome you to the neighbourhood."

"That is kind of you," she said through the closed door. "I am busy. Perhaps another time?"

She wasn't going to open the door.

"Of course. I'll come back later in the week."

"That would be very nice."

"Bye."

Crockett and I walked back to the car. We jumped in the back so we could talk without leaning in windows.

"She's not keen on meeting neighbours," I said.

Ben chuckled. "There's a surprise."

"Did you see the lady?" Emily asked. She'd swivelled in her seat so she could see us in the back. Ben had too.

"No. She spoke through the closed door."

"No visual confirmation," Ben said.

"Now what?" Crockett asked.

"We resume surveillance," I said. "I want to know if she leaves or if someone arrives. I'm curious about the woman you guys saw leaving in that white van."

"Two cars, two teams," Crockett said. "We'll go down the road, you two go up. The only ways in and out are Akatarawa Road or Fairview Drive. There are a few side streets but they're all dead ends."

"Sounds like a plan. Now, about James MacKinnon. Elizabeth Collins was in the house searching for something while James was entertaining Sokolov."

"Shit, that's interesting."

"I know, right? But that's not all. We ran through the CCTV footage and saw Chandler go up to the door. James didn't let him in. Chandler did not look happy when he left."

"Grand Central Station up there?"

"Very much so. There was also an Unknown Subject. A

male. James let him into the library, they discussed something, or many things, for about an hour, and the man left."

Ben spoke, "We got a screenshot but, as yet, no match for our UnSub."

"The thing with Elizabeth or Libby Collins," I said. "Is that she was there twice. Once as a guest, right before Chandler arrived. They must have passed each other on the steps through the bush. That first time."

Crockett shook his head slowly. "She's got herself a fantastic alibi then. Chandler saw her leave. That's brilliant."

"Isn't it? What we don't know is what she was looking for later on. I don't think she found it."

"And why was Sokolov at the house? Was her mission to murder both MacKinnon's?"

"That's what it looks like," I said. "But there's more to it. It has to be tied up with the rug, and people finding out she's working on something with the Chinese and the Taliban. It'd be worth killing to prevent that information getting into anyone's hands. And I think we were right about a bigger target, something on New Zealand soil, that they're intent on pulling off."

"They don't know about the rug," Crockett reminded me.

"No, they don't, but they know there's Intel somewhere, and it's hidden. They must know Zillah had Information and passed it on, just not how."

"If that's true then she's no longer alive," Crockett said.

"Are we still thinking this target is the Prime Minister's wedding?"

I nodded. "More specifically the official reception."

"Where's that being held?"

"Government house," I said. "We don't know if there are other people with whatever it is that Sokolov put in James' cup of tea. We also got the dregs from the cup."

"Who do we get to analyse the tea?" Crockett asked. "And what do we even say? See if you can find teeny tiny robots in the dregs?"

"Something like that," I said. "I have a friend at ESR. I've reached out. She'll meet us." I checked my watch. Nine-thirty. "I'm meeting her back at the office at midday."

"Be interesting to see what she finds, and if there is anything to find. Where's the sample?"

"In the fridge at the office." A car roared down the road going way too fast for the area. "Idiots everywhere," I muttered. "Not just a problem in the city."

Crockett climbed out of the car and opened the driver's door. "Out you get," he said to Ben. "Emily and I are going that way." He pointed the opposite way from where we'd come.

Ben and I said goodbye to Emily. Their doors closed and Crockett drove away.

Ben jumped in the driver's side. We headed back the way we'd come, and parked facing down the road, near the main intersection. That way we could see anyone coming up the road, and hopefully get a decent driver description.

While we watched for cars, I called Steph.

"Anything?"

"Nope. Dead as a Dodo."

"Guess that's a good thing. Seen the old man or Luke?"

"The older gent picked the newspaper up off the lawn at eight-fifteen, then went back inside."

"So, he's alive, that's good. It was the dad?"

"Yes."

"Keep me posted. Check in every hour."

"Will do."

I hung up and called Enzo. He answered on the second ring. "Ronnie, my favourite soon to be cousin-in-law."

"How goes it?"

"Quiet."

"Okay, that's probably good."

"No sign of Zillah's mum."

"Does she get the newspaper delivered?"

"Yes. It was thrown onto the front lawn at about eight this morning."

"And she didn't come out to get it?"

"No."

"One of you should go take the newspaper in. Don't scare the old lady, just be a helpful new neighbour."

"It's me and Art. Which one of us is less scary?"

"You," I replied. "Smile, make those blue eyes of yours sparkle."

Enzo laughed. "I knew I was your type."

I laughed. "If only you weren't so dreadfully gay and

about to marry cousin, Donald."

"You're wicked, Ronnie." The amusement in Enzo's voice lifted my spirits.

"Check in every hour."

"You got it boss lady. I'll pass that along to Art. He's close enough to see me pick up the phone."

"Take care. Don't scare the old lady."

I hung up again.

Four cars followed a small truck down Akatarawa Road causing a car to wait before it turned into Gillespies. Ben and I watched as it made the turn and passed us.

I rang Crockett and spoke as soon as her answered, "Black BMW heading your way. Looked like the server from *Manger*, driving."

We were all too far away to be able to tell if it stopped at the target house, but we'd know if it picked anybody up and tried to leave.

"Roadblock?"

"Yeah, don't let it out. I would like to know who that is. Weird that it looked like the server from *Manger*." Although, it wouldn't be the first time I'd come across the brains of an operation looking like a nobody.

We waited to see if the car would come back our way or go out in Crockett's direction. Time ticked. Maybe it wouldn't leave.

Ben alighted from the car, leaving the keys in the ignition, and leaned in. "I'm walking back to the house."

"Okay, be careful. Call me if the car comes my way, I'll

block the road. Nothing like a pretend accident to cause havoc."

"I'll call. Be safe."

I watched in the rearview mirror as Ben walked up the road and disappeared from sight. I let Crockett know what he was doing, then got out of the car and opened the boot. There were emergency lights and couple of smaller road cones, or gnomes, depending on where you grew up. Enough emergency bits and pieces to create a warning, and protect the car from impact.

I shut the boot and jumped in the driver's side. My phone was quiet. Five minutes later I got a text message from Ben.

Ben: The car is up the driveway of the target house.
I sent the same text to Crockett. Then replied to Ben.
Me: Coming to you.
Crockett: Coming to you.
Me to Crockett: Converge on Ben's location.

I turned around in the intersection and motored up the road until I saw Ben wave. He was walking back toward my position, but only two doors away from the target. I parked. He jumped in. From where we were we could still block the road if needed. I saw Crockett driving toward us. He parked a house back on the other side of the road.

"How many people do you think were in that car?"

"I only saw the driver when he drove up the street. I

saw no more than you did."

"Want to try an entry?"

Ben grinned like a schoolboy offered a free bag of sweets. "Oh baby, you're speaking my language."

"Can we get over that fence into the back?" I pointed at the neighbouring property and the six-foot fence.

"Yes. Might want a distraction out the front though."

I rang Crockett. "You and Emily are the distraction. Ben and I are going over the fence. Two minutes."

"All right. Low key domestic argument right in the driveway."

"That'll work. Just don't get carried away. We don't want cops."

"Okay."

"You armed?"

"Yes."

"Good, because we don't know what's going to happen."

"That just makes this more fun."

"Yep," I said, and hung up.

Ben was waiting. "Ready when you are."

"Just waiting for the distraction to get into position." I could see Emily open her door. "They're getting ready."

The car door slammed.

Ben grinned. "This is going to be good. Wish we could hang around and watch."

Emily stormed off yelling over her shoulder.

And Ben and I headed for the fence. I could hear Emily shouting at Crockett, and Crockett trying to calm her down. If you didn't know them, it sounded quite convincing.

Ben poked his head over the fence, then crouched next to where I was hiding. "Can't see anyone. I think we're good to go."

"Okay."

He poked his head over the fence again. "I'll give you a boost. There's a chair on the other side, it's on a deck, so it's not as big a drop as this side."

"Great."

I put my left foot in Ben's linked hands, grabbed the top of the fence, and climbed over, straddling the capping before I swung my left leg over, and quietly slipped down onto the chair. I moved to a concealed position behind a conservatory. Ben joined me. We could hear Emily and Crockett on the driveway.

A door opened somewhere in the house. Sounded like the other side. A male voice called out, "What's wrong here?"

Crockett's voice lifted, "Mind your business, pal."

The man spoke again. Sounded like he was outside, near the side door. I didn't hear the door shut, so it was probably still open.

Ben moved to the conservatory door. It was a sliding door and unlocked. We entered together. Weapons drawn. From the conservatory there were French doors into the lounge. Again, not locked. Ben opened one. I held my breath until we were both in the lounge room. It had an open plan layout; from the lounge you looked into the dining room and part of the kitchen. I could see a shape outside, through a lace-curtained window. We cleared the rooms and were left with the hallway that led down to the rest of the house. First, there was a short hall containing the door to the laundry, and then the house entrance. The door was open. A shadow lay across the driveway near the door. Must be the man we could hear trying to encourage Crockett to leave his girlfriend alone.

Ben led the way down the hall. First left, a bedroom. Nobody there. First right, bathroom. Empty. Second left, master bedroom. Second right, toilet. The door was closed. Straight ahead, another bedroom. Empty. Good chance our target was in the toilet. We waited concealed in the bedroom next to the toilet. The sound of toilet paper being pulled off a roll followed. Then a flush. A spraying noise. The door opened. Ben looked at me and motioned washing his hands. Water ran. I nodded. Ben and I moved silently to the bathroom. I peered around the open door. A woman stood at the basin with her back to the door. Ben passed me and pressed himself against the wall on the other side of the door. The tap turned off. There was a moment, when she probably dried her hands on a towel, before she walked out the door. I smiled and stepped in front of her. Gun in hand.

"Shush," I said, holding the index finger on my left hand to my lips. "Natalia Sokclov, I presume."

Her pale green eyes widened. Her head moved slowly. "This is not a good idea," she whispered. "Not a good idea at all."

"Nor is killing our colleagues," I replied, spinning her by her right arm and pressing her face into the wall. Ben handed me Plasti-cuffs. I cuffed her, making sure they were nice and tight. Could've been worse, could've been straight up zip-ties. Those things really bite right in. I grabbed her arm and made her walk toward Ben. He turned a tea towel into a gag and tightened it around her head. She wasn't young, and I was planning on going out the way we came. I motioned my intent to Ben, and he nodded. Guess he was okay with throwing an old lady over a fence. Or just this old lady?

Crockett and Emily were still arguing. The shadow was where I saw it last. His voice bellowed. "Leave her alone. You are bullying her."

Crockett yelled back, "Mind your business! Knuckle-head."

We shoved the woman out the French doors and closed them quietly behind us. Then out the conservatory door. Ben forced her to climb up on the chair. He used the arm to swing himself up onto the top of the fence. Then he grabbed the woman by the shoulders and tipped her over, letting her fall onto a grassed strip, narrowly missing a concrete driveway. I holstered my Glock and jumped over after them. It was a much higher drop on the outside. By the time I was ready to walk, Ben had dragged Sokolov to her feet, and shoved her toward our car. Crockett saw and gave a surreptitious hand signal in acknowledgment of my thumbs up. The woman limped to the car. Ben installed her in the backseat. Pushing her down so she couldn't be seen. She was stuck like a weeble-wobble that had lost its power. I jumped in the front passenger side. Ben drove past the house. Emily was already walking back to the car with Crockett making a fuss behind her.

I heard, "Don't be like that. I'm sorry." And then we were out of earshot.

We had a clear run to Pinehaven.

The only interruption to my thought processes were the check-ins from the surveillance crew outside Luke's place. And a phone call from Enzo.

"Bad news," Enzo said. "She didn't pick up the paper because she's dead."

"Bugger. How long?"

"Could've been yesterday, maybe early evening."

"How?"

"No idea. Wasn't violent, but apart from that, I don't know."

"Where was she?"

"On the couch in her living room. There was a tea tray on a table close by. Looked like she was having a cuppa and watching something on the telly."

"Thanks Enzo. You two can carry on with your day."

I hung up. Ben glanced at me and twitched toward the backseat. I wasn't about to say anything with her in the car. She only heard my side of the conversation.

At first I was tempted to go to the office, but if anyone gave a description of us to the guy from the BMW, it might lead to the office. Better to take Sokolov somewhere no one would find her. At least for a while. There was a prison cell at the back of the garage in the safe house. Perfect place for someone like her.

We arrived at the location in Fendalton Crescent to find brown paper bags up against the front door. Groceries. I'd forgotten Art had a grocery delivery ordered for us. Good timing really. At least we didn't arrive at the same time as the delivery guy and have to explain a cuffed and gagged woman in the back of the car.

"I'll put these away, you stick her in the cell," I said to Ben.

He nodded. "Okay. It's not going to take me long. I'll be back to give you a hand running the bags upstairs."

He escorted Sokolov through the downstairs hallway. I picked up four bags by the twisted cord handles, two in each hand, and carried them up the stairs.

Didn't take me long to put the cold things in the fridge, and everything else in the bags somewhere sensible. Ben emerged through the hall door carrying the last two bags. "Pantry for this lot I think," he said, placing them on the bench.

I peered inside the bags. "Tins of fruit, baked beans, spaghetti, and two bags of ground coffee, that's definitely pantry." I swung the pantry doors open. Ben unloaded the last bags. We paused to fold the bags and find where Art kept his paper bag supply.

Ben checked the cameras worked so I could monitor Sokolov on my phone. We were golden. I opened the app. There she was still gagged and cuffed, lying on the bed.

"Breakfast?" I asked.

"Yeah," Ben replied. "What time is it?"

"Nearly lunchtime. We've got to meet a woman about a nanobot at the office at midday."

"McDonalds it is then," Ben said. "Drive thru in Silverstream, here we come."

My stomach growled. "I think two Big Macs and fries will do the job."

On the way back to the office, Ben asked about the conversation earlier.

"Enzo said Zillah's mother is dead."

"Suspicious or not?"

"Very. She died in the living room with a tea tray next to her."

"Ah, the tea. Sokolov must really enjoy putting her little robots in tea."

"Puts a person right off a nice cuppa," I said, cradling the McDonalds bags on my knee. I pinched a fry out of one and munched on it. Being the kind souls we are, we also got burgers and fries for Crockett and Emily. I took another fry and ate it. "I don't think I'll be drinking tea anytime soon."

"Nor will I," Ben said.

We walked up the stairs into the main office and found Crockett and Emily sitting on the couch. I handed them a bag each. "Brunch."

"Thanks," Crockett replied.

"Thank you, Ronnie," Emily said, smiling. "This morning was fun."

"Yeah, it was fun," I said, and sank into the couch next to her. "I'm glad you enjoyed yourself. I like having you back in the field."

"Back in the field," Emily said, watching me closely. "Back in the field."

"Yes, Emily. Back. In. The. Field. Like old times," I told her, then bit into my delicious Big Mac with extra special sauce. I felt the sauce drip down my chin, and it felt good.

Emily nudged Crockett as she opened the paper bag containing her burger and fries. "This is a proper nose-bag. Burgers, not muesli bars."

Crockett wiped the stunned look off his face and bit into his burger. Ben wore a quizzical expression but didn't comment. Nothing else was said until we'd all finished eating. Collectively the mood lightened. Food does that. Also, capturing a fucking bad bitch does that.

"What do we do with Sokolov?" I mused out loud. "We can't let her go. Someone must want her; I doubt she's doing this by herself."

"The Americans want her pretty bad," Crockett said. "She did disappear on their watch."

"True. Then when we're done, let's give her back."

Crockett and Ben nodded.

Emily very quietly said, "If she is a killer, what did she use to kill?"

Oh, shit.

"The male at the house. He could have the nanobots," I said, screwing a napkin into a tight wad. "They might still be in play. Why would they need her to deliver the dose?"

"No reason, I can think of," Crockett said, as he gathered all the wrappers and stuffed then into an empty Maccas bag. "As long as she's under our control, we have a chance of determining the target and stopping it."

"Did you see anyone else surveilling her house?"

"No."

That was something. "*They,* whoever *they* are, might not have known we were onto her, prior to us grabbing the woman."

"I'm picking a few extra layers of surveillance are on Luke's house and Zillah's mother's house," Ben said. "We don't know how deep the layering is."

"I wasn't overly worried about us watching Sokolov. She's not a New Zealander. It's not exactly rural, but it's not suburbia either. If she spotted any of us she wasn't likely to go to police. Would the neighbours? Probably not, and it's a through road. They get traffic, not a huge amount, but they do get traffic," I said.

"We got away with it," Crockett said. "Even if that bloke clocked the rego on Emily's car, he needs the type of access police have to get owner's details?"

"Yes and no," I said. "There are websites that will tell you what type of car has the plate numbers. Then there's CarJam, which will give you a comprehensive report on the vehicle, but since 2011 you can't just wander around in that and get the owner's name and address unless you're an authorised business entity, like for example, *Wherefore Art Thou.*"

"And we don't know if the tall, dark, and handsome, server from *Manger* has access to such a business," Crockett said with a sigh. "Still, we're not going back to Emily's; we'll head to Pinehaven."

"Good call," I said. "As far as I'm concerned the two other surveillance jobs are tricky in comparison. Mostly because they are on New Zealanders in suburban settings, and the neighbours might call police."

None of us wanted to go and say to police, 'hey, we're doing this thing over here' because we shouldn't have been doing that thing over there. What's more, we're probably not the only ones doing that thing over there.

I grinned. "If there's layers, that's where they'll be. That's where the lasagna is. And like all lasagna's it's going to be tricky telling where one layer stops and another starts."

"Zillah's mother?" Crockett asked.

"Dead."

"Shit."

"Yeah, and the only reason to keep surveillance on a dead person is to see who rocks up and what they try to leave with."

I heard footsteps on the stairs, footsteps, and the unmistakeable clunk of a cane. Oh, surely not! How could Nana be clunking her way back up my stairs so soon after the last visit?

The woman would be the death of me!

Chapter Twenty-six:
[Ronnie: Nana's on the warpath]

I swung the office door open and witnessed Nana clunking up the stairs, one hand on the railing, the other on her cane. Fuelled by fury and righteous indignation, she glared at me. Her pale aged eyes sparking.

"Nana, today is not a good day for anything that involves shooting daggers from one's eyes," I said, circling my finger in the air toward her face, as she clunked her way to the door, making disapproving tutting noises.

"Veronica, you have disappointed your cousin, and me. I daren't think what poor Enzo is feeling." She continued into my office with the step, clunk, step, clunk routine. It was showmanship. She didn't need the cane. She liked the cane. She could whack unsuspecting people on a whim, and then play the age card.

"Enzo is fine, Nana."

"I'll be judging that for myself, thank you," Nana snapped. She spotted Crockett on the couch. "Mr Crocker. You missed our game last night."

Ah, good. His turn to squirm.

"Mea culpa, June. I will make it up to you and the ladies."

"You had better young man. Don't let Veronica be a bad influence on you."

That's hardly fair.

"Hello, Nana," Emily said brightly.

Nana tottered closer, then reached out and patted her hand. "Emily, dear. Is the bookshop closed today?"

Emily frowned. "I do not know."

We'd knocked Emily completely out of her daily routine. Of course, she wouldn't know. I stepped in. "Nana, Emily is having the day off to work on a case with me."

"Corrupting dear Emily too, are you?" She took a sharp inward breath, then hissed air out between her false teeth. "You can't leave well enough alone, can you?"

"Hardly Nana. Emily used to work with me. You know that."

"Yes I do. But *she* doesn't remember that does she? And it's for the best."

Wow, Nana was madder than I'd ever seen her. I controlled my tone; no need to cause the old woman to stroke out.

"What brought you to me today?" I tried to inject sweetness into my voice but failed.

"You have missed *every* appointment over the last two weeks. The wedding is important to the family."

"Yes, Nana, I know."

"Is it jealousy, Veronica? Is that why you persistently let us all down?"

"I am not jealous of Donnie and Enzo."

"Veronica!" Nana banged her cane on the floor.

Maybe I shouldn't have called him Donnie instead of Donald. My eyes rolled. "This is not jealousy, Nana. You know me better than that."

"Do I, Veronica? The girl I know would never disappoint her family."

"June," Ben said, with quiet authority. "That is not fair."

Nana shuffled around and locked eyes on Ben. I felt the room energy shift as Ben withered under her gaze. Then another change as he rallied. Good for him.

"June, you are being unfair to Ronnie."

"Benjamin Reynolds. You'll do well to remain silent."

Whoa. Ben put in his place. She was on a roll.

"Nana, shall we discuss how I'm a bitter disappointment later, when I'm not working?"

"Veronica, you are eating junk food with your friends. That's not even a proper meal." She narrowed her old eyes at me. The squint told me she wasn't done yet. "You look like you haven't slept for days." She eyed Crockett, Ben, and Emily. "You all look as though you haven't slept either." She returned to me. "I suppose you are responsible for the bags under their eyes?"

"We're working, Nana," I said, trying very hard to remain reasonable in the face of her anger. "We have a big case and it's taking all our resources."

"When will it be finished?"

I sighed. "You know I can't put a time limit on anything involving people, Nana. It's not like I work in the bookshop and I'm serving a customer."

"Veronica, adjust your tone," she snapped. "I'll be speaking to your father about this."

"No doubt he'll explain, again, what I do for a living,

and you'll end up mad at him too." I took a breath. "You are being unreasonable. I did not mean to miss our last appointment. I was tangled up in a case and I still am."

"That's nonsense. You could've come if you tried. If you *wanted* to come."

"Nana!"

"June," Ben said. "I will see that Ronnie makes it to the next fitting."

"Will you indeed," Nana turned on him. "Are you ever going to put a ring on my granddaughter's finger, young man? Or are you in the habit of stringing women along ad infinitum?"

"Okay, Nana, that's enough," I said firmly. I took her by the elbow and gently turned her toward the door. "How did you get here?"

"Taxi," she replied.

"Then I'll call you a taxi. Where are you going from here?"

"Home," she said, her anger softening to a few levels above annoyance. "There is a treasure hunt this afternoon. The girls and I have entered as a team."

"That sounds like fun," I said, and picked up the phone on the front desk. I dialled the taxi number from memory. Two minutes later, I had a taxi on the way, due to arrive within five minutes. Probably just enough time to escort her down the stairs and make damn sure she got in the car. "I'll help you down the stairs."

"No need, Veronica. I got up here by myself and I am perfectly capable of getting down by myself." She tugged her elbow from my grasp.

Something niggled at me.

"Nana, where is Donald?"

"At work, of course," she replied. "Where else would he be?"

"I'm sure I don't know. Does he know you're in town?"

"I'm not in the habit of clearing my movements with anyone," she said, and gave a sharp click of her tongue.

"I thought you and the ... *girls* ... were joined at the arthritic hip. Why are you flying solo?"

She huffed with annoyance. "We are not joined at the hip."

"Why are you flying solo?"

She started down the stairs, and I stepped down beside her.

"The girls are busy." She wrinkled her nose. "They want a new person to join our circle and are trying to entice her with fruitcake and petit fours."

The plot thickened like cold custard.

"Nana, why aren't you helping them?"

"Stop it at once, Veronica. This interrogation is ridiculous. It's you I came to see; this is nothing to do with me."

"Oh, really. Well, I think we have time to pop around to see Donald. Perhaps he'll have something to say about it."

"The taxi will be waiting."

"I'm happy to pay a fee to have the driver wait. It's the least I can do, after I've been such a dreadful disappointment to you." I checked my pocket, and sure enough I had my wallet. I knew it was the spare and had plenty of cash in it.

Nana hobbled down the last step. I opened the door and held it for her. The taxi waited at the curb. The driver waved. Good fortune smiled on me despite me being such a disappointment. I knew the driver. I'd helped him out with a customer who refused to pay.

I opened the door, blocking it with my body so Nana couldn't squeeze her old bones inside. She suddenly seemed in a hurry to get away.

"Hi Seamus, can you wait for a bit; it'll be worth your while."

"No problem, Ronnie. Gives me a chance to finish another chapter of the book I'm reading." Seamus waved a battered copy of a Wilbur Smith novel in the air.

"Back shortly, then," I said with a smile, and closed the door. "Come on, Nana." I helped her straighten up. She pushed my hand off her arm again, but clunked along beside me. She was not happy about something; I didn't for a minute think it was all about me.

Donald's receptionist greeted us as soon as we stepped over the threshold. "Lovely to see you both. Donald is out the back. Lunch break for him."

"We'll pop out and see him then," I replied with a smile. "Come on Nana, let's surprise Donald."

Nana grumbled under her breath as I led the way through the salon, past people getting shampoos, and someone getting a haircut. I knocked once on the door to the back.

"Come in," Donald said, in his usual sing-song voice. "Hope it's important though."

"It is," I replied, while I opened the door. "I brought Nana with me."

Donald clambered off a red leather lounger. "Nana!" He squealed and kissed both her papery cheeks. "What brings you to town?" He looked past me, then at me, and frowned. "Where are the girls?"

"Exactly," I said. "Nana is out of sorts and the girls are not with her."

Nana being out of sorts was putting it mildly. She was not a happy camper, and I was pretty sure it had something to do with the girls going off without her.

"Let's sit down, shall we?" Donald said, showing Nana to a stylish red leather armchair with chrome legs. "Now, Nana, tell us what's going on."

Donald and I sat opposite Nana on the leather lounger. Both of us leaned our elbows on our knees bringing us closer to Nana.

"You're being silly," she said. "I came to have it out with Veronica for disappointing you, and missing all the wedding appointments, that's it."

Donald turned to look at me. "She did, did she?"

I nodded. "Oh, yes. And she told Crockett and Ben off. Then she asked Ben when he was going to propose."

"Nana! What on earth has gotten into you?" Donald didn't take Nana's side like she'd hoped. It was all turning into day old porridge for her.

"That's enough," Nana said. "It's Veronica that you

should be annoyed at."

Donald nudged me. "Never, Nan, you know that. Ronnie has a job that means she can't always be where we want her. But she'll be at the wedding. I know that for sure."

"Yes, I will." I brought my lips close to his ear and whispered. "We need to talk about that disaster of a frock, Donnie."

Donald threw his arm around my shoulders, laughing, and gave me a squeeze. "Darling Ronnie." He kissed the top of my head. "I've had an awful lot of fun with that dress."

I pulled away and glared at him. "You utter wanker."

"It's the least I could do, after the years of you holding Nana's disapproval over my head. The pair of you having the best time at my expense."

Nana's shoulders shook with suppressed merriment. A smile broke free. "Oh, Donald, we meant nothing by it."

Donald scowled and flipped his fringe away from his face. "You two are so alike."

"I'm sorry, Donald," I said, trying with all my might to appear sorry. But I wasn't, and it was impossible to pull off contrition when there really truly was none.

"You're not, but I don't care, because that dress is exactly what I want you to wear."

I whacked his arm with the back of my hand.

Nana tutted. "No need to resort to violence, Veronica."

"Right, old one, spill the beans. What's up with you and the ... *girls*?" I insisted.

"Nothing. They're simply buttering up a new lady to join our little group."

"And you don't like her?" Donald suggested.

"She seems very nice," Nana said. "She's a bit younger than us. And they seem to think she's the bee's knees and the cat's whiskers."

I could see the problem. I nudged Donald. He too could see the problem.

"So, you're not flavour of the month at the moment. It's not the end of the world," I said. "I'm sure it will all work out."

"What was it you used to tell us, Nan?" Donald paused for effect. "I remember," he said. "Give it three days and you'll have forgotten what the fight was about."

"We're not fighting. We're not children," Nana snapped.

"Then I'm sure they'll be waiting for you when you get back," I added, helpfully.

"No doubt. Waiting to tell me all about the lovely time they had sharing cake with their new best friend and how wonderful she is."

Oh, right, here we go.

"Nana, it's not like you to be threatened by a newcomer. What's so wonderful about this new woman?" I asked.

"She is mysterious and foreign."

"I see," Donald soothed. "It's an infatuation, nothing serious. I bet she can't hold a candle to you, Nan."

"How mysterious and foreign could the woman be?"

"She's lived in America, had an exciting job, and looks

like a million dollars."

"America? What could she have done that was better than being a policeman's wife?" Donald queried.

"A special agent, by all accounts. Some nonsense about the FBI and so forth."

"And now she lives in Upper Hutt. Well, that's not very exciting," Donald said, maintaining his soothing tone. He wasn't bad at wrangling the oldies.

I was stuck on the special agent part, especially since I was fairly sure that Elizabeth Collins was living in Nana's retirement village. And so far, she fitted the bill.

"What's her name?" I asked, trying to keep any stress from my voice.

"Elizabeth Collins."

Of course, it is. Of course. Nana's blue eyes would turn green over Elizabeth Collins. Of course, that woman would be involved with Nana in some manner. That was my fear from the beginning. That is exactly how my luck goes. Extracting Nana from this will be fun, said no granddaughter ever.

"Nana, I don't think you need to worry about the girls liking this new woman and wanting to spend time with her," I said, because she won't be around long.

"Why's that, dear?" Nana wasn't as mean sounding as she had been up to that point.

"Because she's a person of interest in an ongoing investigation," I said, matter-of-factly. "This is strictly a need-to-know situation. I'm breaking so many rules by telling you that." Nana loved to be in on everything. I knew from experience, that if she thought she knew something about someone, she'd be happy as a pig in mud.

Nana's faded blue eyes danced with curiosity. "Veronica, what on earth do you mean? She's retired and living in one of those fancy apartments. She's not in *that* life now."

That's exactly what I'm sure she wants people to think. And yet she was searching MacKinnon's house for something, and we got her on tape.

"Trust me Nana, when I tell you, she *is* a person of interest."

Donald whispered in my ear, "Steady there, double-oh-seven."

I whispered back, "Sadly, it's true. She is. And if Nana and the *Cronies* get involved, it'll be a full-on Titanic-sized disaster."

"They're hardly Bond girls," Donald whispered. "What would the theme song be to that movie?"

"Roll out the barrel?" I suggested.

Donald choked trying not to laugh. I thumped him on the back.

"What were you two whispering about?" Nana asked. "You nearly killed Donald!"

Of course, it was my fault he choked on his own laughter.

"The dress," Donald replied, dragging his amusement back several notches.

"The colour scheme," I replied.

Nana seemed perkier. I was grateful for that, but not sure I'd done the right thing. All I needed was Nana to open her mouth and say something to the Collins woman. An idea formed. We wanted to have the woman under surveillance. I could see so many downsides to my next thought, but ploughed ahead anyway.

"Nana, can I ask you a very important favour?"

She tipped her head to one side, just enough that she looked like a bird of prey eyeing its next meal. "Yes dear."

"I need to put the Collins woman under surveillance. And we don't exactly look like we belong in the retirement village. I don't suppose you could help Crockett, Ben, and me, out?"

She thought for a moment. The cogs lit her faded eyes with possibilities.

"I'm sure I could, Veronica. What would I need to do?"

"Get close to her, but not too close. Maybe, invite her to a game?"

Nana sparkled with instant joy. "I wouldn't be able to tell the girls, would I?"

"I'm afraid not, Nana. It'd have to be just between us."

"I can do that, Veronica. If it's important."

"It is. We're talking life and death, Nana."

"Well, then, I'm on the case, as you say."

I've never said that. Not bloody ever. Good grief.

"Nana, do you think the girls will find it suspicious if you invite Collins to your poker night?"

"Not at all. The more the merrier. Tell Mr Crocker that we'll play tonight. He won't want to miss it."

"Good idea Nana, he can be your backup."

Nana fizzed with excitement. "Oh my, backup!"

"Now, Nana, remember to keep it under your hat. This is national security business."

"Yes, dear. Mum's the word." She drew an imaginary zip across her closed mouth.

I had a bad feeling, but at least Nana's mood was improved.

"Right, let's get you in the taxi and safely home, so you can begin your task," I said, as I stood and offered her my hand. She smiled at me, taut lips over teeth. Terrifying.

"Do you need me to take notes?"

"Only after the fact Nana. When you're alone in your room."

"That's very smart, dear."

Was it? I just involved Nana in our mess to give her something to do. That is not smart. That is certifiable.

Chapter Twenty-seven:
[Crockett: Some ideas are better than others]

I listened as Ronnie told me how she'd placated June by asking her to keep an eye on Elizabeth Collins. That would not have been how I played it, but I understood why she did it. From what I knew of June and the *Cronies of Doom*, I believed they could undertake close surveillance. Whether they'd be sprung or not was a different story. I was fairly certain that June would tell the other two, and they'd help and then they'd get sprung being too nosy. It didn't matter what Ronnie said about keeping Frankie and Ester out of it, June would enlist their help. *The Cronies of Doom* ride at dusk.

Emily sat quietly as we discussed the June and Collins situation. She looked tired. I put my arm around her. She leant her head on my shoulder.

"I guess we need to trust June on this," Ben said. "She's always pretty good when she has a mission, and this time it's not one she invented for herself." He winked at Ronnie.

She nodded. "Right, where are we at with the rest of this mess?"

"James MacKinnon and Zillah's mother are dead. Surveillance continues on Luke," Ben said.

"Art checked in with me while Ronnie was off with

Nana," I said. "He is certain there are two men surveilling Luke. Art said he hasn't seen anyone else, but isn't ruling it out."

"Good to know," Ronnie said, a smile lay on her lips. "I hope that means they still think he has the Intel."

"So do I," I said, adjusting my arm around Emily. She didn't move. "Is she asleep, Ronnie?"

"Looks like it," she said. "We're going to have to get out of here soon. Re-group back in Pinehaven."

"Yes, we are."

We'd need to check for anyone tailing us, or surveillance on us. I was pretty sure there would be some; I'd put money on someone watching the office. Someone would've worked out who we are, or at least who a few of us are, by now. Those Albanians had time to do it. They'd be stupid if they hadn't.

"When is your tech arriving?" I asked Ronnie.

She looked at her watch. "I expected her to be here by now."

"Considering the current climate, that's concerning," I said. "Can you reach out?"

Right then we all heard the door at the bottom of the stairs open and close. Ronnie drew her weapon and went to the main desk. She scooted behind the desk. There was a peephole in the wall beside the door, not in the door. She peered through the peephole, then looked over at us. "It's my contact," she said, while pressing her Glock back into the holster and moving around the desk to open the main door.

She swung the door open before the person knocked.

"Hey, good to see you, come on in," Ronnie said smiling. "I'll introduce you to the team."

Ben stood. "No need to introduce all of us. How are you, Christine?"

"Good thanks, Ben."

The expression of surprise on Ronnie's face faded fast. "You know each other, that's good." She smiled. "On the couch, trapped under Emily, is Crockett."

Christine strode forward and shook my outstretched hand. "Pleasure, Dave Crocker, I presume," she said. "That's the only Crockett I've heard of here."

"Guilty," I replied. I always felt uncomfortable when people recognised my name. Maybe I should be used to it, but I'm not. "Good to meet you."

A brief handshake and she was back talking with Ronnie. I listened. This was Ronnie's deal.

"I have a sample of a cup of tea. I need you to run every test you can and tell me if there is anything in it you wouldn't expect to see."

"Got anything in particular I should look for."

"Nano technology or xenobots. I don't even know how you'd look for those."

"That's why you pay me the big dollars," Christine said with a laugh. "What else, because tea isn't all, is it?"

"Two bodies. One died in Wellington Hospital, and one is still in his house in Ngaio."

"Right, I can get access to the body in the morgue at Wellington Hospital; give me a name." Christine took a notebook and pen from her messenger bag.

"William MacKinnon," Ronnie said.

"And the address and name for body two?"

"James MacKinnon," she said, and then gave the address. "We haven't notified the authorities yet."

"How long has the body been in the house?"

"At least twelve hours," Ronnie said.

I had something to add. "There are usually two staff in attendance during a normal day. The housekeeper and a personal assistant."

"Good point," Ben said. "And we saw no evidence of either person on the CCTV footage we watched."

"That's unusual," I said. "Wonder what that's about."

"Ben, do you know William MacKinnon's PA?" Ronnie asked.

"Yes." He stood and walked to the phone on the reception desk.

Emily stirred.

"Hey, you awake?" I whispered.

"Yes," she replied, her voice thick with sleep. Emily moved back then sat up straighter and rubbed her eyes. "What is happening?"

"Ben is talking to someone on the telephone. We're going to leave soon and go to the house in Pinehaven. Will you come with me?"

"Yes." She looked around the room. "Who is the lady talking to Ronnie?"

"Christine. She's a laboratory tech with ESR. Forensic technician I think."

Ben hung up. His call was conducted in quiet tones. I doubt any of us heard what he was saying. He came over and sat with Emily and me.

"And?"

"MacKinnon senior gave his PA and housekeeper a week off. He said he would be away and there was no need for them to come in while he wasn't at the residence."

"When are they due back?"

"In two days," Ben said. "That gives us time enough to collect any evidence from the body and notify the authorities."

"And scrub the CCTV," I said.

"Yes, and that."

A phone rang. The noise jangled through the room. Ronnie answered it, "Wherefore Art Thou."

She pressed a button, and a disguised voice came from the speaker.

"I know it was you," the distorted voice said.

"I'm sorry, I don't know what you're talking about," Ronnie replied, gesturing to Ben to trace the call. Ben hurried over. I watched him copy the number that had called the business phone, from the screen on the telephone base. He came back and sat next to me, with his phone open. I could see he had pulled up a website.

"You took him," the voice continued.

"I still don't know what you're talking about."

"Don't play games, Ms Tracey. You were seen leaving a restaurant with an actor, and Mr MacKinnon."

We all looked at each other. Ben showed me the screen on his phone. He'd traced the cell phone number to Upper Hutt. What was it with Upper Hutt that made it constantly the centre of nefarious deeds?

"I'm sorry I don't know what restaurant you're referring too," Ronnie said. "If you give me more detail I could possibly help you locate whoever it is you're looking for." Ronnie paused and smiled across the room. "Let's start with your name."

"Ms Tracey, you took something that doesn't belong to you. Give it back before life becomes unbearable."

"I'm sorry, I really don't understand what you want. This is New Zealand, no one owns anyone here. Unless it's not a person that you think I took? Is it a person?"

Heavy breathing rasped from the speaker. "Ms Tracey, you are being difficult. You left the restaurant with someone important."

Ronnie grinned. "He's not that important. He's just an actor. It's not like he's in an award-winning television show or anything."

Ben shook his head, with a smile on his face.

"You are infuriating," the voice said. "Give back what does not belong to you."

"And again, whoever you are, I don't know what you're talking about. What is it that I have?"

"Mr MacKinnon. Return him to *Manger* by five this evening."

"I'm sorry I can't do that."

"Then, Ms Tracey, it is you and your family that will

suffer."

"Okay then, sorry I couldn't help you, random phone voice."

Ronnie hung up. Christine leaned on the reception desk. "You really annoyed that person. Good for you," she said, laughing. "Was that a male or female?"

"That's what I was trying to work out," Ronnie replied. "It felt male, then I doubted myself and thought maybe female. Whatever it was, the voice was altered to disguise it." Ronnie glanced at Ben. "What'd you get from the cell phone number?"

"It's registered to *Manger*. The carrier is Spark. Get this, the account is owned by Elizabeth Collins."

"Buggery bollocks!" Ronnie scowled, picked the phone up again and dialled a number from memory. She tapped her foot while she waited. "Come on, answer the phone." Eventually she hung up. "She always answers."

"Who were you ringing?" I asked, fearing it was June, and she was actually in the lion's den.

"Nana. I wanted to know if Collins made a phone call just now, you know, in case it is her that called me."

Ben spoke, "I've got coordinates for the phone from where the call was placed. Let me see where it points."

He copied something into a map. A second later he jumped to his feet. "We gotta go to June, now."

"Fuck!" Ronnie said.

"We're coming," I said, as Emily and I stood up.

"I'm going to Ngaio, then the morgue," Christine said. "Keep me posted. I'll take some samples and get on with finding out what it was that killed MacKinnon junior, and senior."

She waved as she left the room. Her footsteps echoed in the stairwell but vanished by the time we all charged down the stairs intent on rescuing June and *the Cronies of Doom* from whatever fate was about to befall them.

I had Emily by the hand and took her to the car. One press on the unlock icon on the fob made every light flash. I opened the passenger door for her. She smiled up at me as she settled herself in the seat and pulled the seatbelt across her body. I shut the door firmly and slid into the driver's side. I drove north and turned right into the road by the railway station. Ronnie and Ben were behind me as I re-joined Fergusson Drive heading south. June's retirement village was less than five minutes away. I knew June and the old boilers could hold their own in normal circumstances. But if it was Collins on the phone, if she really thought she could leverage June to get Ronnie to comply with her demands, then shit was going to get ugly. Fast.

Chapter Twenty-eight:
[Ronnie: Nana and the Cronies of Doom]

In some ways Ben driving was good, and in other ways, I wanted to shove him out the car door and take over. Knowing I felt like that meant I should let him drive and keep my mouth shut. It's not his fault I sent Nana into a bad situation. That's on me. This is my guilt to carry. Why am I like that? Couldn't have just placated her and let her be shirty with me for a few days? Oh no, I had to open my mouth and give her a task.

I wrestled my phone from my pocket and was glad it was my phone. I gave Terry O'Sullivan a ring.

He answered on the fourth ring. "Terry speaking."

"It's Ronnie Tracey, Terry. Just checking in. I take it Luke arrived home safely."

"Yes, he did. Thank you for your help."

"No problem. The invoice will be sent out next week. Have you heard from Luke's commanding officer, at all?"

"I'll pay as soon I receive the invoice."

"I appreciate the promptness, and so does our accountant." Otherwise known as Steph and she does excellent nasty office lady when needed. I rearranged my question. "You haven't heard from Luke's boss then?"

"No, not at all."

"Good. If you do, give me a quick bell, please. It's time

I made a decision on a toaster."

"Yes, yes I will." He paused. "Toaster?"

"I was looking at some with Bill Bailey the other day."

"That's Luke's commanding officer's name. I didn't know you knew each other."

"Small world, Mr O'Sullivan. Small world."

"Yes, it is. Thank you again, Ronnie. Goodbye now."

If it was Bill that was listening to O'Sullivan's phone, then he now knew I knew. If it was someone else, they now knew, I knew Bill. I felt in my bones that it wasn't only Bill Bailey behind the electronic surveillance.

My phone screen went dark as Ben pulled into the Quinn's Post car park.

"Probably pays not to advertise our arrival by parking in the retirement home visitor parking," he said.

I glanced to my left and saw Crockett pulling up beside us.

"Strange that Bill Bailey didn't contact O'Sullivan senior to find out if Luke was back," I said, undoing my seatbelt.

Ben swung his door open and climbed out. He leaned into the car before closing the door. "Not really, Ronnie. Not if he's got a team watching the house."

"There's one way to find out," I said. I exited the vehicle and leaned back on the closed door with my phone in my hand. I scrolled quickly through my recent contacts and tapped Bill Bailey's phone number.

Bill answered quickly. "Ronnie, what can I do for you this time?"

"Nothing, Bill. This is a courtesy call. Just wanted you to know that Luke O'Sullivan was safely returned to his father's home, early this morning."

"Ah, thanks for that. I expect he'll be in touch."

"I doubt it, what with him retiring from the army, and moving into the private sector."

Papers shuffled. A door closed. Bill's voice came back, "What are you talking about?"

"He said he's leaving, that the paperwork is done, and he's all but out."

"News to me, Ronnie." He actually sounded sincere, but then, he did tell lies for a living.

I very much doubt he knew nothing about it, more subterfuge. "Anyway, just letting you know I found him, and he's back home."

"He's not injured or anything?"

"No, should he be?"

"I'll be in touch."

I hung up and called Steph right away. "Let me know if there is any movement at all on the target house. I just dropped the cat among the pigeons so we might get some movement."

"Will do. What are you thinking?"

"If nothing happens, you don't see anyone show up, or anything sus, then I'd say Army are already in place watching."

"I'll pass it along to the other team."

"Stay sharp."

I hung up.

Crockett, Emily, and Ben waited for me on the footpath. Nerves jangled. Crockett shifted from foot to foot. Ben rocked on his heels. Emily stood still. Once upon a time she would've rocked back on her left heel. That was a habit she lost to the accident and the artificial right leg.

Everyone switched their phones to silent.

"Okay, let's do this," I said. "In pairs. Ben and I will go in through Nana's ranch slider from the garden. You and Emily go through the front entrance via the main building. Say hello to Margot in reception."

"Got it," Crockett said, taking Emily by the hand. "Let's go visit June."

Emily smiled. "I like June."

Crockett nodded. "So do I."

Crockett and Emily walked toward the retirement village hand in hand. Had to admit they made a good couple. I'd seen more of the old Emily lately, and I suspected it was having Crockett around.

Ben and I went around the corner and entered through the garden gate. We approached Nana's sliding door carefully. I could tell the net curtains were open from where we stopped, one apartment back, and sheltered by bushes. I peeked around the bush.

"We need to be closer." I couldn't see into the apartment, just that the curtains were all open.

Ben pointed to the privacy screen in front of us, that separated the apartment we were near, from Nana's. It came out about a metre. There was no other shelter that close. I nodded. Then looked past Nana's apartment to the next one. It had the same kind of privacy screen/wall arrangement, but also some bushes. I motioned to Ben.

He raised an eyebrow. "Who?"

"You," I said. "I've got a feeling she'll be looking for me."

"By she, you mean, Collins," he said.

"Well, yeah." I took stock of Ben's appearance. "You're too tidy looking. What's under your jersey?" I could see a blue checked collar.

"A shirt." An ah-ha moment flicked across his eyes. He took the jersey off revealing a blue and black checked shirt. He rolled his sleeves up. Untucked a bit of his shirt. Messed his hair up just a smidge. "Better?"

"Yes. Now you look like you've been out here gardening or doing some kind of outdoorsy tidying up."

He smiled. "Outdoorsy huh?"

"Yes."

"Okay." He checked the coast was clear, walked back the way we'd come, and then utilised the middle of the lawn to get into position. I saw him take a sneaky look at Nana's on the way past. He disappeared from view. Then his hand waved once before he hunkered down behind the screen.

My phone buzzed in my pocket. I quickly looked at the screen.

Ben: Nana and the ladies are inside.
I replied: See anyone else?
Ben: No, but it was a quick look.

Just before I pushed my phone back into my back pocket, a message flashed up on the screen. I didn't open, didn't need to.

Donald: My beloved isn't answering his phone. What have you done with him?

Spiky barbs of guilt jabbed into my stomach. I shook it off. Now was not the time to be worrying about anything except the job at hand.

It was quiet in the garden. No birds twittered. Probably because we disturbed them with our presence. I found the quiet surprisingly restful despite my thumping heart. I heard a loud knock, and hoped it was Crockett knocking on Nana's interior door.

I listened, hardly breathing, waiting for a deep male voice. Hoping for a deep male voice. A bee almost hit me when it flew into a purple flower that climbed the dividing screen between the apartments.

Crockett's voice resounded from the apartment, "June, sorry I didn't make the game last night," he said, his tone conveying his apology quite well. I didn't know he was such a good actor.

There was a quiet reply. Straining to listen, I just made out Nana's voice, but not the words.

I figured the attention of the room was on Crockett and Emily. Ben's head poked out from his concealed position. I nodded. We emerged at the same time and approached the sliding door.

Frankie saw us.

She hurried to the door and opened the lock. I slid the door open, and stepped into the room, followed quickly by Ben.

Crockett and I made brief eye contact before I scanned the room. Frankie, Nana, Ester, Emily, Crockett, and there she was, Elizabeth Collins, standing behind Ester. Good choice. Stand behind the slightly wider, former policewoman.

"Ms Collins, I presume," I said across the room.

The woman stepped out from behind Ester. Crockett and Emily were still near the internal door. Collins had remained out of sight from his position. The woman smiled at me, then turned to Crockett.

"Mr Crocker, how nice to see you again."

Again? What the hell?

He didn't respond. Nana did. "Elizabeth, I think you should leave. Seems I have visitors. Perhaps you could come back later this afternoon?"

I swallowed a smile. It takes a lot to rattle Nana.

"Yes, I see," Collins replied, her voice calm and even. "But I think your visitors might know what I want, and where to find it."

"I doubt that," I said. "Come back later. I'm sure we can discuss this further then. Right now, we have wedding preparations to get on with. There's a frock I need to try on."

Nana positively beamed at me, then added, "I'm sure

you can understand that getting everyone in the same room is quite a feat, and this is a gift from God."

Collins balked. "I'm not going anywhere until I have what I want."

Crockett remained silent. He shook his head at me. If I hadn't been staring at him, I would've missed it, the movement was so subtle. How did he know Elizabeth Collins?

"Nana, would you put the jug on, please?" I asked. "Don't know about anyone else, but I'd love a cuppa. And this looks like it's going to drag on."

Nana shuffled a few steps closer to me. "Of course, dear." She adjusted her step and hurried into the kitchen, with Emily close behind.

"I'll help Nana," she said as she walked past me. "Nana, may I have a Milo please?"

Nana's reply didn't reach me, but I was sure it'd be yes. She kept Milo on hand for Emily.

Collins spoke. She sounded more American than Kiwi, "This is all very nice but there is something I require. And we don't want this to get messy, do we?"

Ester and Frankie shook their heads.

"Ladies, have a seat, you look tired," Ben said to them, then glanced at Collins who nodded.

So far she wasn't a monster.

Ester and Frankie took their usual seats on the lounge suite, out of habit. Nana poked her head out from the kitchen area and asked who wanted tea. Frankie and Ester replied saying they would. No one else said a word.

I wanted Nana out of the way for a few minutes. "Nana, could I please have a coffee?"

"Yes, Veronica. Your usual?"

"Yes, thank you."

My manners were on full display.

With the cronies seated and Nana and Emily in the kitchen, the remaining people were Ben, Crockett, Collins, and me. We all stood. I moved closer to Collins, as did Ben.

"Shall we take this into the hallway?" I said and indicated the door near Crockett. "Perhaps you and Crockett can have a lovely catch-up chat out there?"

Collins pursed her lips. For mid to late sixties, she looked in pretty good nick. There was no doubt in my mind that she could still hold her own.

"No one is going anywhere," Collins said. "We're going to sit down in here and you're going to tell me where my property is."

"Okay," I climbed over the back of the couch I was standing behind, and plonked into the soft leather.

Nana's voice rang out, "For goodness sake, Veronica, don't climb all over the furniture. You're not fourteen."

The woman missed nothing. "Sorry, Nana."

Frankie smiled at me. "Wish I could still do that."

Collins interrupted, "Let's get back to the situation at hand, shall we?" She motioned to Crockett. "Sit down Mr Crocker, and you too, Mr Reynolds."

"Yes ma'am," Crockett replied.

He and Ben sat on either side of me which put Crockett closest to where Emily and Nana would sit. The protector. I stopped myself from scoffing out loud. I knew he cared for Emily, and for Nana. But now we knew he had a secret. At which point was he going to say he knew Elizabeth Collins? Never was my bet.

Nana came in with the tea tray just as I said, "What is it you want Collins?"

"MacKinnon."

"He's dead."

"James MacKinnon."

"He's dead."

Collins frowned. "Both dead? How?"

"Why do you want MacKinnon senior?" I asked, not that keen on answering her question, mostly because we didn't have a definite answer yet.

"MacKinnon has something I need."

"Okay, what did he have. Maybe we can help?"

"I doubt that." she replied.

"And the reason you were searching MacKinnon's residence?"

She met my stare, her eyes questioning as thoughts gathered. "You were there?" I could see her trying to work it out. "There was someone with Mackinnon."

"It wasn't me." It was Sokolov. How did she not know that? "The person that was with him was the last person to see him alive."

"Who was it?"

"Someone I think you know," I said, watching her carefully. "Natalia Sokolov."

Collins paled. Her eyes rounded and widened. "She's in New Zealand," she whispered into the room.

"She most assuredly is," Ben replied.

"Do you know where?"

"Yes," I said. "She is at a secure location." I pressed my back into the couch cushions. "How long have you owned *Manger*?"

Surprise registered on her face. "A few years."

"MacKinnon was held there after your flunkies grabbed him, and another man from Upper Hutt."

"I don't have flunkies."

"The hell you don't," Crockett muttered. "Cut the crap, Collins, we know about you. The innocent old Boiler routine went out the window when you threatened people. We. Know."

"What is there to know, Dave?" Collins smiled, but it wasn't pleasant. "I'll wait."

I silenced Crockett with a look.

Nana poured tea and passed teacups on matching saucers to the *Cronies*. "Ladies, can I get you a biscuit."

"No thank you June," Ester said. She glanced around the coffee table and floor. "But I believe I left my notebook on the kitchen bench?"

"Yes, I think I saw it."

Crockett stood. "I'll get it, Ester. Take a load off, June."

Nana smiled up at Crockett. "Thank you dear." She settled herself in her favourite chair with her cup of tea.

So civilised. The whole thing was surreal. Here we were having a bloody cup of tea with a woman who meant to do someone harm if she didn't get what she wanted. Life is strange. My phone rang. I glanced at the screen. Steph.

I shrugged at Crockett, who was back, and had handed Ester her notebook and a pen. He knew she wanted it to take notes. My phone kept ringing. I answered it.

"Steph, what's up."

Collins glared at me then said, "Speaker, thanks."

Bugger.

I touched the speaker icon. "You're on speaker, Steph."

"There's a development," she said.

"Good to know," I replied. "What kind?"

"Bill is parked at the end of the street."

"When did he arrive?"

"Not long after our last communication. I've alerted the team."

"Good work. Keep an eye on him and the magic box. He won't be alone. There'll be another four people somewhere." He's the trigger and they need to find the eyes.

"There's six of us now, we'll be fine."

I hung up before Steph could say anything else. Just in case.

Collins spoke, "Who are you surveilling?"

"That's need to know. You do not," I replied.

"If that has something to do with MacKinnon, then I need to know."

"It doesn't," I said. Not a lie. How could it be anything to do with a dead man?

"So, this is an unrelated job?"

"That's right. I'm a private investigator. I have a business to run and jobs on the books."

She didn't look like she believed me but said nothing.

"How about you tell us what you really want?" Ben said. "You were obviously looking for something at MacKinnon's and you left empty handed. If you tell us, we might be able to help." Sounded very reasonable.

Collins chewed her bottom lip for a moment. "MacKinnon is in possession of a file that belongs to me."

"A file," I said, thinking of the images of her shaking books at MacKinnon's. "And that's all?"

She nodded. "He has a file. It belongs to me."

"Is your former sister-in-law still in New Zealand?" I wasn't quite sure where I was going with that.

"Why?"

"Oh, no reason, I just heard she might be living over the hill."

Suspicion etched into the lines on her face. "Not many people know who my former sister-in-law is."

"Her name came up in conversation a few days ago," I said. It wasn't a lie. It just wasn't the whole story. I could see Nana's curiosity growing. "Nana actually asked me to look her up."

Nana's pale eyes flashed, quick as a wink she said, "Michaela Kennedy-Carlisse, is your sister-in-law, Ms Collins? How delightful."

Ester flipped her notebook open and hurriedly took notes. I knew she used actual shorthand and probably no one in this room apart from her, Nana, and maybe

Frankie, would be able to understand her notes.

Collins said nothing.

Frankie leaned closer. "Oh, Ms Collins, that's very exciting. What was it like having such a famous sister-in-law?"

Ester held her pen paused over a page. Waiting.

"A sister-in-law is a sister-in-law no matter how famous she might be," she replied quietly. "Perhaps when this is resolved I can introduce you."

Frankie oozed delight as she smoothed her shirt and slacks. "That would be lovely."

Maybe Nana and the *Cronies of Doom* weren't in imminent danger.

Nice thought. I watched Collins. She was still standing.

"Sit down," I said to her. "You're making me uncomfortable and this whole nonsense situation is starting to really annoy me."

Crockett and Ben both nudged me. I ignored them.

"There's a stool in the kitchen, why don't you go get that, and sit your old arse down?"

"Veronica!" Nana cautioned. "We don't talk to guests like that."

"Collins is not a guest, she is an intelligence officer, and out of her fucking depth."

"Veronica!"

"Tell her," I said to Collins, as she returned with the kitchen stool and perched on it. "Tell her who you are."

"Elizabeth Collins," she replied.

"The rest," I grumbled. "I'm over this shit. I have

somewhere to be, so, tell my Nana who you bloody well are, and tell me exactly what you fucking want, and get on with it."

"I am Elizabeth Collins," she replied firmly. "And I want a file that belongs to me and that MacKinnon had in his possession."

"You know for sure that he had it?"

"Yes."

"How?"

"He told me."

"Tell Nana who you are."

She took a breath. "I am an intelligence officer."

"And you work for?"

She bit her lip again, then released it. "America."

Great.

"I'm sure you could narrow that down," Ben said quietly.

Frankie's pen scratched on the paper.

"Central Intelligence Agency," she said.

"Just like your ex-husband," I replied. "How nice."

Crockett muttered something about a family business, but no one heard but me.

"So, the file … is it for you personally?" I asked.

"Yes."

"And Sokolov, what's she doing in New Zealand?"

Collins pursed her lips again before answering. "I don't know. I heard there was something coming down the pipeline about Sokolov, but it didn't arrive."

Ah. I think I know where and what that is.

"You heard, or the CIA heard?"

"CIA," she replied, quickly. "The Intel was coming into the country with someone. We didn't know who."

"And the thing you want from MacKinnon, is it the Intel?"

She frowned. Lady, you shouldn't frown. The lines on her face run so deep they look like fault lines. There's about to be a magnitude seven on the Richter scale.

"Not exactly. It is related."

"What if I told you I read a book recently that had some familiar characters in it," I said, because for whatever reason, I thought that might be what she wanted.

"How?"

"Because it was hidden in a spreadsheet, and I was looking for something that would help us make sense of a situation."

"Hidden in a spreadsheet," she repeated. "And where did you get it?"

"MacKinnon," I replied. "He gave it to me."

"When did you find it?"

I didn't really want to say that it was after we rescued MacKinnon and O'Sullivan from her bloody restaurant.

"The other night."

"Was MacKinnon alive or dead?"

"Dead, but I didn't know that at the time."

Collins took another deep breath. "We are on the same side," she said. "I need your help to find Sokolov. You know why if you read the book."

Crockett cleared his throat. "You need our help? You.

Just a little while ago you were threatening us, and these lovely ladies. Now you *need* our help?" He made direct eye contact with Collins. "You are going to have to be a lot nicer, Collins."

"And you might want to tell the class how you know me," she said, almost smiling when she said it, then stopping herself.

"That's not relevant to this situation," he said. "It's true that we've met before, and that's all anyone needs to know."

I gave him a sharp jab in the ribs with my elbow. "We'll talk about it later, won't we?"

He nodded.

Collins attention shifted back to me when she said, "You read the story. You know how dangerous Sokolov is. Do you know what or who, her target is?"

"Apart from the MacKinnon's you mean?"

Another deep frown spidered across her forehead. "MacKinnon's? She killed both MacKinnon's?"

"I think so. Can't prove it until we get the report back from the lab."

"Shall we go somewhere more conducive to this type of conversation?" She asked.

"Enough has been said in front of Nana that if we leave now, she'll just make the rest up and cause havoc," I said, watching Nana out of the corner of my eye. Surprisingly, she didn't refute my statement. A little chuckle from Ester and Frankie sealed the deal. She had witnesses. She couldn't refute my claim without looking like a liar. And that would never do.

"I can't talk any more in front of people without security clearance," Collins stated.

"Fine, then, your apartment?" I suggested.

"Yes."

I leaned toward Nana. "You stay here. I don't want any nonsense. Am I clear?"

Nana sipped at her tea. "I don't know what you are implying Veronica."

I stood at the same time as Crockett and Ben. Now we work in unison? Not creepy at all. Emily placed her mug of Milo on the coffee table before she started to stand. Crockett gently pressed her shoulders downward.

"Wait here with Nana and her friends, Emily. We won't be long," Crockett said gently.

"All right. I like it here," she said and picked her mug back up. "I will wait."

Felt like I'd lost Emily again. For a brief amount of time, she was almost old Emily, and now new Emily had returned. Sadness trickled into my being at the thought of losing my friend again. Brain injuries sucked.

Chapter Twenty-nine:
[Crockett: Collins is a wildcard]

"This is a crapfest, Collins. And you know more than you are saying," I said, making myself at home on the sofa in her living room. "I didn't think you were a bad old boiler, but I'm rapidly changing my mind."

"That's rude, Mr Crocker, and uncalled for. MacKinnon took something that belonged to us. We want it back. Simple really."

"Really, MacKinnon did a job himself? Didn't think he had it in him." Crockett asked. "I had no idea he'd done anything more than sit at his desk for years."

"Ha, ha," Collins replied. "He ordered it, or he did it, same-same. You pedantic fool."

"Fool? Me? Yeah, course; wouldn't be the person who lost something the CIA want control of would it?"

Ronnie circled her finger, subtly. Her cute little way of telling me to wind it up. I grinned at her.

Collins pointed at Ben. "What do you have to do with this disaster?"

"I was called at the same time as the other two. We're all in the same rowboat trying to get to shore before a tsunami hits."

Nice analogy. Maybe I've underestimated Ben.

"Called in?"

"Never mind, Collins, that's now irrelevant. The thing

we want to know is why that book was hidden, and what the deal is with it," I said, pulling her back on track. Ronnie had Sokolov stashed, and we needed to get back to her before anything bad happened or anything worse happened. "We came over to your apartment to hear you out, so, talk."

"We think." She stopped and thought for half a beat. "I think, Sokolov disappeared to The Balkans. I can't prove it. But that's where I think she has been. We've had one report of a tentative sighting near a University in Albania." She paused as if gauging our response. No one said anything. "I've been running down leads for years, and nothing, then I heard something about xenobot research. And it sounded like something she was working on. I thought if I found the missing file, it might help me understand what she wanted. Where she's going with this, and if she was working on a precursor to xenobots."

"Surely you could find out if she was really working on DARPA funded research programs before she vanished," Ronnie said.

"She was, that's the thing. She was. But the research was so highly secretive that no one has seen any reports. It was off-book research."

"Isn't that usually reserved for deniable weapons, like Directed Energy weapons," I said, tapping my fingers on the back of the sofa.

"And super soldiers, if you listen to the conspiracy theorists and gossip," she replied. "I dug around and as far as I could tell, she was working on some off-book, but well-funded research, and then she vanished into the woodwork and no one has seen her since."

"Did she take the research with her?" Ronnie asked.

"We don't know," Collins replied carefully. "We don't know what she had in her possession when she vanished. Everything closed up like a Venus fly trap the minute she disappeared."

"Okay. So, she has evaded the CIA and the fifteen American intelligence agencies for years. Prior to her leaving, she worked on DARPA funded, secret weapon type projects, and you think it was something to do with what we now know as xenobots," I recapped.

Collins nodded. "That's about the size of it."

"What if we told you that we think she has perfected a way of using nanobots, or maybe xenobots, to cause sudden fatal cardiac events," I said.

"Then I'd say the world is in serious trouble. That sounds like the perfect assassination tool."

"Thing is, Collins, you appear to be up to your waist in quicksand and sinking fast. MacKinnon and another man were abducted from Upper Hutt then taken against their will to *your* restaurant in Newtown."

She shook her head. "That's not possible."

"Oh, yes, it is. We broke them out of *Manger*. So, you popping up and threatening us, well, that made us unholy suspicious of your motives."

"I don't know anything about that."

"Huh," Ronnie said. "And yet, you ransacked MacKinnon's home looking for something, and the time frame put you there while he was being held at your restaurant. Did you ask him where it was? Guess you didn't expect to see James there when you rang the doorbell, the first time you called."

"I didn't know anyone had him," she said, shaking her head slowly. "I didn't know."

"The goons at the restaurant aren't yours?" I enquired, with a smile.

"The restaurant is a real restaurant and I'm more of a silent investor than someone involved in the day-to-day. I get quarterly reports."

Bet that hurt then. Someone doing the dirty on her.

"How often do you go there?" Ronnie asked.

"Twice a year."

"That's it? Twice a year?" Ronnie asked. We could all tell she didn't believe the answer.

"Your cell phone is registered to *Manger*. Would you like to rethink your involvement?"

"Yes, it is. One of the perks, that's all, Mr Crockett. I told you, it's an investment."

"Not a very good one," Ronnie said. "I'd hate to invest in something and find my staff were all foreign agents."

Collins chewed her lip again. "This is embarrassing."

"Very," Ronnie said. "You go ahead and deny all knowledge. Meanwhile, someone has planned an attack on New Zealand soil, and whoever is working at your restaurant, or at least using it as a base of operations, has got something to do with it."

"Do you know who the target is?" Even I heard the

hope in her words, and I'm not that good at that kind of stuff.

Ronnie and Ben looked at each other. I saw Ben nod.

"We suspect it's someone, or multiple someone's, at the Prime Minister's wedding."

"That's in less than thirty-six hours."

"Yes, it is," Ronnie said. "And all the security checks have been done, and I have a feeling that if I started poking around I'd find your restaurant was one of the businesses doing the catering."

"We don't have much time." Collins moved from chewing her lip to nibbling on the side of her thumb nail.

"So far, we've had most of the answers," I said. "Time you did some talking."

"When President Carlisse died. Let me change that, he wasn't just POTUS. He was a friend. When Peter died, I suspected Sokolov caused his heart attack with nanobots. She was nearly twenty years ahead of anyone with her research. It was absolutely science fiction stuff back then. The whole thing sounded like a plot from Star Trek. No one believed it was possible. No one looked hard enough."

"Why did you think it was her?"

"I didn't at first. In fact, I think ...," her voice dropped to a whisper, "I thought we were behind it."

"We as in?"

"CIA. To clarify, I wasn't CIA back then. I was a marshal."

"That's huge," Ronnie said. "But I'd already gone down

that path. Wouldn't be the first time, would it?"

"No, it wouldn't."

"So, someone used Sokolov's research to kill, that's what you're saying?"

She nodded.

"All right, then why did nothing show in the autopsy. He was a healthy and fit ..." Ronnie paused for effect. "Healthy and fit and the President of the USA. Why wasn't a foreign whatever found during the autopsy?"

"No one looked for anything like that; if you don't know to look for something, you very rarely find it, especially something that is practically invisible because it's so small."

"And you want the file to see what else is hidden in it ... if there's a link to Carlisse's death and the research conducted by Sokolov."

"Yes. There has to be something. That file, that story, it's not finished. There was no end, at least not when I saw it."

Ronnie looked thoughtful. "There is no end."

"Nothing was added." Collins appeared crestfallen at that news. "I'd hoped someone had found something and added it. So, it's worthless. MacKinnon may as well have destroyed it."

"Not exactly worthless. We know you and O'Hare used the story to share information and compare notes. Who else knew that?" Ronnie said.

"I doubt anyone knew. We were editing the story," she said, putting the editing in air quotes. "It was a shared document. That's how we were passing sensitive information without leaving a trail."

"It's a Windows 98 file, that's what Ronnie said. You could set those up as shared docs?" I asked.

She smiled. "It's not a Windows 98 file; that's how we saved it the last time we accessed it. It was a Pages file. We had shared access via Pages."

I felt the frown on my forehead deepen. "When did you last access the file?"

"Twenty-nineteen," she said. "It was still in our possession when O'Hare died."

"And, then what happened to it?"

"We each saved it as a Windows 98 document. I don't know what happened to O'Hare's version. It was probably destroyed. She had a directive that all her files and computer hard drives were to be destroyed, in the event of her death."

"How did it get to New Zealand, and to MacKinnon?"

"Technically it was already here. I was in New Zealand the whole time we shared the document."

"There're two copies?"

She nodded. "Mine was taken. Someone gained access to my MacBook and removed the file. All trace of it was deleted from the computer and iCloud."

"So, the copy hidden in another file, is the last remaining version?" I asked.

"Yes, and it's probably worthless."

Ronnies head shook slowly. "Not worthless at all. It was that story that made us question MacKinnon's death.

And we saw Sokolov, or we think we saw her, put something into James MacKinnon's cup of tea. She was the last person to see him alive."

"So, she did carry on working on that nano tech," Collins said. "You've given me the first real corroboration that she was still working on something."

"We are in the process of attempting to prove how MacKinnon Senior and Junior were murdered. It could be by either nanobots, or xenobots, or maybe something else entirely."

"Who was in the house when I was there?"

"Sokolov. Sokolov met with James MacKinnon. He invited her in. They had tea. She left. He died."

"Why did he meet with her?"

"We may never know, but I do know that you saw Chandler going up to the house on your way out, that first visit."

"Yes, he passed me. He is a nasty man with an agenda, who is only pleasant when he wants something."

"True, but that's not the point. He was not invited in. He left looking quite annoyed. I think we need to find out what Chandler was doing there the day William MacKinnon died. What did he want?"

Collins rested her head on the back of her chair. "The file."

"Everyone wants the fucking file," I said. "But it appears worthless."

Or is it.

"It's not worthless," Collins said. "It contains *Genesis*

data."

"There was nothing in that story about *Genesis*," Ronnie said. "Nothing."

Collins looked uncomfortable before she said, "Ronnie, I believe there is another file hidden inside that story. That's the only thing that makes sense now." She paused before continuing, "You said the story wasn't finished, there was no end. If no one added to it, then perhaps there is another file. The one with *Genesis* data. The Atlas."

"Holy shit," she mumbled. "I didn't look any further. The book or whatever captured my attention."

My turn. "What makes either of you think MacKinnon, or someone else, hid *Genesis* inside that story?"

Ronnie smiled. It didn't reach her eyes; hell, it barely made it to her lips. "Because that story told us a lot, but it didn't tell us how the information was gathered. It's all very ooky-spooky, but not alphabet soupy."

Collins stared open-mouthed at Ronnie before abruptly closing her mouth.

"That was probably the point," Collins said. "We should go."

"Where?" I asked.

"To wherever you have Sokolov," she replied. "We need to find out everything she knows about the impending attack. And I believe there is one."

Chapter Thirty:
[Ronnie: Sokolov tells tales]

Crockett went back to Nana's for Emily. Ben and I took Collins with us. We weren't taking a direct route to Pine-haven. We'd all run a surveillance detection route, just in case. It gave me plenty of time to mull things over.

I didn't know what to think about Collins. I knew who she was, but not if she was telling the truth about the file. I had the *Genesis* Atlas, but couldn't open it. If that's what was hidden in the story, then we were in the same position. We couldn't open it. And I wasn't at all sure that MacKinnon would want the CIA to get their dirty, sticky fingers on *Genesis*. Other people had tried to escape with the Atlas and were stopped. This seemed like more of the same. She wanted to steal it from MacKinnon, therefore, he didn't want her to have it. He gave me the flash drive for safekeeping, weeks ago. He must've had a reason to get it out of Wellington when he did.

Perhaps Zillah told him something before Luke returned. Or somebody else. One of the analysts? James, he was an analyst. If something had come down the pipeline, he would've known, and if it was as bad as it looks now, he would've warned his father that a storm was coming.

I didn't want whatever real information lived on the flash drive handed to anyone that wasn't involved. Maybe

I just didn't want anyone to ever get it? Did Chandler want the same information or was he stirring the waters to see what would happen? I trusted him as far as I could throw him, and it's very hard to throw something slippery.

I glanced over my shoulder at Collins sitting in the back seat. "How do you know there is a *Genesis* file inside the story?"

"It makes sense."

"Not to me," I said. Not much of anything made sense any more. "Why do you think it makes sense?"

She didn't reply to my question, instead she looked out the window.

"How do you know about *Genesis*?" Ben said. I saw him glance in the rearview mirror.

"Everyone knows about it," Collins said with a sigh. "Or at least has heard the rumours that it exists."

"What do you think it is?" Ben asked.

"A worldwide autonomous, clandestine organisation, that gathers and also acts on intelligence."

Correct.

Neither of us commented. We said nothing else until Ben pulled into the long driveway to Art's safe house.

"Where are we?" Collins asked.

"Our home away from home," I said. "You'll like it; it's comfortable and secluded."

Ben parked right behind the first of the large garage doors, leaving room for Crockett to park on the right of us. I climbed out of the car and opened the front door using the code, then hurried upstairs while Ben escorted Collins inside. I wanted to get the laptop from the safe without exposing the rug. I wasn't ready to share that yet. And anyway, we knew about Sokolov now. She was in the cell in the garage. I opened the secret panel, then the safe, removed the laptop and flash drive, then shut everything again. I pocketed the flash drive. When Ben appeared with Collins, I excused myself, leaving him with the laptop which I'd placed on the dining table.

I quietly went down the stairs and into the small hallway that led to the garage, and an apartment, depending which direction was taken. I entered the code into the electronic lock and opened the garage door, then crossed the shiny concrete floor to the cell, situated at the very back, and on the far side of, the massive two car garage workshop.

I peered in the steel-barred, small glass window at the top of the door. Sokolov sat on the army cot and leant on the wall. She lifted her head and glared at me. I waved and left.

She was alive, that's all I wanted to know at this stage. I could've looked at the app on my phone, but I wanted her to react to my presence.

Carefully, I closed the interior door to the garage which locked it automatically. Halfway up the stairs my phone rang. Donald. It was a FaceTime call. I scurried to the master bedroom and answered the call.

"What's up Donald?"

"I texted you and you didn't answer." He flicked his

hair. The white streak bobbed then slid back over his forehead. "What's going on, Ronnie?"

"I'm working. So should you be." Behind him I could see he was in the back room of the hair salon.

"I am having a break and a crisis. Where is my intended?"

"Working," I said with a smile. "He's helping me on a job."

"Why isn't he answering his phone? Are you covering for him, Ronnie? Has he got cold feet?" Panic was setting in quickly. "Is it something I've done, or not done?"

"Settle Petal. His feet are not my concern, but last I heard he was excited about the wedding."

Donald pouted, then sighed. "It's not like him to be out of touch."

"Donald. You know who he is and what he does." But probably not what his special skill set is. "He can't always talk about it, or answer his phone, nor can I. You know this."

He let loose another large sigh then smiled. "All right, Ronnie. I trust you. If you say everything is fine then it is." His spark returned. "I just never thought I'd be marrying the spy who shagged me."

And just like that the wedding theme made sense.

"I've got to go. I'm sure you'll hear from him soon. No more teetering on the edge of imaginary cliffs, Donald."

Donald waved. I hung up and hurried back to the dining room. As I opened the kitchen door, I heard car tyres crunching on gravel outside. Ben looked at me. He was sitting at the end of the dining table and could see anyone entering the kitchen.

"Car," I said. "Hopefully, Crockett."

"I'll check."

Ben disappeared as I flicked the jug on in the kitchen.

"Collins, do you want coffee?" Look at me being the best hostess in the spy world.

"That'd be great. Real or instant?"

"Real," I replied. I was tempted to make her drink instant.

Ben emerged from the kitchen door. He'd gone through the lounge into the hallway and back around. "It is Crockett, he'll probably want coffee. He has Emily."

"There's Milo in the pantry," I replied, adding extra mugs. Ben rinsed the French press and scooped coffee grounds into it. He spooned Milo into one of the mugs.

We gave the impression that we had all the time in the world, even though, we knew we did not. There was no sense getting all flustered and panicky over the impending attack. I poured the boiling water into the French press and filled the Milo mug as well. My thoughts centred on Nana and her wisdom, while I waited for the coffee to brew. No sense getting all bent out of shape over the prospect of a targeted terror attack. It'd still be impending regardless. Calm heads would prevail. If Nana taught me anything over my lifetime, it was that panic helped no one.

Get the facts.

Make a plan.

Handle it.

Don't rush at anything.

Moscow rules surfaced: Assume nothing. Listen to your gut. Everyone is potentially under opposition control. Do not look back; you are never completely alone. Go with the flow and blend in. Vary your pattern and stay within your cover. Lull them into a sense of complacency. Do not harass the opposition. Pick the time and place for your action. Keep your eyes open.

The way the intelligence regarding Sokolov, and her bedfellows, was delivered was about as analogue as it could get. Dead drops are so last century - why not encode a rug? Back in the day, troop movement intelligence was coded and knitted into scarves and jerseys. Voices filled the adjoining room. I pressed the plunger down on the French press.

"Coffee is ready."

Ben appeared to help me carry the cups. I loaded cups onto a tray I found in the pantry.

"Everything all right?" He asked.

"Fine and dandy," I replied. "Shall we?" I nodded my head in the direction of the voices.

Coffee cups were passed around the large dark-stained wooden table. I handed Emily her Milo last. She thanked me. Always polite, always correct.

Through one of the large windows, I saw dark grey clouds gathering. It seemed fitting. A storm was coming. Ben turned the dining room lights on as the clouds blocked the weak winter sun.

"Where is Sokolov?" Collins asked. She turned her cup, so the handle was on her left.

"Safe," I replied. "We'll get to her soon. First coffee."

Collins lifted the cup with her left hand and took a sip. "It's good. New Zealand always has had good coffee."

"Better than that muck they have in the US, that's for sure."

"Don't tell me you spent time in the US and never had Peet's?" Collins said, placing her cup back on the table.

"Oh, I had Peet's in San Francisco," I replied. "As I said, we have better coffee."

Ben laughed. He knew not to argue with me about coffee and he was American, not pretend American like Collins.

Crockett grumbled into his cup about Tim Hortons, but no one took any real notice. Collins pointed a finger at the laptop.

"Is that the laptop? And the files are on it?"

"Yes that is a laptop, but no the files are not on it," I said.

"Where are they? Where is the flash drive?"

"Safe. Will you tell me why you wanted the flash drive so badly?"

"It contains something I need."

"You might need it, but I don't think you are supposed to have it," I said, smiling. "MacKinnon trusted me with this. He didn't send it to you. He didn't give it to Chandler."

"And you think you can keep this out of everyone's

hands?"

I nodded. "You bet I do."

She looked around the table. No one disagreed with me. Two of us were armed. She wasn't. Guess that also factored into her thinking.

"It might help us get to the bottom of this situation with Sokolov," she said.

"It won't. Talking to her will." She wasn't going to get that file from me. "If we're all done with our coffee, perhaps Crockett and Ben will bring Sokolov to us."

Crockett stood. He gathered the empty coffee cups and put them on the tray. "Come on Ben," he said. "Let's get the old trout."

The mugs rattled when he put the tray on the kitchen bench. Ben winked at me and followed Crockett. Emily sipped her Milo.

"Where's the flash drive?" Collins asked again.

"Safe," I replied. "I can assure you it will not fall into the wrong hands." Or her hands. Pretty sure they were the wrong hands. *Genesis* is not for people like her. It is not for any one organisation to control. It sure as hell is not going to be handed to the bollocking CIA. "We don't even know for sure that the drive contains *Genesis* info. I got as much from that strange novel as I could. We have Sokolov. We don't need anything else at this point."

Crockett brought Sokolov into the room right on cue. I could see Ben behind Sokolov.

"Have a seat," Crockett said, pulling an empty chair out.

The woman sat. She wasn't happy. Who would be in her situation? Frowning wasn't doing her any favours. She and Collins could have a face-roadmap, fault line competition.

"Natalia Sokolov," Collins said.

"Elizabeth Collins," she replied, with barely a trace of a Russian accent. "So nice to see you again."

"I doubt that, Natalia. I doubt that very much."

"I hoped you would find me."

"Why?"

"Because, Elizabeth, I need help."

Oh, nice, it's a reunion.

"You need help?" Collins said, incredulousness evident in her tone. "You disappeared from the US with research and now You. Need. Help."

"Yes. I am in a difficult situation."

"I have no doubt it's of your own making. You're going to need to explain why you think I should help you."

"People will die if you do not."

"People have already died at your hand," I said. She turned her head to look at me. "Sorry, I haven't introduced myself. I'm Veronica Tracey." I did not offer her my hand.

"What people?"

I smiled. "Come now, really? You want to pretend you don't know about James MacKinnon?"

Her face clouded, defining more wrinkles. "James is not dead. I had tea with him."

"And you put something in his tea, and now he's

dead."

Her head shook slightly as she said, "No, that is not true."

"Okay. Then Ben and I must've shared a hallucination when we saw you put something in James MacKinnon's tea." I gave her a cool smile. "I've heard such things are possible, but not generally while watching CCTV, and stone cold sober."

"This is a misunderstanding," she said.

"Which bit? You being here? You needing help? You killing MacKinnon?"

Her frown lines deepened; those things were impressive. No doubt with a set of lines like that, life had not been kind.

Collins tapped her fingernails rhythmically on the table. "You left the US with research that belonged to the government. Where is it now?"

Sokolov folded her hands in front of her. "It has grown considerably since we parted ways."

"When you say it like that, it sounds like it was mutual. It was not. We have been looking for you for years."

Sokolov smiled. "In all the wrong places."

"This little reunion is wonderful. Touching even. But let's get down to the nitty gritty," I said. "You're here Sokolov, and healthy people are dying of sudden heart failure. Your research into bioweapons, in particular, nanobots and xenobots, has us curious."

"Many scientists are conducting research into nano particles and the application in the health sector," she replied. "I can't be held responsible for every nanobot in the world."

"I'm sure you're not responsible for every nanobot, or nanotech device," I replied. My phone buzzed. I pulled it out and looked at the screen.

A text from Christine.

Christine: Foreign bodies found in James' blood and heart. Initial findings put the cause of death as sudden cardiac death. Ring me.

"What is it?" Ben asked me.

"Christine. She found something. I'm going to give her a ring." I excused myself and took my phone into the lounge. I stood by the large windows that overlooked the driveway, watching rain tumble from the sky and made the call.

"Hi, Christine, what was it you found?"

"Potentially the cause of death. Tiny things that are shaped like Pac-Man. When I say tiny, they're less than a millimetre wide and they also seem to work in groups."

"And they shouldn't be there?"

"They definitely should not be there. I'm pretty sure these are biological. I'm convince that I'm looking at xenobots. And I did not expect to see these inside anyone for at least ten years."

"How long do they live?"

"From what I can gather from research papers I've read in the last hour, they biodegrade after seven days, and they wouldn't be found if we didn't know to look."

"You're sure? They're not some kind of weird cell mutation created by his own body?"

"I'm a hundred percent sure that they are foreign to his body."

"And they caused his death?"

"That I cannot prove. But his medical records say he was healthy, his heart was healthy, there is no reason for his heart to stop beating by itself. He has no indicators for sudden cardiac arrest, or sudden cardiac death. No family history to suggest any heart disease."

"You have his medical history?"

"Yes. As I said, he was in good health. He routinely had heart checks as part of his yearly exam."

I knew that was true, it was part of the job. I used to have regular checks when I was employed by the Government as an intelligence officer. We were monitored closely for anything that could impede our ability to work. It would be tricky if a spy dropped dead in the field. If they knew we were healthy then sudden death could mean murder.

"How could those little nano doodads stop his heart?"

"If they were programmed to cause interference in the electrical circuit of the heart. For instance, if they caused arrhythmia. Ventricular fibrillation. A person could die in that instance, especially if they were alone."

"It's possible to survive ventricular fibrillation?"

"Yes, it is. In a hospital setting with a defibrillator to shock the heart back into its normal rhythm."

"Always?"

"No, not always."

"If that's what killed MacKinnon senior, we were in the hospital. Help was right there, and he died."

"This is going to sound a bit Star Trekky, but if these are xenobots or nanobots or whatever, they could continue working. If they are programmed to upset the heart's ability to beat properly, they could keep doing their job. Regardless of how hard the ED doctors and nurses try to save the patient, they never will. The bots will keep on doing what their programming tells them to do until they decompose. And the really scary thing is that these things can reproduce, after a fashion."

The sound changed. A little more background noise encroached, I was on speaker. I sat on the couch and stared at the wood-burner on the opposite side of the room.

"So even if you could keep shocking a person back to life for seven days, it wouldn't matter because there would already be a new batch of bots to keep killing." Buggery bollocks we were really and truly up against it.

"Yes," Christine said. "Be careful, Ronnie. Whoever is behind this is ruthless. If you get close, do not eat or drink anything. In fact, don't even touch the person. I can't be a hundred precent sure how the bots got inside James MacKinnon, so avoid all contact." There was a definite hollowness to her voice.

"The sample of tea I gave you, have you looked at it?" I asked. That was what my money was on as the entry point.

"I have a drop under the microscope now," she said. There was silence for a beat. "I wish you could see this. I'm looking at a couple of one-mil wide Pac-Man chaps. They don't look overly happy. Tea revives us, but perhaps isn't the liquid of choice for these little chaps."

"They sound fascinating."

"They are. They really are." She sounded happy to have made the discovery. "This is the most interesting cause of death I've ever come across." Trust a pathologist to get excited over new ways to kill people.

"It's possible that William MacKinnon drank some in a glass of water."

"Protect yourself and tell the others to do the same," Christine said. "I'm about to weasel my way into William MacKinnon's autopsy. Once that's over, I should be able to confirm if any sort of bots were responsible."

"Authorities?"

"I collected as much evidence as I could from the house. Then called police. They'll notify whoever needs telling."

"And ..."

"Nobody knows you were there. I said I dropped in for a visit. Old friends and all that."

"Thank you."

"I'll be back in touch when I know what killed MacKinnon senior. Stay safe. Catch the person, will you?"

"Will do."

I hung up and let everything Christine told me, sink in.

Death by teeny tiny bots. Good grief! Whatever next?

The voices in the dining room drifted my way. No words just tone. It wasn't unpleasant. I took a breath and rejoined the gang.

Collins looked up at me as I entered. "Everything all right?"

"We have a cause of death," I said. All eyes were on me as I took my seat, and my attention was on Sokolov. "Natalia Sokolov, you just became the prime suspect in a murder investigation." Only the police don't know that. They'll go with the coroners findings of sudden cardiac death, once the death is referred to the coroner, because they don't know any different. No one else knows to look for nanobots. But Sokolov doesn't know that she's not a prime murder suspect, as far as police are concerned. And that worked in our favour.

"Police will not keep me safe," she said.

"Why do you need to be kept safe? You committed murder."

"I had no choice," she said.

"That's not how life works," Crockett said. "Everything is a choice. You had a choice."

"The people I work for do not see life that way," she replied. "I don't do what they want, and they kill me, and do it anyway."

"I think the choice you missed, Sokolov, was the one where you created nanobot tech to murder people. You could've stopped before that point. Chosen to be a better person," I said with a small smile. "You chose to kill. That was your choice. I can assure you that your cohorts will not be getting what they really want."

"And what do you think that is?" Collins said.

"You know very well what it is," I replied. "As far as I'm concerned, you're as bad as she is."

Ben's leg touched mine causing me to look at him. One eyebrow rose at me. I ignored his questioning glance. "Who are the targets?"

Sokolov frowned. Deepening her wrinkles until they resembled fault-lines on her map of hard knocks.

"They didn't tell me." she said.

"I find that very hard to believe. You killed James. You. I saw you do that. Why wouldn't they tell you who else to kill?"

"I am not their assassin," she said.

Wrong.

"Who are they?" I asked. Knowing full well she was working for the Chinese and the Taliban. "Who. Are. They?"

She shook her head. "I can't tell you that."

"You can and you will." I looked at Crockett. "We need Enzo here."

Crockett nodded and left the room with his phone in his hand.

Collins moved in her chair attracting my attention. When I looked at her she spoke, "What are we doing here now?"

"Getting relevant information before the attack. Stopping a terrorist. Not letting this old woman get away with anymore nonsense."

Sokolov spoke, "I want asylum."

My own laughter caught me by surprise. "I'm sorry, you want what?"

"Asylum."

Asylum. Not something that was in my wheelhouse. Private investigator. Private citizen. I stood and walked into the kitchen, followed by Collins and Ben.

Emily called out, "Me?"

I raised my voice slightly and said, "Go to Crockett, Emily. He's in the lounge."

I watched her go past the kitchen doorway and into the lounge. Sokolov was alone in the dining room.

I leaned on the kitchen bench. "She has no grounds for asylum, right?"

"None," Collins replied. "She's on the run from the US. She can't ask for political asylum. And she's potentially a terrorist."

"She's what, nearly seventy?"

"Yes," Collins replied. "Sixty-nine. And she carried on creating havoc and working for the wrong people."

"Are there right people? We're talking about someone creating nano-weapons ... there are no right people to make those for," I said. "What is wrong with people?"

Ben grinned. "Why are they like this?"

I laughed. "You sound like Donald." I wondered if Donald was all right. He might be a massive pain in the bum, but I loved him. He was blood. "We need this sorted. I need to get to Donald's and try that ugly dress on."

Ben chuckled. "You must really miss him."

"Yeah, I do. I can't tease anyone else like I can him."

Ben chuckled some more. "I call bullshit on that."

I laughed. "It is what it is."

Collins interrupted us. "I don't know what this is," she said waving her hand at us. "But I'm a third wheel. I'll go back in there with Sokolov."

We watched her as she tried to walk away. I called out, "Stop. You are not going to be alone with her. Turn right into the lounge."

She glared, it did nothing for her. To her credit she turned right. I heard Crockett tell her to sit on the couch and stay.

"We need to get this done and get the Russian into custody," I said quietly to Ben.

"Custody ... novel approach," Ben replied. "I suppose without MacKinnon around to give alternate instructions to his clean-up guy, it will be custody."

My eyes hit his. "Crockett."

"The elephant in the room."

The elephant in the lounge.

"I liked it better when we didn't say it out loud." I liked it better when I could pretend that's not what Crockett did. I liked it better when he was just a problem solver. "What do we do with her?"

"Police. Have her charged with terrorism or something, but don't let the CIA get their hands on her."

"That's a no brainer." But hard to pull off. She'd end up in custody and they'd petition the courts saying she belonged to them. "Who is Collins working for now?"

"Maybe us," Ben said.

"You sure?"

"No."

"Chandler?"

"Well, it wasn't old MacKinnon," he said.

Buggery bollocks. "Does it make her a double agent if it's New Zealand, and the US?"

"Two states — two countries. Yes."

"And we're right in the middle," I replied, because we were all working for MacKinnon this time. All of us. Working for the Aussies. "What's that song?"

"Stuck in the middle with you." His lips brushed mine. "There are worse places."

A loud cough interrupted our moment. Crockett.

"All right, break it up. We've got work to do."

I grinned at him. "Life is short, we have to seize the moments."

Ben's arms tightened around me for one last hug.

"Enzo?" Ben asked as he let me go.

"On his way. He's leaving Art with the surveillance crew. I told Art to pull back from the dead woman's house and join Steph and Jenn on Luke."

"Excellent," I said. "I bet they're getting tired of that job."

"Yes," Crockett said. "How much danger do you think Luke is in now?"

"Enough that we should keep an eye on him," I said. "We have Sokolov. They could go after him again to trade."

"True."

"Who are they?" Crockett said. "Who are we actually going up against?"

"The man we saw when we grabbed Sokolov was Asian," I said.

"How did they get Sokolov here?" Ben asked.

"I think Enzo might get the answers for us," Crockett said. "To that, and so much more."

"He was effective last time we used his skill set," I said. "I don't much care for it, but he's productive and we don't have time for banter and niceties."

Before we joined Sokolov back at the table, I ducked my head around the lounge room door, and beckoned to Collins. I looked around the room. Emily wasn't there. Odd.

Collins passed me and sat at the table.

"Emily?" I asked looking at Crockett before I sat down.

"She's looking for a book to read," Crockett said. "She needs a distraction to re-charge."

Fair enough. This wasn't her thing anymore. This new version of Emily was easily overwhelmed. Old Emily was a different kettle of fish. Kettle of fish reminded me of Nana.

"While we're waiting, I'm going to ring someone," I said, and hurried into the lounge, then the study, and pushed the door to. Nana answered on the fourth ring. "Nana?"

"Veronica. Is everything all right?"

"Yes, Nana. I'm checking to see if you and the ladies are okay."

"Of course, we are dear. Now, we found someone who might be able to help you."

My heart sank. What could they have done?

"How's that, Nana?"

"Well, you see, dear. We were looking for Michaela Kennedy-Carlisse, and it turns out she is Michaela Falacco now, and she knows that dreadful Collins woman."

They're related by marriage, but whatever.

"Nana, you shouldn't be stalking people."

She tutted down the phone line. "Don't be silly, dear. We're not stalking anyone. We're talking to her."

"How Nana?"

"She's here, dear, with us. Having a cup of tea and a slice of fruitcake." Nana's voice rang with joy. "She's an absolute delight, Veronica. Did you know she has three pen names?"

"No, Nana. I certainly did not." I couldn't imagine what Nana and the *Cronies of Doom* were playing at, but it smacked of danger. "Can you please try and stay out of trouble?"

"Veronica, we're having a fine time with our new friend. Donald is calling in soon."

Oh, goody. It's a family affair.

"Nana, please, don't do anything else."

"We're not doing anything at all, Veronica. We're just chatting over tea. No harm in tea, dear."

If only that were true.

"I'll talk to you soon, Nana."

I hung up.

Emily was sitting on the couch engrossed in a book. She didn't look up as I passed her. I don't know when she resumed her place on the couch or where she found the book and it didn't much matter.

As soon as I sat down, Crockett and Ben said, "What's wrong?"

"Oh, good, men in stereo," I replied.

"Well?" Crockett said.

"Nana," I replied. "Just more Nana."

"Is it important?" He asked.

I nodded. "More than likely, you know how the old one operates." I couldn't exactly say she'd tracked down Collins' former sister-in-law and was having tea with her. Not out loud and not in this company. "Bear with." I extracted my phone from my pocket and texted them the predicament.

Ben shook his head when he read the text. Crockett smiled when he read his.

"Typical June," he said.

"Disaster," I replied.

"You don't give her nearly enough credit for knowing what she's doing," Crockett said quietly.

"And you think this is okay?"

"That's not what I said. I merely suggested that you don't give her enough credit. She's not a silly woman, Ronnie."

A motorbike roared up the road.

"Saved by the Harley," I said to Crockett, as the bike rumbled up the long driveway toward us.

Crockett stood and motioned to Sokolov to do the same. He held her firmly by the elbow and moved her to the kitchen with him. "I'll take her downstairs," Crockett said. "Let Enzo get right on with it."

I nodded. I remembered feeling quite squeamish about how Enzo gets people to talk, once upon a time. Yet here I was turning over a sixty-nine-year-old woman to him, without even breaking a sweat. What was different?

She killed the MacKinnon's, and she planned to kill many more people, and she wanted the *Genesis* files. *Genesis* was hot property. No one could have it. Too much was at stake. Too many good intelligence officers would die or be maimed. Not to mention the strike teams and support personnel. And the families of those officers. The files had to be safely turned over to James MacKinnon's replacement. I was sure he had one, someone standing in the wings who could run *Genesis*. I didn't know who that person was, but I knew who it wasn't. It wasn't Chandler. He was just another set of sticky mitts trying to make a grab for the intelligence gathering capability of *Genesis*. Whoever took over became a target. That person would need security and an understanding that life was fleeting.

Chapter Thirty-one:
[Ronnie: Why do you care?]

Collins placed her hands palm down on the tabletop, a shoulder width apart. She appeared to study her own fingers for a moment, and then she lifted her eyes, and looked at Ben.

"What is going to happen to Sokolov?"

"I don't know," Ben said. "I do know that Enzo has little trouble getting the truth from people."

"And this is fine with you two?"

"Yes," he said, speaking for both of us. "Sometimes the end justifies the means."

Today, now, it did.

"You're talking about enhanced interrogation?"

"We're not CIA," Ben said, quietly. "He probably won't waterboard her."

"She's sixty-nine," Collins said.

"Yes," I said. "Maybe she shouldn't go around killing people with nanobots, or xenobots, or whatever the fuck she killed them with."

"What happened to innocent until proven guilty?

"That doesn't apply to terrorists. And there's no alleged offence. We witnessed her put something in James MacKinnon's drink and then he died. That's one hell of a coincidence don't you think?" Doesn't matter how much she denies it. We saw her do it.

Collins removed her hands from the table and folded them into her lap. For a moment there she looked sixty-fiveish. "Where did you take her from?"

"A house in Akatarawa," Ben said.

"Is anyone watching the house?"

"No."

"Wouldn't that have been a good idea?"

"Limited resources," I said. "We had her. We have someone else under surveillance."

"Someone else," she repeated. "Luke O'Sullivan."

Ben and I made eye contact.

I picked up my phone and opened an email app. Not my usual one, but one I shared with Steph and Jenn. I wrote an email dictating what I wanted done with my third of the agency should this job go pear shaped and saved it in the draft folder. It was to go to Donald and Enzo.

"Collins, if these little beasties can live for seven days, how do we know they're not already incorporated into whatever they are being delivered in?" It seemed like a sensible question considering what Christine told me, and considering we suspected Collins restaurant was one of the restaurants catering the wedding.

She looked confused for a second. She looked at her watch. "Approximately thirty hours until the wedding. We're looking at food made ahead of time."

The bloody cake.

"Ben, the ..."

"Cake," he said. "But everyone will eat the cake, or at

least most people."

"Can these things be baked into something and survive?" I wondered out loud. "Heat usually kills bugs."

"Icing isn't hot," Collins said.

"We need to know who is making the cake."

Ben piped in, "It wouldn't be *Manger*, would it?"

"I wouldn't think so," I said, and pulled up the *Manger* website on my phone. "It doesn't mention cake as a specialty. Collins, does *Manger* have a top-notch baker?"

"They have a patisserie chef. It is possible, but I wouldn't think likely."

"What do we do now, call every bakery in the region and ask if they have the contract for the wedding cake for the Prime Minister's wedding? No one is going to say yes. The security would be extreme," Ben said.

"It doesn't have to be the cake," Collins said. "Any cold dessert."

"Can we find out what *Manger* was asked to deliver?"

She nodded. "Can I use the phone?" She pointed to the landline in the alcove at the end of the breakfast bar.

"Yes," I replied. "If you don't mind me listening on the other end."

"Go ahead." I hurried down to the main bedroom. Collins called out when she'd dialled, and I lifted the receiver. I could hear the phone ringing. Seemed to take forever before it was answered.

"*Manger*, Admir speaking."

"Admir, this is Elizabeth Collins. Can please you tell me what desserts *Manger* is supplying for the Prime

Minister's wedding?"

I heard a page turn. They used paper instead of an electronic tablet to keep track of things. Old school. Another page turned.

"Honey and nut cake," he said. "Enough for one-hundred and fifty servings."

"Anything else?"

"Baklava."

"What is being made first?"

"Honey and nut cake," he replied. "The cake will be made today so it has time to cool before the syrup is added, and then the cake will chill in our fridge until delivery."

"Thank you, Admir. Tell chef I look forward to tasting his shendetlie at the wedding."

"I will pass your message to chef."

"Thank you." Collins hung up, and so did I.

I hurried down to the dining room. "You have an invitation to the wedding?" I said from the doorway.

She shrugged and smiled. "Don't you?"

"No."

"Ladies. Never mind the invitation status. What came of the call?" Ben said.

"*Manger* are making two desserts. The first is a honey and walnut cake called shendetlie. It has a sugar syrup poured over it once it's cooled."

"Could that be the method they use to get the bots into people?"

"I don't know. How do you think boiling in sugar water

would be for them?"

"Probably not great," I said. "But it sits in the fridge after the syrup is poured over it?"

"Yes."

"So, the little buggers could be sprinkled on it then," I said.

"Yes," she said.

"Isn't chewing going to destroy them?" Ben asked.

"Good point. We don't know." We don't know anywhere near enough about these little killers. "Drinks? They're not chewed, generally."

"We know they survived in tea and that would've been warm, so, any drink I guess," Ben said.

"Bar staff?" Collins asked.

"It would only take one person behind the bar to add bots to drinks. Who would notice? They could be put in anything and everything."

"What are you saying?" Ben sank in his chair. He seemed deflated almost.

"Don't eat, and don't drink," I said. "Nothing is safe."

"How exactly do we go about telling the Prime Minister that her wedding is a potential terror attack?" Ben asked.

"Carefully?" With all the security checks already done, this was going to be a nightmare. No one would want to admit the possibility of an attack. We could prove there were nanobots involved in James death, but could we prove the wedding reception was under attack? We'd have to talk to Chandler. He had the PM's ear. Why did it have to be Chandler? Of all the people. It'd cost us too much to deal with him.

I sat back in the chair and gave the mess some real thought.

Bill Bailey. He was option number two, and potentially the better choice. I bumped him to option number one, knocking Chandler out of the running.

"We can go to Bill Bailey," I said.

Collins frowned. I wished old women would stop the frowning, it did them no favours.

"He's Army Intelligence; how do you know him?" She asked.

Really?

"This is New Zealand. Have you forgotten that everyone knows everyone, or at least someone who does," I said with a smile. "Bill and I go a long way back. I don't necessarily trust him in the grand scheme of things, but this involves the PM, and he has the reach." And he's not Chandler, so he won't make anyone feel dirty just by talking to him.

"We have to be one hundred percent about the impending attack, and what it entails," Collins said. "Have you heard from your colleague about William MacKinnon?"

I shook my head. "Not yet. I'll give her a ring shortly."

"Ideally, we need Sokolov to talk. She developed these nanobots; she must know what they intend on doing with them," Ben said. "I don't believe she doesn't know."

"I imagine she does," I said. "Enzo will find out."

Ben and I looked at each other. He'll find out, and unless Sokolov is smart enough to talk, she won't like how. I shoved those thoughts away. Wouldn't help thinking about his methods especially when we need answers. It wasn't as if we had days to interrogate her.

"We need a wedding countdown. We need to know exactly when everything will be in place. Especially when the caterers are expected to deliver. Who do we know with that access?" Collins asked.

The wedding planner. They would've needed one.

"Don't suppose anyone knows what wedding planner the PM used?"

Ben held a finger up. "I know how to find out." He dragged his phone from his pocket and made a call. A one-sided conversation ensued. Ben charmed whoever the recipient of the call was. Quite the talent. After two minutes he held his hand out, and indicated he wanted a pen and paper. I handed him a pen, and Collins slid a notepad across the table. Ben thanked the person, hung up, and then wrote a name and number on the notepad.

"The wedding planner," he said, pushing the notebook to me. "She's a friend of a friend."

New Zealand is a great place when you want to locate someone.

"One of us needs to meet with this person. I doubt she's going to want to give out the details we need over the phone."

"Make contact, and we'll take it from there," Ben said.

My phone rang. Christine. "This might be what we

need," I said, as I answered the call. "Christine, what have you got?"

"MacKinnon died the same way as his son. I found evidence of bots in his heart."

"And we have anecdotal evidence that he drank water given to him at *Manger,* prior to his sudden death."

"I've written my report," she said. "I take it, it is to go to Chandler."

"Yes. Their deaths were on New Zealand soil. He has to be told. Could you send me a copy? I know it goes against protocol, but I'm going to need it to convince someone in Army intelligence to help us stop this disaster." I wanted another favour. "Can you hold off on notifying Chandler? We need twenty-four hours to try and get ahead of this before he interferes." And he will interfere and screw it all up and then blame everyone else.

The sudden silence on the line didn't fill me with confidence.

"I can do that," she said quietly. "I'll hold the report for twenty-four hours, but I'll send you a copy now."

"Thank you. Actually, I'll give you access to my email. Put it in drafts, don't send. That way your head isn't on the chopping block."

"Okay."

"Texting you the login details now. Thanks for your help."

I hung up and texted her everything she needed to get the report safely stored in my drafts folder. When my email chimed, Ben and Collins looked at me expectantly.

I checked the email knowing it would not be from Christine. Drafts do not have an alert.

"Junk email," I told them. "But there is a new email in the draft folder." I opened the folder. The attachment was the report from Christine. I downloaded it to my phone. Nothing was sent. No electronic trail.

"Right, I need to go meet Bill, and we need to set up a meeting with the wedding planner. What was her name?"

"Karen," Ben said. "Karen Simons."

"You set up a meeting with her. I need to see Bill. He won't meet with anyone but me, and you're the famous actor."

I took my phone and went into the kitchen. I made a call, then hung up, and waited. Two minutes later my phone rang. "Bill?"

"Trouble." It wasn't a question; it was more like a nickname.

"Sometimes."

"What do you need?"

"Face to face. Urgently."

"Same place as before. See you in fifteen."

He hung up. I rejoined Collins and Ben. "I've got a meet."

"We're both meeting with Karen Simons to plan our wedding."

"Never tell Nana that," I said. "Never."

"When are you meeting your guy?"

"In fifteen minutes at Briscoes."

"We're meeting Karen in an hour."

"Where?"

"The bakery in Silverstream."

"Okay, good, that's handy."

"What am I doing?" Collins asked.

"Coming, I suppose," I replied. "Can't leave you here alone with Emily." Then I remembered Crockett was still here. "Nah, I'll grab Crockett and he can babysit you."

Yes, that would work.

"Fine," she replied. "One of us should be here to collect the information from Enzo."

"Ah, you're not one of us. Don't think we're handing you anything," Ben said. "You're an interloper who initially threatened a group of old ladies."

"You know I wouldn't hurt them, right? I enjoy their company."

"We don't know that. Your behaviour did not suggest kindness. We don't know you from Adam," I said. "You're the stranger Nana always warned me about when I was a kid."

Collins smiled. "That's going a bit far."

"Not for me. You threatened my Nana. We are not going to be friends, lady."

Not ever.

Chapter Thirty-two:
[Ronnie: Briscoes and Bill]

I parked in the alleyway behind the agency on Fergusson Drive. Walked across the road and used the subway to get to Briscoes.

Felt weird walking there without Romeo. I knew he was fine with Donald and was probably at the hair salon with him. I could duck around the corner later and have a quick visit.

I took my sunglasses off, pushed them into my jacket pocket, and walked into the shop. Why was the interior so much darker than outside? Someone called out hello. I turned and saw a familiar face at the cash register.

"Hi," I said.

"No Romeo today. Is he all right?"

"He's at work with Donald today."

She smiled. "I'll see him later then. I've got an appointment to have my hair coloured after work."

"Great." Donald was an expert colourist. I shut down my thoughts, hoping to prevent his colouring escapade on Jenn a wee while ago, from surfacing. Too late. Clown hair. "See you later," I said, trying to control the rising mirth. A sure sign I was in need of sleep.

I walked toward the kitchen appliances and saw Bill by the toasters.

I stood on the other side of the display. We were face

to face.

"What is it?" Bill asked, without looking at me.

"We have a problem. A big one," I replied, turning an electric beater box around to see the price. "Bigger than the price tag on this thing."

"O'Sullivan is back where he belongs, what is the problem?"

"First, you could tell the truth about why you were watching him?"

"We're not the only people watching."

"I know that. But why were *you* watching?" I just wanted him to admit he knew about the intelligence. Just tell the truth Bill, so I know I can trust you with our problem.

"Grapevine stuff. He was fully debriefed overseas, but then we heard a whisper that he was returning with Intel for MacKinnon."

"And?"

"That's it."

"All right." I picked up a smaller electric beater, looked at it, and put it down before moving a few steps down the aisle to make it look like I was browsing. Bill did the same. "I have the Intel."

His eyes flicked up to mine. "And?"

"We need to work together to stop something from happening."

"Do we, indeed?" he muttered.

Both our phones alerted at the same time. I glanced at mine and saw Bill do the same. It was a news alert. A protest outside the Governor General's residence in the city. A group of twenty or so anti-vax and anti-mask people were causing a disturbance.

"Protestors," I said to Bill.

"At the wedding reception venue," he replied. "There is a police cordon. They're checking all cars and trucks going in before the wedding."

Good to know.

"Bill, we think the wedding is the target of a terror attack, but not the usual kind. No one's going to shoot anyone and there won't be IEDs."

"What kind of attack are you talking about. Are you talking DE?"

Shit, I hadn't thought of a Directed Energy attack, even though I knew that was part of Sokolov's research.

"I wasn't. But maybe I am. That could be part of it," I replied. "I'm talking about nanotech deployed to cause sudden cardiac death."

"Deployed how?"

"In food or drink."

"Can we detect these nanobots with anything?"

"No. We need to stop it before they get into the venue."

"Circle back to the DE," Bill said. "Do the terrorists have that tech?"

I nodded. "They have control of a scientist who worked on DE and nanobots."

A customer turned down the aisle I was in. I moved two over, Bill followed. He was right behind me when I whispered, "My office."

"I'll meet you there in five," he replied.

I left. I stepped into the weak winter sun. At least the rain had stopped. I put my sunglasses on, then followed the path to the subway. Once safely in the office, I rang Ben.

"What's with the protest in town?"

"Saw the news bulletin on my phone too. I'll see if there is some television coverage," he said. "All okay with you?"

"Yeah. He might help."

I heard the television fire up. "Live broadcast, having the protest outside the PM's wedding venue guaranteed that."

"How many people?"

"Looks to be thirty or so. There is a van there, white, unmarked." He paused. "It's the one that was at the place with Sokolov."

"You sure?"

"Just glimpsed the rego. I'm sure."

"And the van is doing what? Trying to gain access or just sitting?"

"Parked half on the curb. The side is open. Trying to see, but I need the camera to swing back to the van."

The office door opened, and Bill walked in.

"Nice space," he said.

"Have a seat." I pointed to the couch and armchairs under the window. Ben's voice came back. "They're handing out bottles of water."

"To?"

"The protestors."

"I don't think that'll be good."

"Nor do I. I don't think there's much we can do."

"Keep watching, I've got a visitor."

I hung up and joined Bill under the window.

"What's going on?"

"That protest. Someone is handing out bottles of water from a van we saw earlier."

"And?"

"Do you know who Natalia Sokolov is?"

Bill nodded his head. "Everyone has been looking for her for years."

"We found her. I think the water in the bottles has nanobots in it. Those protesters will be dead in forty-five minutes to an hour."

"They cannot die in front of the Governor General's residence," he said slowly. "What can we do?"

"It'll take us too long to get into town." I thought about the implications of letting them die there. It would be bad. Imagine thirty or so anti-vax protestors dropping dead in front of a couple of news crews? "Why would they kill people in front of the residence?" It was rhetorical.

I knew the why. Impact. A warning of things to come. People will die, and no one will know what caused so many people to die of heart failure, at once.

Bill said nothing. He sat staring at the phone in his hands. "You're one hundred percent sure about the attack?"

"Yes."

"Have you seen the guest list?"

"No. Hoping we will soon. Do you have access?"

He shook his head. "No need for any of us to be involved with that. That was all Security Intelligence Service, and police diplomatic protection, with monitoring by GCSG."

"Chandler." There was no way for me to say his name without a grimace.

"Yes." Bill half-smiled. "The biggest arse of them all."

"Won't the protest trigger a response?"

"Of course. Police are already there. There is a cordon to stop those radicals getting into the Governor General's grounds, but they're not going to stop do-gooders handing out bottles of water."

Bill scrolled through his phone, paused, then tapped the screen. I waited. He touched the speaker icon. Ringing reverberated around the room.

"Office of the Police Commissioner."

"Is Charlie in? This is Bill Bailey."

"Yes, sir, putting you through now."

A click. Another ring, and then the call was answered.

"Bill, good to hear from you, man."

"Circumstances aren't the best, Charlie."

"Regardless, it's always good to hear from you." The commissioner's voice sounded upbeat. I knew Bill was about to ruin that.

"Might not be when I tell you what I have for you, Charlie."

"You better tell me then."

"The protestors making a fuss outside the Governor General's; they're going to die."

"Of?"

"Apparently natural causes." Bill chose his words carefully. "There is a white van and someone handing out bottles of water; the water is poisoned. We have reason to believe this is part of a terror attack."

I mouthed the words 'poisoned' and 'what the fuck?'

Bill shook his head at me.

The commissioner said, "Leave it with me, Bill."

He hung up.

"Can we watch?" Bill said, putting his phone on the table. I was ahead of his request and had the television remote in my hand.

The television on the wall sprang into life. I channel surfed to the news channel. Sure enough, there was live coverage of the protest. Big news, the day before the wedding. A reporter talked on camera about the impact protestors would have on the nuptials. Behind her we could see the front bumper of the white van. Confirmation it was still there.

"How many people do you think have water bottles?" I said, not expecting Bill to reply.

He did. "Over half."

The reporter announced police had moved in on the van. She turned. The camera moved to film the new situation. Police swamped the van; they had the person, a dark-haired woman, in handcuffs. We could see more water bottles in the van. Police asked protestors to put the water down.

Someone yelled, "You can't stop us drinking water!"

Police again asked for people to put the water down. Sirens whooped and whined.

"Ambulances are arriving," the reporter said. "This has something to do with the water bottles." She stopped speaking as a police officer spoke quietly in her ear. "I've just been told the water may contain a poison."

Chaos erupted behind her. Paramedics came into view. The reporter and camera operator moved out of the way. That's when I saw the road was closed by police cars.

"Okay so they told them this was a poison, and they're transporting anyone who drank the water to hospital," I said. "They will still die. If I'm right about the nanobots, they will still die."

"But they won't die in front of the residence. They won't die on camera."

And will the world miss a bunch of anti-vax weirdos who dodged the latest COVID mutation by sheer luck. I know I wouldn't. They seemed determined to spread germs and endanger the vulnerable. Their deaths were no loss in my eyes. Not sure when I turned the corner into not giving a shit about protestors lives, but I had. Probably something I should keep to myself. Bit jaded perhaps.

"Now what, Bill?"

"Do you want my help?"

"Yes."

"Then I will help."

"You'd better come with me. Ben set up a meeting with

the wedding planner, and ..." I checked the time. "We need to go now, or we'll be late."

"How did you get access to the wedding planner?" Bill asked.

I shrugged. "I'm resourceful."

"Clearly."

I locked the main office door behind us, and walked Bill to my car, parked in the alley behind the building.

Chapter Thirty-three:
[Ronnie: The wedding planner]

I parked in the New World carpark. Plenty of parks there. We put our masks back on and walked to the bakery. We scanned in. It used to be a bigger place, but now there was an extra wall, and fewer tables. Ben sat in the furthest corner. A woman sat with him.

"Over there," I said to Bill.

We pulled our chairs out at the same time and sat.

"Hi, I'm Ronnie," I said to the woman, as I took my mask off. "This is my brother, Bill."

She smiled. "Pleased to meet you. I'm Karen Simons. You'd be the bride then."

Not in this lifetime.

"Yes," I replied. "I hear you do some pretty fancy weddings."

"I've done a few big ones. Have one tomorrow, actually. Today is hectic. Lucky I was out this way picking up some last-minute bits and pieces for the bride and groom's table."

Ben smiled. "We're looking at one hundred and fifty seated guests, a lot of celebrities. What sort of security do you have to safeguard seating plans and guest lists?"

Bill gave the appearance of a distracted non-listener as he fiddled with a glass of water in front of him. I knew better.

"And what about the caterers," I said. "We wouldn't want anything to find its way into the tabloids."

"I can assure you that I am the only person with access to sensitive information."

Right person then. Except in this case, NZSIS also had the guest list for vetting purposes.

"Sounds good so far," Ben said.

"We need to move this along." I looked at my watch. "Time is ticking."

"Tell me what you need to know," Karen said.

I leaned across the table. "We need to know who is doing the catering for tomorrow's wedding."

Surprise registered on her features. "I'm sorry. I can't talk about tomorrow's wedding."

"Yes you can. This is a security issue. And we need you to tell us exactly who is doing all the catering, and where the bar staff are coming from."

She started to stand. Ben grabbed her by the wrist and encouraged her to sit back down.

"I will not talk to you, or anyone, about this."

At that point Bill slid his identification across the table to her. "You will."

I smiled at the worried woman. "You have back-ups, just in case, right?"

She nodded. "Yes. Do I need to call them in?"

"No. You can't use them either. You're going to have to find a whole new crew and have them vetted by police in time for the wedding," Ben said.

I glanced at Bill. He nodded. Guess my question to him

was obvious.

"We have an alternative for you," Bill said. "We can supply the catering, servers, and bar staff. They will be military and therefore good to go."

"But what do I do now?"

"Tell us the caterers names, give us the menu, and the name of the company that is providing the bar staff."

"I'm using a restaurant that the PM likes. They could provide everything we needed, and keep it in house, so there was less security risk."

How handy.

"It's *Manger*, isn't it?" Ben said, keeping his voice low.

"Yes."

"Has anything been delivered?"

She shook her head. "No, delivery won't happen until three tomorrow afternoon. The reception begins at six-thirty."

"Think very carefully before you answer," Bill said. "Are you sure nothing, not even bottled water, was delivered today."

"Yes, I'm sure."

"We're going to provide you an escort when you go back to your office," Bill said. "Please don't try anything silly, like evading them. They are there to keep you safe."

Visibly shaken, Karen nodded. "What do I do about *Manger*?"

"Absolutely nothing. That's now our problem," I said, with a friendly smile. "Do you have access to the catering menu, now?"

"Yes, it's all on my iPad."

She started to bend down. "I'll do that," Ben said. He reached for her bag, and lifted it to the tabletop. "It's in here?"

"Yes, inside the device pocket."

Her phone was on the table near her left hand. I picked it up. She looked at me. I was holding her phone, so the screen faced her. It unlocked. I turned the phone toward me.

"Thanks."

"Why do you want my phone?"

Seriously?

"We need to make sure you aren't working with anyone to cause chaos," I said.

Ben had the iPad. He asked Karen to unlock it.

We now had full access to her devices. Ben found the menu. He passed the iPad to Bill. Bill read the menu then took several screenshots with his phone. He emailed someone the images, then he made a phone call.

"It's Bill. I've got a catering job for you. Needs to be delivered and set up by fifteen hundred hours. We also need wait staff and bar staff from you. Dress uniforms, please."

I couldn't hear the reply, but I assumed it was affirmative.

"I've emailed the menu." There was a pause. Maybe the other person was looking at the menu. "Excellent. I'll be in touch tomorrow."

Karen watched me going through her phone messages.

It must be a horrible feeling having someone violate your privacy like I was. There was a text message thread I wasn't sure about. It was messages about flowers. Cold icy fingers clawed at my spine.

"What's this?" I said, showing her some of the texts.

"A client was asking about flowers."

No, the client wasn't. I recognised too many of them from the rug.

Ben showed me the screen on the iPad. He'd opened her messages and found the same thread. "This is a little too familiar," he said.

"That's what I thought."

"Flowers?" Bill questioned. "How are they relevant to this?"

"It's code, Bill. She's involved with more than wedding planning."

Karen blanched. Her once healthy complexion washed out until she looked quite ill.

"And it says?"

"It's not exact, but the gist is here. Karen doesn't much like the PM and she has communicated this to someone called Admir. I know that name." I'd heard Collins use it. "He works at *Manger*."

"She would've passed a NZSIS check," Bill grumbled. "This is a disaster."

"No, Bill, it was. But we're going to fix it, and no one will ever know."

"They'll know. They're going to know. This should never have gotten this far." He stood up and motioned me to go with him. We walked out the door into a courtyard area. He spun around and glared at me. "Where the fuck is MacKinnon? Don't you work for him?"

"I don't think we can make this an Aussie problem, Bill. And anyway, the Albanians killed him."

"What?"

"He's dead. So is his son."

"How did you get involved in this mess?"

"You know how. Your man, Luke O'Sullivan, pulled me into it with a phone call. MacKinnon asked him to make that call, by the way. And I'm still not convinced that some of this hasn't come from your branch."

"I assure you, Ronnie, it has not. I've been all over. No leaks. Nothing."

"Why did you plant bugs in Luke's house?"

"We don't have time for this now. Let's get *Manger* shut down, and that bloody woman in there under lock and key, before we have an international incident on our hands."

"It's too late for that, Bill."

Bill made another call. I stood there with my hands in my jacket pockets listening to him give orders. The next phone call he made fascinated me. He said, "Prime Minister, we've made some changes to the wedding reception due to a security leak." A pause. "Ma'am everything is under control and will go ahead as planned, but instead of your chosen caterer and staff, Army will provide the catering and the staff needed." Bill shrugged one shoulder at me. "Dress uniform of course, ma'am."

There was a long pause before Bill spoke again. "Congratulations again, ma'am. I look forward to seeing you and your husband tomorrow evening."

He hung up.

"Nicely done, Bill."

Maybe I'd been a little harsh with him earlier.

"Where's Sokolov?"

"You're about to find out. I suppose we're taking Karen with us?"

"Yes, we are."

The five-minute drive took fifteen because we ran an SDR before going to the house, once we were sure we weren't followed. Karen was popped into the cage, without her bag, phone, or iPad.

Enzo emerged from the downstairs room, wiping his hands on a cloth.

"Ah, just the person I want to see," he said to me, then eyeballed Bill. "Bailey, what are you doing here?"

"About to ask you the same question, Enzo."

"I'm working, what's your excuse?" He finished wiping his hands, and balled the cloth up in one hand.

"So am I."

"Can we take this happy little reunion upstairs?" Ben said. Then he pulled Enzo closer by his left arm. "Where is she?"

"In there," he tipped his head to the concrete block wall beside the stairs. On the other side of the wall was an apartment. "Alive, in case that was your next question."

"It wasn't, but good to know."

"I take it she's not going anywhere?" I said, with one foot on the bottom step of the stairs.

"Nope."

I climbed the stairs. Bill and Ben followed me, and then Enzo joined the procession.

Collins was in the dining room with Crockett.

She startled when Bill walked in. Interesting reaction.

He stared straight at her. "Elizabeth."

"Bill." She regained her composure. "Nice to see you again."

"I somehow doubt that," he said, and sat opposite her.

"Does everyone know everyone here now?" Ben muttered to me.

"I think so," I whispered back.

The silence at the table was deafening for a split second, then Crockett spoke. "Isn't this nice?" He thumped the side of his fist against the table. "Does anyone want to know what Sokolov had to say, or have we moved on?"

"I'd be interested in hearing her point of view, and how she developed nanobots that kill people, then went right ahead and killed people. No doubt she's the victim here," I said.

Enzo perched on the table between me and Crockett. I glared at him. "Move your backside. We don't sit on tables. You need to learn that."

He jumped off and leaned against the table between us. "Better?"

"Yes."

"Victim is stretching things, Ronnie," Crockett said.

"What did she say, Enzo?" I gave him a nudge.

"The guy you saw at the house in Birchville; Chinese national. Xiang Chan. Here on a student visa."

"Great. Who was the chick in the white van?"

"Laila Kemendi. Albanian national. Here on a student visa."

"I'm seeing a pattern," I said.

Enzo adjusted his position. He was facing me and Crockett, not the table. Clearly he was not bothered about letting everyone in on his findings.

"The restaurant, that the old slag over there part-owns," He tipped his head toward Collins. "is mostly staffed by students, except for the manager who was serving tables when you were there."

"How'd you know we saw the manager?"

"Sokolov; she told me the manager was waiting tables last night."

"Because she would know when she was in Birchville ..." Except I sensed her energy at the restaurant when I dowsed. "She was there when we were. Wasn't she?"

Crockett leaned closer. "Sounds like it."

"What was she doing there?"

"Slipping nanobots into water glasses," Enzo replied. "She was there for one reason and that was to kill William MacKinnon."

"I don't get why she couldn't let the school kids do it," I said. "Seems over the top to have a scientist deliver a killer dose of whatever."

"I pushed that point," Enzo said. "They lost two servers

at the restaurant because they ingested nanobots."

"Oh, for God's sake, that's just stupid. Who are these fuckwits? Have they come up with a catchy name for their little terror cell?"

Enzo scoffed. "Not that Sokolov knew about."

"Okay, what else, apart from killing students because they're utter dumb arses?"

"The bodies of the students are in the walk-in freezer."

"Excellent."

"Sokolov asked for asylum."

"What the fuck for?" Crockett said. "She's a terrorist on the run from how many agencies?"

"All of them," I said. "All. Of. Them."

"She said *Manger* were catering the wedding of the year and providing the bar staff."

"That we know already."

"Did she give us anything apart from a couple of dead bodies?" Ben asked.

"The protest was planned and executed by Laila Kemendi. They wanted the protestors to die on camera to prove that no one can evade them, and that they do have an untraceable deadly poison."

"Foiled again. They'll die all right, but in hospital, away from prying eyes and cameras. Nothing will be made public."

"Okay, so, they want people to be scared of dropping dead, and the perfect time to create fear is on the eve of the wedding. Did they release a manifesto or a video demanding anything?" I asked, tapping my fingernails on the table. The conspiracy theorists would lap up sudden deaths.

"Do you have to tap?" Collins snapped at me.

I continued tapping.

"No. She didn't know of one, or if there would be a statement or demand made."

The rest of the table listened in silence to Enzo telling us what was learnt from Sokolov. It wasn't until he said something about Elizabeth Collins again, that all ears appeared to prick up.

"Collins bought a large interest in that restaurant for another party," he said. "It's an off-shore interest."

"CIA," I said. "How would Sokolov know that? I doubt the CIA are in the business of consulting terrorists for advice." I stopped. Or are they? Enzo stood and moved so I had a clear view of Collins. "You had to know we'd find out," I said, stabbing my index finger in the air toward Collins.

"I don't know what you're talking about. Find out what? What is it?" Collins said, her cool eyes locked on mine. "You seem a little distraught. Perhaps a nap?"

Enzo smiled, but it didn't reach his eyes. "Sokolov had a lot to say about how the CIA brought her here to kill a few people, and make it look like a spate of sudden cardiac arrests."

That made sense. How else would she get into the country?

Bill jumped to his feet with his phone in his hand. Ben lurched into a standing position.

"Enzo, who are the main targets?"

"Heads of State attending the wedding, other guests, the newlyweds." He stared at me for a beat. "The more the merrier. They had multiple ways of delivering the nanobots. Sprinkled on the cake with cake glitter. In the champagne for the toasts. Drinks poured by the bar staff. Some kind of syrup that goes on a particular cake. In the bottles of sparkling water on each table."

I took a breath. "Chandler?"

Enzo shook his head. "From what I could tell, he wasn't involved. He might be the only person, apart from Bill here, that we can trust."

Surely not?

I leaned close to Enzo and whispered, "What did she know about the Atlas?"

"Nothing. She wasn't privy to those conversations."

So that was Collins task. Kill the MacKinnon's and grab the Atlas.

I watched Collins for a moment. A half-smile lay on her lips. "I suppose you think you're clever," she said.

"Not at all," I replied. "But I think you're done."

Bill was on the phone. I couldn't hear his conversation, but it seemed like everyone was talking at once, and the air buzzed with words.

"You can't hold me." Collins words cut through the noise.

"Wrong," Bill replied. He walked around the table to me. "AOS are at the restaurant."

"Good. We need the bodies. We need the food. I need

345

to talk to my mate at ESR, and so do you. She's done all the evidence gathering so far. She can help the pathologist look for the nanobots. She knows what they look like."

I thought about the bodies. If they were dead for longer than seven days the nanobots would've self-destructed. It was worth a shot though.

I rang Christine. She picked up on the fifth ring. "Ronnie, what's up?"

"Two more bodies, in the restaurant walk in freezer. We have almost everything now. Can you make yourself available for the police pathologist?"

"Absolutely. I've worked with Sarah Talbot many times."

"Thank you, for everything you've done."

"Did you find out what the goal was?"

"Yes. I'll tell you all about it over a drink next time you're out this way."

"I'll look forward to it."

Bill's phone rang. He looked from the phone to me. "Police Commissioner."

He answered while walking into the kitchen. When he returned he said, "Sixteen anti-vaxers have died so far. And the news crew."

"Oops a daisy," I replied. Collateral damage.

"How are we going to keep this under wraps with a bunch of people dying?" Ben asked.

"No doubt that's why they killed the protestors, to make it hard for anyone to keep it quiet," Crockett replied.

"It's going to be a challenge, for sure," Bill said. "I doubt all those people will die of 'sudden heart failure'. I'm sure there will be other causes of death, and they'll be staggered."

"But they have families," Ben said. "People will miss them."

"COVID's a bitch," Bill said. "It affects so many people in different ways, and those new variants are hard to keep up with."

Crockett grabbed Collins by the shoulder and marched her out from behind the table and into the lounge. He sat her in an armchair where we could see her from the dining room.

Crockett rejoined us at the table and said, "Bill, what do we do with her?".

"Collateral damage," he replied. "Looks like she ate the cake."

"And what about the wedding planner and Sokolov?" Crockett asked.

"I hear the cake was delicious," Bill said quietly.

The sound of a heavy vehicle on the driveway interrupted the conversation. I looked out the lounge window. A dark-green armoured vehicle.

"Army have arrived," I said to Bill, as he stepped up next to me. "What do you call that truck they're in?"

"Pinzgauer. A light operational vehicle, LOV. Except today is an armoured version."

"Take no chances?"

"Something like that," he replied. Bill turned and extended his hand to me. We shook briefly. "Thanks."

"Thank you, Bill."

"That toaster is probably on sale by now."

"Probably."

Bill hoisted Collins to her feet. Enzo and Crockett went with them. No doubt to help get the other two women safely into the hands of the Army.

Emily got up, stretched, and walked to me at the window.

"Good book?" I asked, while watching soldiers cuff and shackle the women.

"Yes." She pointed at the truck. "Do they expect an IED on the way to joint command headquarters?"

I turned slowly to see Emily grin at me. "They're not very trusting," I replied.

"Trust no one," Emily said.

"Did you hear what happened?"

"No. I was reading."

I filled her in. On and off I saw glimpses of old Emily. Maybe she was starting to come back.

My phone rang.

Nana's picture stared at me from the screen. FaceTime. Wonderful. I tapped accept and there she was in my hand.

"Nana, everything all right?"

"Yes, dear. Our new friend, Mikki, is a delight. I just wanted to tell you something that we've just discovered."

"I'm all ears Nana."

Emily stood beside me and waved at the screen. Nana waved back.

"Did you know you have some of Mikki's work in your bookshop?"

I shook my head slowly side-to-side. "I did not. How about you Emily?"

"I did not know either."

Nana's lips stretched tight over her teeth as she smiled. "Look at that, Ronnie. I know something that you didn't. Isn't that the pip?"

I sighed. "Nana, I'll be over in the morning to try that frock on."

"You'll shower first won't you, Veronica? And change?"

"Yes, Nana." I rolled my eyes.

"Don't be like that, Veronica. You're wearing the same clothes I saw you in earlier this week. Goodness knows what gets into you. And those bags under your eyes!"

"It's been a busy week, Nana. I'll see you tomorrow."

"Will you stay to watch the wedding?"

"Wouldn't miss it Nana."

The End.

[Acknowledgments]

Writing is a strange process when viewed from the out-side, mostly because writers spend an awful lot of time in their own heads having conversations with characters that no one else can see, and then there is the creating of complex stories that bring those characters to life, so we can share them with the world.

I am grateful for the people in my life that allow me room to write and to be me in the process.

Super thankful to the two people who put their hands up early for beta reading and note giving. Margot Kinberg and Pete Turner made this story better even before my editor got her hands on it! (And I'm pretty sure she appreciates the hell out of you both!)

Which brings me to Nicky Hurle; we've known each other for a very long time (as school photos can attest). Friends don't usually become editors, but you have, and I appreciate every comment and suggestion.

The usual suspects are next in line with a few modifications:

My dad - when dad says something is "not bad" I know I've done a good job. I've heard a lot of "not bad's" over the years. Fun fact: As a kid I thought my dad was a spy because he never talked about work, and I also thought he didn't know mum's name, because he used nicknames when he talked to her. I was wrong on both counts ... or was I?

Geoff - it's been a tricky time for us with borders closed and COVID restrictions, but we've done hard yards before and this isn't even close. Geoff gets some odd questions from me while I'm writing, random things that I don't know, but I know he does. He always gives a well-thought-out response no matter what I throw at him. Thank you for helping me with Crockett.

And now to my kids - are you ready?

Caleb & Lizzie, Rebekah & Joshua-Luke, Patricia & Tim, Josephine, Joshua & Jenna, Caoilfhionn, and Brianna.

And grandchildren ... Isaac, Deaglán, Caeden, Connaire, Tori, David, Corey, Lily, Xanthea, Violet and Aspyn.

Thank you all for being there, and understanding that most people don't discuss manner or cause of death, at mealtimes, but we do and that's okay, and by now you should all be able to get away with murder.

Violet was the first person to hear any of this story because I read to her a lot while she was asleep in my arms as a newborn. I suspect she'll have good foundations to grow up and become a police officer or a spy. We'll see.

Thanks to Chrissy (and Mike) for having my back since day one. 40/45 is everything.

Robbie and Duigald; I know you're there, cheering and drinking, and I love it.

As always, my Admins are never far from the keyboard to wrangle the loonies. Without you, Admin One and Admin Bubbles life wouldn't half as amusing! How many people understand "Letterbox Olympics"?

[Leave a message] is the third book in this short Kiwi series.

I may have just started another. It's true, there will be another.

And about dowsing ... it works not just for water but for whatever you want to find. And yes, I can dowse. It's a family thing.

[About the Author]

The more things change the more they stay the same.

Do they though?

Cat Connor is a multi-published crime thriller author. A tequila aficionado, long black drinker, music lover, fruitcake maker, traveller, murderer of perfectly happy characters, and teacher of crime writing via CEC at Wellington High School.

She's also a mother, pretty good ex-wife, an amazing partner, a fairly decent friend, a spectacular daughter, and a very proud Grandma.

Cat has a deep love of animals and very much enjoys the company of Diesel her lab x mastiff and Patrick the tuxedo cat while writing, Netflixing, or reading.

Surely by now Netflixing is a word?

Other works by Cat Connor:
The Byte Series first published by Rebel ePublishers:
Killerbyte (2009)
Terrorbyte (2010)
Exacerbyte (2011)
Flashbyte (2012)
Soundbyte (2013)
Snakebyte (2013 9mm Press)
Databyte (2014)
Eraserbyte (2015)

Psychobyte (2016)

Metabyte (2017)

Qubyte (2018)

First published by 9mm Press:

Cryptobyte (2019)

Vaporbyte red (2020)

Vaporbyte purple (2020)

Raidbyte (2021)

Kiwi books:

1. [Nothing happens here] 2020

2. [Lure the Lie] 2021

3. [Leave a message] 2022

4. [Whiskey Tango Foxtrot] 2023

And numerous short stories, poems, and other things (which would be radio and screenplays)

You can contact Cat in the following places:

www.catconnor.com
Twitter: @catconnor
Instagram: @catconnorauthor
Facebook: @cat.connor

She's always happy to talk writing and whatnot!

As always, if you enjoyed this book let people know.
It only takes a few minutes to write a review.

If you purchased [Leave a message] from Writers Plot
Bookshop - please leave a review on the bookshop website: www.writersplot.org.nz

Thank you!

www.ingramcontent.com/pod-product-compliance
Lightning Source LLC
Chambersburg PA
CBHW022349020726
47500CB00002B/189